WE RULE THE WORLD

THIS IS A WORK OF FICTION
BUILT ON A FRAMEWORK
OF NON-FICTION.

WE RULE THE WORLD

DOUG TURNER

TURPENTINE PUBLICATIONS INC.
BOX 4284
QUESNEL, B.C.
CANADA, V2J J3J

PUBLISHED BY TURPENTINE PUBLICATIONS
INC.
BOX 4284
QUESNEL, B.C.
CANADA   V2J 3J3
(NO UNSOLICITED MANUSCRIPTS)

COVER DESIGN AND TYPESETTING BY
S.FONTAINE

Canadian Cataloguing in Publication Data
Turner, Doug, 1949-
We Rule the world

Printed in Canada

ISBN 0-9683804-0-9

I.. Title.
PS8589.U746W4 1998   C813'.54   C98-910607-1
PR9199.3.T832W4 1998

**THIS BOOK IS DEDICATED
TO
THE MEMORY OF
ANN TURNER
1918 - 1996**

SPECIAL THANKS TO SHERILL

WE RULE THE WORLD

~

That's right. We (a fifteen-member main-council and twenty-one smaller sub-councils) rule the world, and have for fifty-three years, or sixty-seven, if the years previous to gaining final — or "fission" — control are included.

Naturally, we don't "officially" exist, and anyone not in the council who has some knowledge of us won't acknowledge it — unless they don't care about themselves — and loved ones — living any longer... and even if they did decide to tell what little they know, their information wouldn't reach the public because, after all, we have eyes and ears — and "control" — "everywhere." (Besides, the great majority don't "really" want to know that we "really" exist because, as T.S. Eliot once correctly observed: Humankind can't bear much reality.)

This might make us sound like some kind of "evil" organization — but we aren't. Certainly, we've been responsible for the deaths of "many" millions — as well as "much" suffering. But there's "never" been "any" malice, hatred, anger, or greed in our actions. Everything we've done — or haven't done — has been "necessary."

For example, had we not obtained the atomic bomb before Nazi Germany, "many" more deaths and "much" more suffering would've occurred. And this is a "fact," since a number of council members (including myself) personally spent many hours listening to Hitler's plans for a global *New*

1

Order after he'd — using "any" means available, including atomic weapons and germ warfare — skewered (and screwed) the world with the swastika. (Hitler, of course, never knew about the council; he believed we were simply American businessmen sympathetic to his cause and desired to be part of his *New Order*; some council members even joined — "pretended" to join — the Nazi party.)

His plans basically boiled down to one plan: The world — which was going to be renamed, *The Third Reich* — was to be "cleansed" of "all" those he deemed "inferior." First on his list, of course, were Jews and Negroes (and even .01% Negro blood in someone made him/her a "Negro"; he claimed his scientists had actually developed a machine that could determine if someone had "any" Negro blood in him/her). They were to be "totally" exterminated and "every" trace of their existence (such as historical and religious writings, artwork, etc.) was to be destroyed. It'd be as though they'd never existed.

Also on the list were all those — including Aryans — who were deemed physically and/or mentally and/or morally and/or spiritually inferior... and all those fortunate enough to be declared "fit" were to have the "honor" of becoming "servants," on one level or another, of *The Third Reich*, the greatest nation in history.

At the very top would be people like Hitler (oh, yes, he'd only be a "humble servant" of the *Reich*), and at the very bottom would be those whose duties would mainly consist of refuse management, particularly in the disposal — or "processing" (such as grinding up bones for fertilizer) — of the many millions of corpses that'd be created by the cleansing programs. (Hitler estimated that a "minimum" of 300 million inferiors would be eliminated in the first five years following the beginning of his *New Order*.)This mass slaughter was going to be carried out mainly through the use of deadly chemicals, such as Kyklon B, Tabun, Sarin, Soman...and whatever other lethal concoctions Hitler's chemists could come up with.

In many areas, those condemned — "judged by due process of law to be unworthy of citizenship in *The Third Reich*" (everything had to be "legal," of course; and if something was "legal," it must also then be "moral," so the "reasoning" went) — were to be picked out of the population and placed in camps, where they'd be exterminated in gas chambers. An example (a "small" example) of this was seen in World War Two Europe.

In other areas, however — particularly Africa (the "world's biggest human cesspool," Hitler called it) — the plan called for the aerial spraying of the chemicals, with the amount and number of planes depending on population density. A low population density area, for instance, might receive a couple hundred gallons by one single-engine plane, whereas a high population density area might receive a couple million gallons by a large formation of multi-engine planes. (During talks with Hitler — with him doing most of the talking and council members doing most of the listening — he'd often get extremely excited as he talked about his "purifying angels," and the numbers would rise. He'd talk — "rave" — about huge planes — 6, 8, 10 engines — in formations of one, two, three, four thousand, etc., etc. — spraying hundreds of millions — even billions! — tens of billions! — of gallons during a single operation.)

And...well, hell, nothing more really has to be said, does it? I believe it's been made clear enough what would've happened had Hitler been the first to get the bomb — and why we — or "America" — "had" to get it before him, or anyone. It was a "necessity" — an "absolute" necessity.

There were, however, a few problems.

One was that a "reason" was needed for America to build such a weapon. Or, more accurately, a reason was needed that people could "understand" and, more importantly, "accept." And making such a weapon for "self-defense" — even to avoid possible domination (and possible extermination) by someone like Hitler — simply wasn't an acceptable/understandable reason. America wasn't being threatened by anyone at the time, and many Americans couldn't see a time — not even in the far-distant future — when it would. The popular feeling was: As long as we leave people alone, they'll leave us alone.

Another problem was that many Americans couldn't really even begin to comprehend what an "atomic" bomb was — it was something "unreal"; something out of "science fiction". So they couldn't really begin to understand what might happen if another nation had one (or two, three, four, etc.) — especially one with a leader like Hitler. (Although, in all fairness to the American people at the time, it must be remembered that they didn't know Hitler like we did. Most saw him as more of a cartoon character than anything else.)

Consequently, since it would be virtually impossible to undertake such a massive project in peacetime — especially since it'd have to be top-secret — what was needed in order to justify building an atomic bomb was a war. A "major" war.

But before America could have a major war, it needed a "major" enemy — and it had to be one that the new weapon could be used on once it was completed because, in order to "prove" just how devastating the atomic bomb "really" was (and that America wasn't afraid to use it), there "had" to be a "live-firing" of the weapon.

And it was quickly determined that the perfect country

4

for this was Japan, since there weren't many Americans of Japanese descent (at least compared to Americans of German descent; Nazi Germany was, naturally — because of Hitler — our first choice). Plus, more importantly, many Americans were "extremely" prejudiced against the Japanese, viewing them as little, slant-eyed, buck-toothed, funny-talking, funny-walking, "monkey" people (or "creatures") who — perhaps worst of all — had yellow skin (which made them, in the eyes of many Americans, even lower than black/brown skinned people). Therefore, it certainly wouldn't be any great tragedy should they have an atomic bomb or two dropped on them — especially if they'd done something to deserve it.

At the time, however, they, like the Germans, weren't America's enemy, or even a "potential" enemy. Sure, they were conquering, raping, torturing, oppressing, and killing in Korea and China. But that was 5,000 miles from America, and since many Americans also regarded the Chinese and Koreans as "monkey" people/creatures, what the Japanese were doing to them certainly wasn't any great calamity; many, in fact, felt that it was much needed birth control in that part of the world.

Therefore, something had to be done to make the Japanese an enemy of America...like maybe somehow manipulating them into attacking an American military base...like maybe the one in the Hawaiian Islands, only 2,400 miles from mainland America...yes, that's correct...we orchestrated the 7 December 1941 Japanese attack on Pearl Harbor.

We accomplished this by manipulating American government/military personnel (using money, fear, blackmail, violence..."anything" that was needed), and inserting agents into Japan, where they manipulated (in the same way American government/military personnel were manipulated)

5

the Japanese High Command (including the Emperor). It was an "extremely" difficult operation — especially as regards the Japanese — since it was, after all, quite clear (at least to us) that it was suicidal for Japan to start a war with America. Certainly, Japan had a large, well-equipped military and Japanese soldiers, with their *Code of Bushido* (which forbid surrender; they must fight to the death), were formidable fighters. At the same time, however, American soldiers, though lacking a *Code of Bushido*, certainly weren't slouches when it came to combat. And America also had a large, well-equipped military (its warship tonnage at the start of the war, for example, was about 1,345,000 as compared to Japan's approximate 1,016,000), with the potential to be "much" bigger than anything Japan could produce.

Or, better yet, look at it from the perspective of each country's size, population, and mineral resources. Japan was a small country (about sixteen thousand square miles smaller than California) with a population of about 60 million, and its mineral resources were negligible (all its minerals had to be imported; a "major" weakness). America, on the other hand, had a "huge" wealth of mineral resources and a population of about 130 million.

As well, Japan was an island nation, which made it very vulnerable to enemy encirclement — especially since it didn't have any close allies. Actually, it didn't have "any" allies, since we were also manipulating Italy and Germany. In May 1940, for example, Hitler had about 370,000 British, French, and Belgian troops trapped on the beaches of Dunkirk, France. They didn't have a chance. Hitler's forces could've "easily" annihilated/captured them. We, however, convinced him to order his ground forces to halt their advance on those trapped on the beaches by telling him it'd show the world what a great "humanitarian" he was. At the same time, however, we also urged him to let his crack air force, the Luftwaffe, keep up its attack, assuring him that there was such a thing as being "too much" of a humanitarian; England and France, after all, had started the war with Germany — they were the ones who'd "officially" declared war (thanks to our manipulations, of course) — so they had to pay some kind of price (actually, urging him to let the Luftwaffe keep attacking was part of a plan to manipulate Hermann Goering, the commander of the Luftwaffe, and the second most important person in Germany; if Hitler suddenly died, he'd be the one to take control — and we wanted to be prepared).

We then manipulated Hitler into not invading England (had he invaded as planned, we calculated that most of the country would've fallen in ten weeks or less because, even though about 340,000 of those trapped on the Dunkirk beaches were allowed to escape to England in the famous *Dunkirk Evacuation*, nearly all their weapons were left behind, which meant that England's defense capabilities were at an all-time low). Instead, we urged him to "completely" crush British morale by concentrating his bombing of England on the urban centers, and not on the Royal Air Force (RAF) bases in southern England as he'd been doing (they were practically finished anyway, we said; which was true — another month or two of bombing would've finished them). This he did, thereby giving the British military (especially the badly battered RAF) time to regroup.

And we also manipulated Hitler into not securing the strategically crucial Strait of Gibralter, which would've given Germany control of the western entrance to the Mediterranean Sea (and securing the strait would've been "extremely" easy, since it's only about 30 miles long and only between 8 and 23 miles wide). As well, we manipulated Hitler into not giving top priority to the construction of the atomic bomb and other important weapons, such as the awesome *Messerschmitt 262* jet fighter and *V-2* ballistic missile (and our manipulations also prevented maximum use of important weapons, such as the *262, V-2,* and U-boats; U-boats, for example, would've sunk "much" more Allied shipping than they did had we not interfered and, in fact, would've been able — in combination with the Luftwaffe — to completely isolate England from all Allied shipping).

Our two most important manipulations of Hitler, however, were convincing him to invade Russia in June 1941, thus creating a two-front war for Germany (which would be "suicide" for Germany, Hitler had once said; was he ever right!), and getting him to sign — and honor — a mutual assistance treaty with Japan, in which he agreed that any enemy of Japan was also Germany's enemy. (Convincing him to honor this treaty was "extremely" difficult, since he loathed the Japanese almost as much as Jews and Negroes.)

We convinced him that, after the united forces of Germany, Italy, and Japan defeated America — and everyone else — Germany and Italy could then defeat Japan (and "cleanse" it), and Germany would then be in total control of the world (with Italy in a definite subservient position). So he declared war on America immediately after Japan attacked Pearl Harbor.

So then, with America now at war with two formidable foes — in a struggle for its very existence — building the atomic bomb was a "necessity."

Consequently, America built the atomic bomb and, while doing so, defeated Hitler — with the help, of course, of Russia, Great Britain, Canada, and others (who, naturally, we were also manipulating). Then, on 16 July 1945, at Alamogordo, New Mexico, it tested its first atomic bomb (it was one of the highlights of my life; a "religious" experience of the most intense kind). (Something needs to be said here. I'm sure that many — but especially those of the Jewish faith — are wondering: if we were manipulating Hitler like I say, why didn't we prevent him from carrying out his genocidal program against the Jews? The answer is — very sadly — we didn't because we might've needed all that blood on his — and Germany's — hands. It was a trump card in case something went wrong — like some unbelievably good luck on Hitler's part, such as a successful invasion of Russia. It would make him — and the Nazis/Germans, in general — "irrevocably" — "monsters" who deserved whatever they got — such as an atomic bomb or two.)

Then the day following the test, the *Potsdam Conference* began at Potsdam, a small city near Berlin. It was attended by President Harry S. Truman of the U.S., Prime Minister Winston Churchill of Great Britain (who was replaced during the conference by Clement Attlee after a general election in Great Britain), and Premier Joseph Stalin of the Soviet Union, and — "unofficially" — a few members of the council (including myself; it was another great highlight of my life).

The "official" purpose of the conference was to settle problems in postwar Europe, plan the occupation of Germany, and issue an ultimatum of unconditional surrender to Japan (which meant nothing; Japan was going to get A-bombed, no matter what), and — "unofficially" — inform Churchill, Attlee, and Stalin that America, because it had the atomic bomb (and the air power to deliver it "anywhere" in the world), was now in control — "total" control — of the world.

It was a bombshell (no pun intended). Churchill, Attlee, and Stalin — particularly Stalin — were outraged. They said — screamed — that America couldn't just take over the world! It wasn't fair! It wasn't right!

9

After seeing film of the test, however, they knew it was pointless to argue. (And they also knew that much — or all — of their anger stemmed from jealousy. Were positions reversed — had Great Britain or Russia gotten the bomb first — they would've done exactly what America was doing; it would've been "completely" idiotic not to have taken the advantage.)

Then, on 6 August 1945, four days following the end of the conference, to show them — and the rest of the world — just how devastating the atomic bomb "really" was — and that America wasn't afraid to use it — the Japanese city of Hiroshima was atom-bombed. This was followed three days later — to show that the atomic bomb was a "reliable" weapon and that the U.S. "really" wasn't afraid of using it — by the atom-bombing of Nagasaki. (A note here: The atom-bombing of Hiroshima and Nagasaki is considered by many to be "terrible" — "beyond" terrible — and indeed it was. At the same time, however, it must be remembered that the Japanese, as a "nation," "really" deserved the bombs since, long before council manipulations, they'd committed "terrible" atrocities in Korea and China. As well, it could've been "much" worse, since we originally planned to drop more than two bombs. A last minute decision saved Tokyo, Yokohama, Kobe, and Osaka from A-bombs.)

Both bombings were, of course, spectacular successes, establishing us ("America," that is) as "the" world power. We had "fission" control (and "fusion" control was soon to follow). We were, therefore, in a position to assume overt global control.

There would then be world peace — or at least, "major" world peace — because there'd still be a certain amount of fighting, since violent conflict definitely appears to be a natural human trait. But there wouldn't be anymore "major" wars like World War One and Two.

And, yes, the world would've been under a "dictatorship," since we — "America" — would've been in "total" control. And yes, I know "many" will say that such a thing would've been terrible. It wouldn't have been, however, since it would've only been a "limited" dictatorship, with a major part of the new country's foundation being the greatest governmental document ever written, the Constitution of the United States of America, so there would've been much room for democratic voting (and "dissent").

But, to our absolute horror, our plans collapsed when we realized that, with just one group in power — those possessing atomic weapons — the power would be concentrated in just one place (in the "mental" sense; the weapons themselves could be in different locations around the world, but they'd still be under the control of just one group) — which, of course, would be a tempting target for a Hitler. And if a Hitler — or a Stalin — got control of the atomic arsenal...

However, if it appeared that the world's atomic arsenal was in widely separated areas — being controlled by two different/opposing groups — it'd be obvious that getting control of one-half of the world's atomic arsenal wouldn't also mean getting control of the whole world. (Many times we've discussed eliminating the problem of a Hitler, a Stalin, etc., getting control of the atomic arsenal by simply getting rid of the arsenal, but have always concluded that such a move would be foolish because it wouldn't make the world any safer, since it'd mean that we'd lose our control — and it'd be back to square one.)

Therefore, what was needed was some kind of "conflict"...yes, we created the *Cold War*. We turned America and the Soviet Union into deadly foes who were amassing

11

huge arsenals of nuclear weapons in a nuclear arms "race." It was all pure theater, with most of the actors having "no" idea of the truth and the nuclear arsenals of both countries (and everyone else) being, for the most part (the council, of course, had — and has — a small number of live weapons), simply illusions, such as big steel tubes painted with military insignias, fitted with pointed nosecaps, and filled with concrete to make them heavy (although the great majority of them were/are much more complicated than that). And, naturally, these illusions — or "props" — were/are protected by the highest level of "national security" (and breaking national security laws — especially those on the highest level — can be "extremely" dangerous to one's health).

This all might sound totally unbelievable. What's unbelievable, however, is how easy it all was. We, of course, greatly added to the drama by having both sides (including a number of allied countries) conduct tests of nuclear weapons (all controlled by us, naturally), as well as engaging in a conventional arms race, much of which was used — and is being used — in "hot" conflicts/wars (Korea, Vietnam, Afghanistan, etc.) that we also — regretfully — had to create.

This greatly pained us because we didn't want to see anyone killed or maimed — or suffer in any manner — and we had some extremely heated discussions about it (blows were almost exchanged on a few occasions; the only time that's ever happened in the council). Finally, however, it was decided that we didn't have any other choice. A *Cold War* without some "hot" conflict (including some non-*Cold War* conflict such as the Arab-Israeli wars, the Iraq-Iran war, and the Gulf War) would simply look ridiculous.

So why did we then allow communism in Russia (and other places) to collapse and the *Cold War* and nuclear arms race to end (and the conventional arms race to be considerably slowed down)?

The answer is: The *Cold War* and nuclear arms race haven't really "ended." It only "appears" that way. They're really only in a state of "suspension" (and the conventional arms race slowdown may only be "temporary") while the council makes some difficult decisions regarding the future. It's become increasingly apparent that our *Cold War* and nuclear/conventional arms race plan is destroying the environment (pollution, ozone depletion, deforestation, etc., etc.). Therefore, it appears that the council is eventually going to have to abandon that plan altogether and take a chance that it can retain control of the nuclear arsenal (and as I've said before, the nuclear arsenal must be kept; destroying it would be pure folly), and assume overt control of the world and turn it into *The United States Of The World*.

However, as a few council members (Seats Seven, Eight, and Fourteen, to be precise) have suggested, it might be a good idea for the council to step back for a number of years before taking overt control and allow the world's present economic/social system to collapse. (The council would, of course, retain control of the world's nuclear arsenal and nuclear weapons manufacturing capabilities, as well as keeping control of the world's major conventional weapons, such as modern combat aircraft and warships.)

This would create a period of utter chaos — "violent" chaos — for "the people" of the world, which would "cleanse" — or "help" to cleanse — the world of much of the hatred, frustration, hopelessness, jealousy, greed, anger, etc., that's accumulated over the years — as well as helping to curb the world's uncontrolled population growth (Seat Four, a statistical and probability expert, has determined that, should the council step back for five years, the global death toll from violence of all kinds, diseases of all kinds, and starvation will be between 2.85 and 4.58 billion above the normal death rate). (The council wouldn't, of course, be affected by this nightmare since it, and a few hundred million select support staff, would retire to various"safe areas," where it would stay until it took overt global control.)

I realize this sounds terrible — "beyond" terrible. But it must be remembered that in the big picture — "ze cozmik pikzur," as Albert (Einstein, that is) used to say to me — it really doesn't matter what the council does, or doesn't do. It won't change the ultimate ending by one iota — which, of course, is that everyone is eventually going to die. And one day, billions of years from now, even the Earth itself is going to die, since it's going to get fried to a crisp as the sun swells toward burnout.

And so what?

The reality, after all, is that Earth — and the human species — are nothing more than mosquito farts in "ze cozmik pikzur."

Many, of course, find it extremely difficult accepting this fact...hell, many absolutely refuse to accept it at all. As previously stated, T.S.Eliot was absolutely correct when he said that humankind can't bear much reality — although, generally speaking, humankind often has "much" trouble distinguishing reality from nonreality. How many, for example, have ever considered — even for a "moment" — that the *Cold War*/nuclear arms race might not have been "real"? Very few, I can assure you.

Or take the *Missile Crisis* — the *Cuban Missile Crisis*, that is. It was a terrifying time for the world's people because they believed that America and Russia were on the verge of a world-destroying nuclear war. It was THE END!!!

It, however, wasn't THE END!!! It wasn't even "close." It was simply an illusion — a Hollywood movie, so to speak (and a grade B, or C, one at that). But no one (to the best of our knowledge) ever questioned its authenticity.

~

he "crisis" began on 22 October 1962, when JFK (John Fitzgerald Kennedy, 35th President of the United States) announced that Soviet-built and supplied nuclear missiles were being installed in Cuba...no, that's not quite accurate. It all actually began much earlier, in August 1951, when the council decided that, in order to make the American people feel they were "really" being threatened by the evil beast of communism, a communist "threat" had to be established close to America.

And it was quickly decided that the perfect location for such a threat was Cuba, just 90 miles south of Florida. It was a small island (about 44,000 square miles), which meant that the operation could easily be contained/controlled — especially since America had a large naval base (a "permanent" base, as guaranteed by a 1903 treaty) at Guantanamo Bay in Oriente province, about 50 miles from the eastern end of Cuba's southern coast. It was from there that the Cuban part of *Operation Crimson Cube* would be directed.

Now all that was needed was a dynamic, charismatic, "revolutionary" leader with excellent oratorical skills who could "capture the hearts and minds" of "the people" of Cuba ("brainwash" them, in other words) with his passion for "justice" and "equality" and "freedom from tyranny," and lead them in a struggle against the oppressive regime of the evil dictator Fulgencio Batista. (At the time this plan was conceived, Batista wasn't "evil" or "oppressive" — "corrupt," yes; a bit "heavy-handed" at times, yes — but not "evil/oppressive." He would, however, as the operation progressed, become extremely "evil" and "oppressive"; the council would make certain of that.)

Enter Fidel Castro. He was a lawyer in his mid-twenties who possessed everything we were looking for — including a   ravenous lust for power (which made manipulating him "extremely" easy). The idea of being the leader of Cuba — the "absolute" leader — was a dream come true. It was winning the big lottery. Sure, in the global picture, Cuba definitely wasn't a big deal. To Castro, however, it was "everything." It'd be his kingdom and he'd be able to do almost anything he wanted (remember, the council would be controlling him). He'd be able to play army with his own real army, complete with artillery, tanks, ships, and planes. He'd be able to imprison/torture/execute people who annoyed him. He'd be able to screw all the young, teenage girls he wanted. He'd get to be in the world news as a "world leader." He'd be a "somebody" — a "big" somebody. And if he had to become a "communist" — a "Marxist-Leninist," to be precise — in order to get the big prize — so be it.

He knew that the ideas of Marx and Lenin (but especially Marx, since he started communism with *The Communist Manifesto*) were, generally speaking, bullshit. But he also knew that "the people," generally speaking, preferred bullshit to the truth, or "reality." And the reality was (and is) that, no matter what happens, "the people" are "always" going to be on the bottom.

It's exactly as George Orwell wrote in his novel, *1984*. Throughout history there have only been three kinds of people — the High, The Middle, and the Low — and no matter what's happened (wars, revolutions, elections, famines, epidemics, etc.), the basic social structure of High, Middle,

17

and Low has always remained the same.

And the goals of the three groups have always remained the same. The High strive to remain where they are (or get even Higher). The Middle try to become the High (while also trying to avoid becoming the Low). And the Low — "the people" — seek to get rid of all distinctions between people and create a society in which all people are "equal" (that is, when the Low have a goal regarding the structure of the society they're living in, since they're often too pressured by the forces of simply trying to survive — getting and keeping a job, paying the bills, etc. — to have much "real" interest in what's going on outside their daily lives — or they simply don't give a damn).

It's a wonderful thought — a society where there aren't "any" distinctions between people; where "everyone" is "equal"; a "classless," or "one-class," society. Unfortunately, however, it's a utopian dream. And always will be, no matter how many Marxs' or Lenins' insist that it's possible. For one thing, people are "naturally" born "unequal" (some, for instance, are born physically stronger/healthier than others).

And for another thing, in their perpetual war with the High, the Middle constantly manipulate the Low into believing that they (the Middle) are fighting for "equality/justice/freedom."They promise the Low all kinds of "changes/reforms" when the struggle is over and the High have been defeated. (Sometimes this struggle is called a "revolution," and is often accompanied by much violence; many times it's called an "election" — a "democratic" election — and is "always" accompanied by much bullshit.) But if the High are indeed defeated, the Middle then become the High, and the great majority of the Low will find that all that's "really" changed for them is the names of their masters (or "leaders").

And, as stated before, Castro knew this. But he was, of course, more than willing to become a "Marxist-Leninist," a fighter for "the people," spewing out utopian dream rhetoric ("Power to the People!") to "the people" of Cuba in order to become one of the High (or, in Castro's case, as regarded Cuba, "the" High) — although he didn't "officially" become a Marxist-Leninist until a few years after overthrowing Batista.

The reason for this, of course, was had he declared himself a communist/Marxist-Leninist while fighting Batista, America wouldn't have had any other choice but to aid Batista and squash Castro — although America should've destroyed Castro regardless of politics, since American citizens/businesspeople had hundreds of millions invested in Cuba at the time (plus the U.S. military had the base at Guantanamo Bay), and if Batista (a longtime American "ally") was being threatened, so were those investments (and base).

And it would've been "extremely" easy for American forces ("assisting" Batista, of course) to have destroyed Castro. People ("the people" of America, to be precise) were manipulated into believing that Castro was very hard to get at because he fought most of his revolution from the Sierra Maestra mountain range, an extremely rugged ("impregnable" was a word often used in the media) area in southeast Cuba — which, to a degree, was true. The Sierra Maestra's "were" indeed "extremely" rugged.

At the same time, however, they were also very close to the American base at Guantanamo Bay (for most of his "revolution" Castro was never much more than 100 miles from the base), and American military power — especially air power (such as B-52s with 30 ton bombloads) — would've

19

made the Sierra Maestra's "much" less "impregnable." Hell, it wouldn't have mattered where Castro had fought his revolution from in Cuba; he "always" would've been within "easy" range of the American military (and, of course, since Cuba was an island, Castro was trapped; he couldn't flee across a border to a friendly country).

And it wouldn't have been anything unusual for America to have given Batista "direct" military aid (the aid it was giving him was "indirect"; weapons, ammunition, supplies, etc.), since it'd given combat aid to foreign countries in the past to help keep governments ("dictatorships") in power, as well as protecting American business interests/lives(for example, four times in Nicaragua between 1910 and 1933). And it could've easily done this in Cuba — especially after late June 1958, when Castro kidnaped ten American citizens and 28 U.S. naval personnel from near the base at Guantanamo Bay in retaliation against America for refueling Batista's planes at the base.

America, however, only scolded Castro as though he'd simply played a childish prank and demanded that he release the hostages — which was understandable as long as Castro had the hostages — but wasn't understandable after he released them the following month.

The U.S. had promised it wouldn't retaliate against Castro if he returned the hostages unharmed. After their release, however, America could've "easily" said the promise wasn't binding because it'd been made under duress, then, after labeling Castro a communist, it could've blasted Castro and his tiny force into a fine red mist.

But, of course, it didn't. Instead, "bowing to public pressure" (by this time, we'd turned Batista into a world-class tyrant), it stopped "all" military aid to Batista and even imposed an arms embargo on Cuba to prevent Batista from getting military aid from other countries. This allowed (in the most literal sense) Castro to overthrow Batista on 1 January 1959 — which, in turn, led to 1 May 1961, when Castro officially declared that he was a communist (a "Marxist-Leninist," to be precise) and Cuba was a communist country — which meant that there was now a communist threat — THREAT!!! — just 90 miles from America, the "free" world's main bulwark against the evil communists.

Before Castro's announcement, the hot spot (though non-violent) in the *Cold War* — as "directly" concerned America and Russia — was in Europe (especially in the Berlin area), and if a major war broke out between the two, chances were that it'd be confined to Europe and the Soviet Union, since America had superior (and better positioned) forces/firepower. It'd be able to act so fast that the war wouldn't have a chance of reaching America (except perhaps for a little radiation from the smoldering ruins of the Soviet Union and Europe).

Now, however, the enemy wasn't just "way over there." It was now also "right here" — just 90 miles from America — only about ten minutes by combat aircraft — maybe a couple minutes by nuclear missile...the FEAR!!! was incredible — especially since relations between Cuba and America had greatly deteriorated in the 28 months since Castro had overthrown Batista...no, that isn't quite accurate. Relations between Cuba and America — and Russia and America — had greatly deteriorated in the 28 months since Castro had ousted Batista because Russia had become involved when it began trade relations with Cuba in February 1960. It then became "much" more involved in July 1960 when Nikita Khrushchev, Premier of the Soviet Union, threatened America with a "rocket attack" if it attacked Cuba (which had been rumored for months — especially since Ike;

21

Dwight Eisenhower, the U.S. President at the time — had approved Central Intelligence Agency — CIA — training of Cuban exiles who were plotting to overthrow Castro).

Khrushchev's threat was shocking, to say the least, since the rockets in question were nuclear missiles and, if Russia fired nuclear missiles at America, America would then fire nuclear missiles at Russia, and it'd be...THE END!!!

Or so it appeared...remember, none of this was for real. It was "all" an "illusion" created by the council. And at times the illusion became so absurd that it was unbelievable to the council — even knowing the difficulty people often have telling the difference between reality and nonreality — that people were so easily fooled.

Take Khrushchev's threat to attack America with nuclear missiles, for instance. It was absolutely ludicrous (had everything been for "real") that Russia would be willing to go to war with America — "end-of- the- world" war — over a little country like Cuba — especially since it didn't have any military forces close to America (unless one counted the Soviet Union-Alaska area, and Alaska certainly couldn't be considered a "major" target). America, however, had forces very close to Russia — especially in Europe — so an attack against America would've been suicidal for the Soviets, but not vice versa. (Something should be noted here: Both America and Russia were often called "superpowers" because of their huge militaries — yet Russia "openly" lacked a "key" ingredient for superpower status. It didn't, like America, have a fleet of aircraft carriers.

The reason for this was simple. It was a council experiment. We wanted to see how many would notice this "obvious" military flaw. It was an "intelligence" test, so to speak.

And very few noticed this "vital" missing piece in the

Soviet arsenal. And most of those who did — and wrote about it — came to the conclusion that the Soviets regarded carriers, because of their size, as being obsolete in a nuclear military, and had instead decided to build a large submarine fleet.

This made some sense. However, aircraft carriers can — and do — carry aircraft specifically designed to detect — and destroy — submarines, and a large fleet of carriers, such as America had, would be able to keep track of Russian subs "anywhere" in the world and, along with other anti-submarine weapons — such as destroyers — attack and destroy them should war occur.

Consequently, without a carrier fleet, Russia was "clearly"never a "superpower.")

Khrushchev's threat, however, did set the stage perfectly for the next scene, which was Castro's seizure (or "nationalization," as he called it) of "all" American-owned Cuban property — worth about a billion dollars — in August 1960. (Castro, of course, was quick to point out that he wasn't "stealing" the property; the former owners would be compensated over the next fifty years with bonds at 2% interest — which was the equivalent of spitting into America's face.)

Castro's action enraged many Americans (and not just former Cuban property owners), and they wanted America to invade Cuba and take care of Castro, once and for all. And if it meant nuclear war with the Russians — do it to them before they can do it to us! Enough is enough! Show those commie bastards that America isn't going to be pushed around anymore!

But, of course, cooler heads prevailed (after all, Castro wasn't yet "officially" a communist) and America didn't attack Cuba...but it also didn't sit still. It fired off barrage

23

after barrage of verbal condemnation against Castro (and Khrushchev), and mobilized military forces and shuffled them around. Then, on 19 October 1960, it imposed a partial trade embargo against Cuba, followed by a complete severing of diplomatic relations in January 1961.

Then relations between America and Cuba/Russia hit a new — and dangerous — low when, on 17 April 1961, CIA-trained and supplied Cuban exiles invaded Cuba, in what quickly became known as the *Bay of Pigs Invasion* (because the Bahia de Cochinos — "Bay of Pigs" — had been chosen for the landing site).

It was, of course, a total disaster — and a joke — because, while the invasion was supposedly a "secret," pre-invasion preparations had been reported in the American media for months prior to the attack (including "on-the-spot" reports from "secret" bases), and all Castro had to do to keep informed of the activities of the exiles was to keep tuned-in to the American media — although, of course, he didn't even have to do that, since the council made sure he knew exactly when and where the invasion was going to occur.

As well, the council also made sure that the exiles made all kinds of serious "mistakes," such as not landing in the proper locations; failing to check-out landing craft properly before they were launched (like making sure they had enough fuel); not having enough ammunition (or having the "wrong" ammunition); failing to begin the invasion on time and thus landing in daylight instead of semi-darkness...they didn't have a chance. Castro's troops (well-armed with Soviet weapons) defeated the exiles in a couple of days, killing a few hundred and taking the rest — about 1,200 — prisoner.

The failed invasion terrified, not just Americans — or others in the Western Hemisphere — but people all over the world because the popular belief was that Khrushchev would make good on his threat to launch nuclear missiles at America, since the Bay of Pigs invaders had been trained and supplied by the CIA. Then America would fire nuclear missiles at Russia, and it'd be...THE END!!!

But, of course, he didn't — because, after all, that would've spoiled the next scene (not to mention modern civilization): Castro's declaration on 1 May 1961 ("May Day"; the big communist holiday) that he was a communist ("Marxist-Leninist") and Cuba was now "officially" a communist country, and was "officially" aligned with the Soviet Union and the rest of the communist world.

So now, for the first time in the *Cold War*, America — and the whole Western Hemisphere — was vulnerable to a sneak attack by the evil commies. Cuba was like a monstrous enemy warship permanently moored just 90 miles from America — and there was plenty of room on that warship for "many" big bombers and large nuclear missiles. As stated before, the FEAR!!!was incredible as the specter of Pearl Harbor loomed huge — and mushroom-shaped — over America and the rest of the Western Hemisphere.

And the FEAR!!! was intensified in July 1961, when both America and Russia announced that they were boosting their military budgets by $3.5 billion (a "lot" of money at the time; a doctor in the U.S., for example, only made about $15,000 yearly, and a new Ford could be had for about $2,000).

Then, in the months following, Kennedy, Khrushchev, and Castro kept the FEAR!!! level as high as possible with intense verbal skirmishing (and they made it sound "real," because the council had manipulated them into believing it was for "real"; they knew there were people "behind-the-scenes" who were "really" controlling everything — but they didn't have any idea of what was "really" happening; they didn't, for instance, know that the *Cold War* was fake — but one thing they did know for certain, however, was that they'd better do as they were told); Castro challenged America's right to retain the base at Guantanamo Bay, making it clear that they — "the people" of Cuba — the "liberated" people of Cuba — wanted the "Yankee Imperialists!" out of Cuba, and threatening that Cuba might use force to push them out (which, of course — had everything been for "real" — was an absolutely ridiculous threat; it was like a goldfish threatening a large school of sharks); Kennedy said that America wouldn't leave Guantanamo Bay, and if Cuba used force against America, America would respond with force; Khrushchev said that if America used force against Cuba, Russia would use force against America (adding that Russia was going to increase its arming and training of the Cuban military); Kennedy condemned the Soviet-assisted Cuban military build-up and again warned that if Russia attacked America, America would respond "accordingly," and pledged to use "any" measures to combat Cuban aggression — and communist aggression, in general — in the West; Khrushchev said that an American attack on Cuba would mean war — nuclear war — between Russia and America...Kennedy warned...Khrushchev threatened...Castro condemned...it all actually started getting a little boring; people actually began getting used to it...so the really BIG!!! scene began...

In October 1962, Kennedy announced that the U.S. had received reports that short and/or intermediate-range nuclear missiles were being shipped to Cuba from Russia, and that bases for the missiles were being constructed by Soviet technicians. Naturally, both Khrushchev and Castro vehemently denied the charges. Kennedy, however, produced pictures taken by American U-2 spy planes that "proved beyond any doubt" that the charges were true (and no one in the "free" world questioned the authenticity of the pictures, or thought about how easy it is to fake pictures, or build fake missile sites, or build fake missiles).

And it was: THE WEEK THAT SHOOK THE WORLD!!!

Kennedy stated that the installation of the missiles in Cuba was a "provocative threat to world peace." He warned that if even one missile was fired from Cuba at America — or any other country in the Western Hemisphere — America would launch a massive retaliatory attack against not only Cuba, but the Soviet Union as well, since that's where the missiles had originated.

He then announced that he was imposing a naval and air "quarantine" on Cuba to stop the shipment of anymore missiles/missile launching equipment, and other "offensive" weapons/equipment/supplies to Cuba. And he also demanded that "all" of the "offensive" weapons that'd been supplied to Cuba from Russia be removed from Cuba and returned to Russia.

Khrushchev and Castro argued that there weren't any "offensive" weapons from the Soviet Union, or anywhere else, in Cuba; "all" the weapons in Cuba were "defensive," not "offensive." But Kennedy insisted that certain weapons — especially the missiles — "were" offensive and repeated his demand: Get them — and all other offensive weapons — out of Cuba and back to the Soviet Union or wherever else they came from...or else!

Angry words snapped back and forth between Kennedy, Khrushchev, and Castro for a few days, with no one willing to budge from their position. The militaries of the U.S., Soviet Union, and Cuba were put on red-alert — as was every other military in the world because this was leading to

27

the ultimate confrontation and was going to affect "everyone" in the world. This was going to be a "global" war — a global "nuclear" war.

It was then reported that Soviet cargo ships, reportedly carrying "offensive" weapons to Cuba, were approaching the U.S. warships that were enforcing Kennedy's quarantine.

This was it! Showdown! High noon! And maybe — very likely — THE END OF THE WORLD!!!

People who had bomb shelters headed for them (if they weren't already in them). Freeways, highways, streets, and roads started grid-locking as people fled cities and towns (especially those considered primary target areas).

The Soviet ships kept getting closer to the American warships — and they weren't slowing down. Contact was only an hour away!

People got on their knees and prayed harder and faster and louder than they'd ever prayed before. And those who'd never prayed before — those who'd scoffed at the existence of God — prayed for the first time, pleading with Him, or It, to save them from the coming holocaust.

Forty-five minutes to contact!

American Intercontinental Ballistic Missile — ICBM — silo doors began sliding open; B-52 strategic bombers laden (supposedly) with nuclear bombs were approaching Soviet airspace; anti-missile batteries were ready to shoot down the coming rain of Soviet nuclear missiles. (It was assumed that similar activities were taking place on the Soviet side.)

Thirty minutes until the Soviet cargo ships arrived at the quarantine line!

ICBMs began rising out of their silos into final pre-launch positions; once there, all that was needed was to turn the dual launch keys and they'd be on their way to devastate

28

the Soviets (at least that's what everyone believed; in fact, of course, turning the launch keys wouldn't launch anything).

Ten minutes!

The Soviet ships weren't slowing down, or altering course.

People were sobbing their last good-byes and prayers, and cursing their last curses at mankind's insanity...this was it! THE END!!!

Five! Four! Three! Two! One!...then the Soviet ships slowed, and turned away from the American warships — and it was over!

Or, more accurately, the "climax" was over because, while the Soviets backed down and returned the "missiles" and other weapons to the Soviet Union, Cuba was still a communist country (just 90 miles away!) filled with evil commie monsters who could "never" be trusted — so America would have to be "extremely" vigilant — which it has for the 36 years since the "crisis."

Yes, it's been a long and profitable operation — a fantastic success, to say the least. But, of course, everything we do is, to one degree or another, "successful." There isn't any failure when you're the Highest of the High — only varying degrees of success.

Take the Vietnam conflict, for example. The popular belief is that it was a total failure for America. In reality, however, it was a great success.

~

𝕮alling the Vietnam conflict a great success for America might sound like something from Orwell's *Newspeak* in *1984* (*War Is Peace* and *Freedom Is Slavery*, for instance). It must be remembered, however, as I've said before, the Vietnam conflict, like the *Cuban Missile Crisis* and the *Cold War*/nuclear arms race, was an "illusion" created by the council (and it also must be remembered that the Vietnam conflict was never "official"; the U.S. never "officially" declared war on the communists in Vietnam — so it therefore couldn't "officially" lose/fail).

Had it been for "real" — had it "really" been a fight against communism — America never would've become involved the way it did (forgetting for a moment that, had there "really" been a fight against communism, it would've began right after the end of World War Two and would've been over in a few months, with America — because it had the atomic bomb — being the victor). It would've sold/loaned/given weapons, ammunition, equipment, and supplies to South Vietnam, but it certainly wouldn't have become a combatant. It was, after all, "obviously" a fight that couldn't be won, or even "stalemated," by America/South Vietnam (unless, of course, nuclear weapons were used; and if they were, there wouldn't be any excuse for not using them to fight communism in other parts of the world — which would've meant a "very" quick end to the *Cold War*).

The reason for this was that South Vietnam (unlike Cuba and South Korea) couldn't be isolated. The Vietnamese communists, who were based in North Vietnam, simply couldn't be prevented from infiltrating South Vietnam. It was an "impossible" task.

A quick look at a map of the area (when Vietnam was still divided into North and South, of course) clearly shows that one didn't just have the border between North and South Vietnam to contend with. One also had to deal with the borders between South Vietnam and Laos/Cambodia — and that was a "major" problem. The border between North and South Vietnam was only about 40 miles across fairly decent terrain, but the border between South Vietnam and Laos/Cambodia was about 800 miles, through some of the roughest country (jungle/swamp/mountains) in the world. American/South Vietnamese forces — even with America's awesome air power — simply couldn't keep that border sealed.

As well, North Vietnam couldn't be isolated from its huge communist ally — and neighbour (sharing a border of about 600 miles) — China. (China also shared a border with Laos — about 150 miles — so weapons, ammunition, etc., could go from China to communists in South Vietnam without even having to go through North Vietnam.)

So how can the Vietnam conflict be called a "great success" for America?

Simple. After America failed (supposedly)to prevent Cuba from becoming communist, the morale of the American people hit an all-time low. American involvement in Vietnam (as well as making the Soviets back down in the *Cuban Missile Crisis*) was a much needed patriotic boost. Their great country was again vigorously fighting the evil beast of communism (and killing plenty of evil commies).

And it also helped keep "the people" of America diverted, to one degree or another, from internal problems (like racism, poverty, crime, and political corruption), as well as proving to them and everyone else in the world — especially regarding protests against American involvement in the conflict — that America was "truly" a "free" country, since open dissent was allowed.

But the greatest success for America in the Vietnam conflict was in the area of employment.

Many condemn spending on armaments as a waste of money, saying it can be used for much better things, like finding cures for diseases, feeding the hungry, housing the homeless, educating the uneducated, protecting the environment, etc., etc.

Spending on armaments, however, "isn't" a "waste" of money, since the armaments industry provides "much" employment which, in turn, generates consumer spending and tax revenue which, in turn, generates more employment, consumer spending, and tax revenue which, in turn, generates more employment, consumer spending, and tax revenue, and so on and so on. (And much of the tax revenue is used for social programs, like education, health and welfare, protecting the environment, etc. — which, of course, creates more employment, consumer spending, and tax revenue, and so on and so on.)

And since much of what the arms industry produces is meant to be "consumed," or "destroyed" (anything that goes Bang! or Boom!), a certain amount of "live" conflict is — from a strictly economic perspective — "good," because peacetime militaries simply can't use/consume large amounts of armaments — at least, not without it looking very strange.

In the Third Battle of Ypres in World War One, for example, the British, before attacking the Germans, shelled the German positions for 19 days, consuming an astonishing 4,300,000 artillery rounds (one year's production for 55,000 workers!) — an amount which, if consumed during a training exercise of 19 days — or even 19 weeks — or even 19 months — would look very odd.

Or, going to the Vietnam conflict...in the years 1965-1973, American B-52 bombers flew about 126,500 sorties, during which they dropped more than 2,600,000 "tons" of bombs. Now, let's say that each ton of bombs equals 200 person hours of work. That comes to a total of 520,000,000 person hours of work, or 260,000 full-time jobs — and full-time taxpayers/consumers — for one year.

Then there's the employment that was created by the manufacture/maintenance of the bombers; and the construction/maintenance of the facilities where the bombers were made; and the manufacture of the tools/ equipment needed to make the bombers; and the obtaining of the raw materials needed for the making of the tools/equipment and facilities and bombers; and the creation/harnessing of the huge amounts of electricity needed for everything; and the production of the fuel the bombers used (each B-52 could carry a minimum of 46,000 gallons).

And, of course, the B-52 was just one of "many" different aircraft America used during the Vietnam conflict — and bombs were just one type of ammunition that was used. A "huge" assortment of ammunition — and weapons — were used/consumed during the conflict. (And it must be remembered that America wasn't the only country using/consuming — or "supplying" — armaments in the conflict.)

As well, "enormous" quantities of all kinds of non-armament equipment and supplies (such as food, clothing, tires, building materials, etc., etc.) were used/consumed — and "are" used/consumed — since militaries (especially "modern" ones, like America's) are much more than simply troops with weapons. They're actually "separate societies" (in that they can — or "should" be able to — function independently of "regular" society) that need everything that's needed in "regular" society (such as food, clothing, and shelter) — the production/sale/distribution of which, of course, creates jobs, tax revenue, and consumer spending, etc., etc.

Furthermore, military personnel also create jobs, since they're taxpayers and, on a "personal" level, consumers. They go into the marketplace and buy the same things civilians do — houses, appliances, cars, clothing, food, entertainment, etc., etc.

Then why, if the Vietnam conflict was so successful, did we end it?

Simple. It'd run its course. It was becoming ridiculous. The great United States of America couldn't beat a bunch of lowly peasants whose war machine was "much" inferior to America's. Even the most patriotic anti-communist Americans were tired of it. They increasingly demanded: Win the damn thing, or get the hell out!

Consequently, we pretended to bow to the wishes of "the people" and got the hell out — and it was an extremely successful retreat (or "rearward advance," as the government/military liked to call it). It made America look "good" in the eyes of the world (or at least in "many" eyes), and the Republicans were able to use the withdrawal as an election platform to keep them in the White House (with our "approval," of course, since we, after all, are the ones who "really" decide who gets into — and stays in — the White House; elections are held simply to make "the people" believe that they're living in a "democracy," and that they — "the people" — are "important"). And all those who'd for years been protesting American involvement in Vietnam were able

34

to boast that they'd "stopped the war" (never realizing that much of the anti-war protest had been financed by the council; had it not been for us, the anti-war protest, both in America and the rest of the world, wouldn't have been nearly as strong as it was).

And yes, many Americans experienced a loss of morale — the great United States of America had been defeated (call it a "rearward advance" if you want — it still meant "defeat"). But a humbling experience every once in awhile is good for people (and good for the council, because people who've had a humbling experience tend to be — especially in a "collective" sense — much easier to control/manipulate, since they hunger to have their pride restored and, generally speaking, people with such a hunger are fools).

And yes, many Americans were killed and maimed and suffered in the conflict (or suffered because loved ones were killed/maimed/suffered in the conflict), but that simply couldn't be helped; it was, after all, an "armed" conflict (and besides, tears/anguish also tend to make people — especially in a "collective" sense — easier to control/manipulate because, generally speaking, tears/anguish tend to turn people's intellect into mush).

As well, it must be remembered that, despite America's "rearward advance" in Vietnam, the *Cold War* was still on — there were still plenty of dirty commies to fight (and kill) — so the American armaments/military force industry was kept busy (even busier, since the American military had a lot of replacing/rebuilding to do after the conflict).

Of course, as I've previously mentioned, this cycle of conflict = employment = taxpayers/consumers = employment = taxpayers/consumers, etc., etc., that we created after World

35

War Two has created an extremely serious problem: It's destroying the environment (pollution, deforestation, ozone depletion, etc.) — and, as I've also previously mentioned, we're eventually going to have to do something about it.

Actually, the "big" problem isn't the economic cycle we created with the *Cold War* and nuclear/conventional arms race. The "big" problem is the human species itself. It's the most unstable/destructive species on the planet, and it doesn't appear that it's going to change. (And before anyone blames the council — accuses it of promoting violence and preventing change — it should be remembered that the human species was unstable/destructive/violent "long" before the council was formed. Also, as I've clearly illustrated, were it not for the council, the world would've experienced "much" more violence/destruction than it has.)

Many will undoubtedly argue that the human species can indeed change. All humans have to do is learn more about themselves. They'll then be in a much better position to prevent, or at least "control," all, or much — or even just "some" — of the destructive things they do — such as aggressive violence.

This definitely makes sense. It's highly unlikely, however, that humans will ever "really" know themselves to any "great" degree, since research into human behavior is impeded by the fact that, in order to "really" study the subject, humans have to be used in "exactly" the same way guinea pigs and other animals are used in scientific research (including breeding humans specifically for such use and, in order to insure the "purity" of the research, denying them "any" kind of " rights"). This, of course, is something most find — even if it could greatly improve the human condition — to be morally wrong (to the "extreme"). Many will no doubt even say that simply "thinking" about such research is morally wrong (to the "extreme"), perhaps pointing at the Nazi "research/experiments" conducted on humans during World War Two as an example of the "evilness" of treating humans "exactly" like research animals.

Nonetheless, the "only" way humans can "really" learn about themselves, both individually and collectively, is to use fellow humans as research subjects in "exactly" the same way research animals are used, since animals, no matter how humanlike they might be, are still only human "like"; they aren't "human."

Although, even if such research was conducted, it might not be successful, or "totally" successful, since it might be that the human brain — no matter how "superior" it might be — is incapable of understanding ("totally" understanding) itself. It is, after all, that same brain that's judging itself to be "superior."

Perhaps the human brain — and the human species — isn't as "superior" as many believe? Maybe the human species is actually a "lower" life-form, instead of a "higher" — or "the" highest — life-form?

Many will no doubt argue that that simply can't be true, pointing at all the technological advances humans have made (tools, machines, etc.), and saying that only a "higher" — or "the" highest — life-form could've done all that.

However, while humans have indeed made many remarkable technological advances, it doesn't appear that any of them have made the human species any less violent/destructive. In fact, it seems that they've only helped make humans more violent/destructive; aircraft, for example, while revolutionizing transportation in a major way, also revolutionized warfare in a major way (as well as being a major contributor to pollution, both in their use and manufacture).

As well, what humans have "achieved" — all the "progress" they've made — might be very misleading, in that humankind might not be moving linearly. It might be moving circularly. Instead of going from primitive to "advanced" — and staying   advanced and/or getting more advanced — it might be going from primitive to advanced to primitive.

Perhaps a thousand — or two or three or four thousand, etc. — years from now (or much less), no matter what's done or isn't done by humans (including the council), the human species (if it isn't already extinct) will be much like, or maybe "exactly" like, the human species of one, two, three, four thousand, etc., years ago?

This might sound ridiculous, but it must be remembered that there are already "many" (hundreds of millions, even billions) who are currently living ("surviving" would probably be more accurate) much like humans did thousands of years ago. Many will undoubtedly be quick to point out that the council is responsible for the way these people are living — and suffering/dying. Which is true. The council is indeed responsible.

On the other hand, however, were it not for the council, "many" of these people wouldn't have even had a chance at living, since the great majority of their ancestors would've been victims of Hitler's "cleansing" programs...and perhaps the council made a mistake there? Maybe it should have let Hitler win the war and carry out his cleansing programs...

~

These were Seat Nine's words at a meeting a number of years ago:"Perhaps we should have let Hitler get the bomb, win the war, take control of the world, and carry out his cleansing programs. Then we could've overthrown him and taken overt control — and we wouldn't have the mess we currently have — or at least, it wouldn't be nearly as serious as it is."

Now, while this might sound like a horrible thing to say, the council has to think about and discuss "everything/anything" pertaining to the human condition, no matter how horrible/unpleasant some of these things might be. And, as unpleasant — as "terrible/horrible" — as it might sound, it indeed "might" have been for the best if the council had let Hitler win (which we "easily" could've done), and then overthrown him after he'd "cleansed" the world.

Consider for a moment what the world would be like — or "might" be like — had Hitler got the bomb first, conquered the world, and carried out his cleansing programs. Forget — or try to put aside — the hundreds of millions who would've been slaughtered. I know this might be "extremely" difficult — especially if one is a Jew or has dark skin pigmentation. But try looking at it in a purely "scientific" manner.

For one thing, there'd be "much" less racial strife/hatred in the world — at least as regards black/white relations — since there wouldn't be any black/Negro people in the world. And there also wouldn't be any hatred for

39

Jewish people because there wouldn't be any Jewish people in the world. And there also wouldn't be "any" religious hatred in the world because there'd only be one religion — Nazism.

And there also wouldn't be any wars/conflicts in the world, since Nazi domination would've ended all wars/conflicts (at least on a "large" scale; there still would've been conflicts on a "small/personal" level). And because — or "especially" because — there wouldn't have been a *Cold War* and nuclear/conventional arms race, the world also wouldn't be in the danger it's presently in from pollution, deforestation, ozone depletion, etc., etc.

Or, more simply put — "all" things considered — looking at it from a purely "scientific" perspective (or an "emotionless" perspective) — it does appear that today's world would be a "much" better place had Hitler won the war (been "allowed" to win; remember, the council would've still been controlling everything) and carried out his cleansing programs, followed by the council taking overt control and "saving" the world. (Of course, from a purely "scientific" perspective, the world would undoubtedly be an even "much" better place if the human species weren't living on it; from the perspective of plants and non-human animals/creatures, the human species must be like some kind of monstrous cancerous growth.)

I realize this sounds terrible — "beyond" terrible. But before condemning me, or the council, consider this "fact": Had Hitler indeed conquered the world and carried out his cleansing programs, the great majority of the world's population today wouldn't have "any" idea of what "really" happened prior to his conquest and cleansing, since part of his plan involved rewriting the history books.

As I've already mentioned, not only was Hitler going

40

to get rid of "all" Jews and blacks/browns, he was also going to get rid of "every" trace of their existence — which means that today, one wouldn't be able to find even the "slightest" mention of Jews or blacks/browns "anywhere." They would've "completely" disappeared from history — except, of course, in the memories of those old enough to remember — and it would've been punishable by death (and torture, of course) to have transmitted those memories, in "any" form, to "anyone."

And the same with "all" religions (except for the "religion" of Nazism, of course). Every Bible, Koran, Torah — "every" piece of religious writing — was going to be destroyed, along with "every" religious artifact and building. And "any" mention of any religion other than Nazism — even simply saying, "Jesus," or "Christ," or "Bible," etc. — would've been an offence punishable by torture and/or death (torture and death for those who spoke/communicated the forbidden words/thoughts); simple death for those who became "contaminated" by the words/thoughts).

Which brings up something interesting. The philosopher George Santayana gave the world this often-quoted thought: "Those who cannot remember the past are condemned to repeat it." This "sounds" good, or "wise" — but is it really such a good idea to remember the past?

Consider what writer Sholem Asch had to say about remembering the past: "Not the power to remember, but its very opposite, the power to forget, is a necessary condition for our existence."

Or, put another way: Remembering the past isn't necessarily good because, in "remembering" — in preserving and/or spreading "knowledge" — certain facets of that knowledge can prove to be "extremely" harmful.

Take the Nazi persecution/extermination of the Jews,

41

for example. Many feel what Hitler and the Nazis did to the Jews should never be forgotten, so it'll never happen again. Which definitely makes sense. At the same time, however, it can also be very destructive, since "knowledge," or "education," can be a double-edged sword of the sharpest kind. In learning about the Holocaust, for example (which, incidentally, contrary to what today's Nazis say, did "really" happen — it wasn't a "hoax"; I personally saw Jews being gassed and cremated), one can't also help learning about Nazis/Nazism. And because of that — or at least "partially" because of that — Nazis/Nazism continues to exist because, for one reason or another (perhaps it begins simply with such superficial things as flags, uniforms, weapons, etc.), some find Nazis/Nazism very appealing — which reminds me of an idea the council briefly considered in early 1945.

We called it *Operation Third Strike*. It was a plan that called for the elimination of every Nazi — and Nazi "sympathizer" — in the world. They'd be hunted like vermin and killed. And every record of their existence — such as Hitler's *Mein Kampf* — would be destroyed, and "any" mention of Nazis/Nazism would be strictly prohibited.

We quickly realized, however, that such a plan was far more complicated than it appeared. Certainly, we would've had the power and resources to implement such a plan because, after all, we would've been in complete control of the world. Such a plan, however, would've also meant having to oppress the Jewish people, in that they wouldn't have been allowed to legally remember the Holocaust, since it couldn't be remembered without also remembering the Nazis. And we simply couldn't do that to them — or the rest of the world's people, for that matter — because we felt, despite the double-edged sword of "remembering/knowledge/education," that the

Nazis should never be forgotten because they're one of modern history's greatest examples of the danger of patriotism — or "blind" patriotism, to be precise.

Unfortunately, however, it appears that "many" have failed to get the message because a popular belief (especially among those who, in one way or another, experienced World War Two from the Allied side) is that a "good" citizen is one who's "patriotic," in that he/she is willing to "serve their country" (go to war) without question or complaint should their country "call upon them" (never mind that the "country" doing the calling is actually a small number of politicians who get to declare and fight wars from the comfort/safety of offices and homes far away from the battlefields).

Of course, as Seat Nine once suggested, perhaps this leaning towards blind patriotism/obedience is only "natural," since it definitely seems, generally speaking, that the human species is, to one degree or another, afflicted with an inherent stupidity — and this includes those who are supposedly "educated/intelligent." (In fact, those who are supposedly "educated/intelligent," such as those with college/university educations, often have a far higher level of stupidity than those who aren't nearly as "educated/intelligent," since formal education systems tend to suppress "creative" thinking in favor of promoting established/accepted ideas and traditions — even though there might be "much" stupidity in those ideas and traditions.)

Consider, for instance, the attitude many have regarding violence. They'll insist that, "violence doesn't solve anything,"even though it's "clearly" a "fact" that violence can indeed solve problems. (The problem of Hitler and Nazi Germany, for example, was solved by using violence...yes, the council helped create that problem, but if it hadn't, the war would've happened anyway; Hitler was determined to conquer — and "cleanse" — the world long before the council came into existence.)

And they'll also insist that words — talking, discussing, reasoning, etc. — can solve "all" problems, when it's "clearly" a "fact" that words are sometimes simply inadequate when it comes to problem-solving. For example, words might not work if people can't speak/understand the same language, and translators aren't available, or they're unreliable (especially in the sense that they might not be neutral), or there simply isn't any time for translating; or if people have difficulty in understanding what others mean, even though the same language is being used (especially if people are playing word "games"); or if people aren't able to speak well, or listen well (and listening is just as important — many times even "more" important — than talking); or if people aren't allowed to speak freely (such as in a dictatorship, or a bullying relationship); or if people aren't willing to listen because of prejudice, narrow-mindedness, closed-mindedness, etc.; or if people lose control of their emotions (anger, for example, can end a discussion very quickly); or if people have mental abnormalities/differences (trying to "reason" with a psychotic or a psychopath, for instance, can be like trying to stop an earthquake with duct tape)...no, words sometimes just can't solve problems and violence might be the "only" recourse (especially if one isn't able to flee or buy their way out of the situation).

Violence, after all, is a "basic" form of "communication." It's a "universal language" that everyone understands — and the "only" one that some will "really" listen to (such as a Hitler).

Many will undoubtedly try reinforcing their ridiculous argument that violence is never the answer to problems of any kind by saying that using violence is "wrong." The

44

"right/wrong" of violence, however, isn't relevant to whether or not violence solves problems, since the issue of "right/wrong" is a "philosophical/moral" issue, whereas, whether or not violence solves problems is a matter of simple "physics" — an area where philosophical/moral "right/wrong" doesn't (or "shouldn't") apply.

A criminal, for example, is committing a crime and a police officer suddenly appears. The police officer is a big problem for the criminal. The criminal kills the police officer. Now, what the criminal did might be morally "wrong," but that doesn't — or "shouldn't" — factor into the equation as concerns simple "physics." The criminal "did" solve a problem. Violence, no matter how "wrong" it might've been, "was" a solution (although not necessarily a "permanent" solution, since using violence isn't any "guarantee" of a permanent solution).

But many will continue arguing that non-violent actions are "always" the "only" way to solve problems...and chances are, to reinforce their argument, they'll start talking about Gandhi, who believed that violence should never be used to effect social change. But Gandhi's success with non-violent civil disobedience, or "passive resistance," doesn't mean that it'll work in all cases.

Had he been facing the government of Nazi Germany instead of the government of Great Britain, for example, Hitler would've destroyed Gandhi and his followers without a moment's hesitation (which I know for a "fact," since Hitler personally told me that, after he conquered the world, he was going to cleanse the world of that "filthy little man and all the vermin who follow him").

Furthermore, all those who hero-worship Gandhi because of his beliefs/actions (or "non-actions/beliefs") should remember that Gandhi and his followers, while vastly outnumbering the British, lacked — by a "huge" margin — the weapons and combat knowledge (weapons alone don't make an effective fighting force) necessary to defeat the British.

Had Gandhi been able to arm his followers — and train them — to a point of equality with the British (or at least to a point where they could've put up a "strong" fight; strong enough to "seriously" hurt the British), I'm quite certain he would've quickly abandoned non-violent civil disobedience/passive resistance in favor of violence. And same with one of Gandhi's most famous disciples: Martin Luther King Jr. Had he been able to arm his followers to a point of equality with the American government (or to the point where they could've put up a strong enough fight to "seriously" hurt the government/military), I believe he would've been a lot less peaceful.

And perhaps, had violence been used, King and Gandhi and/or their followers — or at least "some" of them — might've found (especially if they began scoring "big" victories) that they actually "liked" (or even "loved") it, since the use of violence (or even just threatening its use) can produce an "intoxicating" feeling — a feeling of "power" (particularly when a "righteous" cause is involved — and especially when your opponent begins showing fear; the feeling that can result from scaring people can be as addictive as "any" drug) — which is something that's existed for thousands of years — and still exists. (I know that on a number of occasions, when the council has had to threaten certain individuals/groups with violence if they/he/she didn't do what the council demanded, I — and other council members — have definitely felt an intoxicating feeling of power. But we know about — and can control — that feeling. We don't let it control us. It's when people don't realize what's happening to themselves that problems arise; Hitler, Mussolini, and Stalin, for example, were hopelessly addicted to the feeling produced by threatening/terrorizing others.)

And by all indications, it'll continue to exist for as long as humans exist because, despite all the technological progress they've made over the centuries — and despite all the philosophical/metaphysical exploring that's been done — and despite all the spiritual searching/awareness that's occurred — it appears that humans, generally speaking, are still basically the same "emotionally" (anger, fear, and hate, for instance) and "instinctually" (the "survival instinct," for example) as they were thousands of years ago.

Or, as some have put it: Even the most "modern/civilized" humans — ones with all the latest technology and access to huge amounts of knowledge — aren't far from loincloths and spears.

Consider what would happen, for example, should the council decide to implement *Operation Crystal*...

peration Crystal is the council stepback I mentioned earlier, where, in order to save the world's environment (and the human race), the council allows the world's economic/social system to collapse, then takes overt global control after a period of cataclysmic disorder.

A major part of this operation involves controlling the lifeblood of modern civilization: electricity. Many forget just how important it "really" is. They take it for granted. Just flick a switch or push in a plug, and there it is. It's as natural as the sky, or the sun. But, of course, it isn't. The electricity that powers the world isn't "natural," since it's been created by humans. And because of that, it can also be "decreated" by humans.

The council, for example, has the power to shut off approximately 90% of the world's electricity in about seventy-two hours (that is, without doing damage — or "serious" damage — to equipment/machinery/people; if "serious" damage to equipment/machinery/people isn't a consideration, it can be done in less than twenty-four hours). And, more importantly, it also has the power to keep it off — for a week, a month, a year, two years, three years...for as long as the council desires. As well, the council has the power to shut down about 98% of the world's telephone service, and approximately 80% of major fuel sources — gasoline, diesel fuel, aviation fuel, natural gas, propane, and coal — in about ninety-six hours (or about thirty-six if damage to equipment/machinery/people isn't a consideration). (These shutdowns wouldn't, of course, affect the council and its support staff, which includes the American military and other select militaries.)

And should these shutdowns be "lengthy"(such as five, or ten, or twenty, etc, years, for instance), the world's people will find themselves in a "loincloths and spears" condition — "literally" — because such shutdowns will create, as previously mentioned, a global nightmare of proportions never before experienced. And all those who believe that "violence doesn't solve anything" — that "words can be used to solve all problems" — will suddenly find themselves faced with bands of human predators who'll quickly appear — on a "large" scale (they already exist on a small scale) — and begin rioting, destroying, robbing, raping, torturing, killing...

They'll be those who, for one reason or another (victims of racism, for example), are filled with hatred, frustration, hopelessness, jealousy...and want to strike out against someone or "something" (like "society," in general). And once their adrenaline gets pumping (especially in a "collective" sense) — once the glass starts shattering and the buildings and cars start burning and the blood begins spurting — only violence will be able to stop them. Weapons, not words, will be needed. And because there won't be any government/police/military to stop them (the council will make certain of that), it'll be up to "the people" to do it. They'll be on their own. It'll be "survival of the fittest." And those wanting to survive will "need" to use violence.

Operation Crystal, of course, is only one of a number of options the council has. There's also *Operation Tranquility,* where the council, as previously mentioned, takes a chance that it can retain control of the nuclear arsenal — that another Hitler, Stalin, Mao, etc., won't get their hands on

49

it — and turns the world into "The United States of the World," with the council, based in America, in total control (but allowing as much democracy as possible — such as voting for regional governors, for instance — as well as allowing as much dissent as possible; we abhor tyranny, but should we take overt control of the world, we realize that we're going to have to use a "firm" hand — an "extremely" firm hand).

A big problem with this option, however, is that many in the world, for one reason or another (jealousy, for example), hate America/Americans. And because of this, they'd likely go on a "suicidal" rampage after the council made its announcement — even though we'd make it "absolutely" clear that any resistance would be "totally" futile.

Consider, for instance, the huge number of "fundamentalist" Moslems who consider America to be the "Great Satan," and would gladly die fighting it in a "holy war" (especially since, according to the Koran, such a sacrifice guarantees an instant spot in Heaven). No amount of "reasoning" would stop them from fighting...although, they could perhaps be manipulated into believing that America isn't the "Great Satan." They could perhaps be manipulated into believing the exact opposite — that America is really the "Great Savior." They, after all, were manipulated into believing that America is the "Great Satan" in the first place (and yes, the council was/is behind that manipulation; we did it — and are doing it — because there might come a time when Moslem fundamentalists will have to be eliminated because, long before the council appeared, Moslem fundamentalists believed they had the right — the "God-given" right — to convert non-Moslems into Moslems through violence, and that belief is stronger than ever, and it simply can't be tolerated in the council's new society).

Or maybe it'd be better to simply destroy them — or "it" (just "fundamentalist" Moslem, that is, not the entire faith) — or at least damage it as much as possible — before the council makes its announcement of global control? Or, perhaps better yet, manipulate them into damaging/destroying each other?

It'd be easy — as easy as starting the Iraq-Iran War in 1980 and the Gulf War in 1990...no, it'd be far easier because there's much more hate ("internal" hate, that is) in the fundamentalist Moslem world than there was even five years ago.

Iraq, for example, hates its Moslem neighbor, Syria, because it sided with the American-led "Coalition" during the Gulf War (or more accurately, Iraq hates Syria "more," since it hated Syria — and vice versa — long before the Gulf War). And Iran harbors a hatred for its Moslem neighbor, Iraq, because it started the war in 1980 (or "appeared" to; as I've already said, it was the council who actually started that war).

So, a little scenario: Iraq is manipulated into attacking Syria. They fight for a couple of months and really hammer the crap out of each other. Then Iran is manipulated into attacking Iraq. Then, after a few more months of intense fighting, Iraq, unable to withstand both Syria and Iran, uses nuclear weapons (supplied and "controlled/used" by the council, of course) against both countries who, in response, use nuclear weapons (also council supplied and controlled/used) against Iraq. (It should be noted that all the nuclear weapons would be smaller — and "cleaner" — than the ones used on Japan in World War Two.) This horrifies the world and a United Nations force (led by America, of course) intervenes and occupies all three countries, placing them under "strict" martial law.

51

Or another scenario: Syria, a longtime enemy of Israel, is manipulated into attacking Israel, and the two fight (are "allowed" to fight) for a couple of weeks. Then Iraq, seeking revenge for Syria's actions in the Gulf War, takes advantage of Syria's weakened condition (Israel will, of course, quickly gain the upper hand) and attacks it (is "manipulated" into attacking it). Then a month or so later, Iran, seeking ("supposedly") revenge on Iraq for the Iraq-Iran war, is manipulated into attacking Iraq and, at the same time, is also manipulated into attacking Saudia Arabia because it gave aid to Iraq during that war. Iraq then uses nuclear weapons on Syria and Iran, and Iran and Syria use nuclear weapons on Iraq — and Iran also uses nuclear weapons on Saudia Arabia. A United Nations force then intervenes and occupies Syria, Iraq, Iran, and Saudia Arabia — and Sudan, Libya, and Egypt since, while the Syria/Israel/Iraq/Iran/Saudia Arabia conflict is taking place, Libya and Sudan will be manipulated into mounting a joint-attack against Egypt, with nuclear weapons being used by all three countries. As well, while all this is taking place, Moslems (especially "fundamentalist" Moslems) in other countries (particularly Afghanistan, Pakistan, Algeria, Bangladesh, Ethiopa, Morocco, and Turkey) will be manipulated into fighting and damaging/destroying each other — which, of course, will justify United Nations intervention/occupation.

Yes, it all sounds "terrible" — "beyond" terrible (Seat Four has determined that between 32.43 and 46.89 million will perish in such a conflict). But look at it from another perspective: Should fundamentalist Moslems somehow infiltrate and overthrow the council and get control of the nuclear arsenal, they wouldn't hesitate for a second to use it to turn the world into a fundamentalist Moslem state, or "dictatorship," since that's what it'd really be (and it wouldn't matter to them how many non-Moslems were killed; in fact, fundamentalist Moslems would love to see "all" non-Moslems dead — or converted to Islam). (The chance of such a takeover happening is, of course, "extremely" slim; Seat Four has calculated the odds at about 950,000,000 to 1 against it happening — but it could happen....)

Although that wouldn't necessarily be a "bad" thing since, in some respects, a world under fundamentalist Moslem control probably wouldn't be any worse than a world under overt council control (particularly if one was born into it, and didn't have to "convert"). In a fundamentalist Moslem world, for example, there wouldn't be any religious freedom; everyone would have to be Moslem — "fundamentalist" Moslem — which, to many, would be a definite violation of human "rights/freedom".

In a world overtly controlled by the council, however, religious rights/freedom would also be violated since, in creating a peaceful new society, religion would "need" to be "strictly" controlled.

Many will undoubtedly scoff at this, saying that it'd be "impossible" to "strictly" control religion, especially Christianity and Islam because they're just too powerful. However, should the council first step back and allow the world's economic/social system to collapse, resulting in five, ten, fifteen, twenty, etc., years of chaos, the world would be "much" different than it is today, and organized religion wouldn't be "organized"anymore (especially since council-financed agents would've created a great deal of "deorganization" even before the economic/social collapse; actually, council-financed agents are already working at "deorganizing" organized religion — especially in the Christian and Moslem worlds — particularly in the "fundamentalist" regions; and some of these agents hold "very" important positions in both worlds and are making it appear as though they're working hard — "very" hard — to strengthen their particular faiths, rather than weaken/destroy them).And when the council emerged from its "safe areas" and took control, it'd make certain that Christians and Moslems stayed deorganized. (Of course, it must be remembered that "many" of the world's Christians and Moslems would perish in the years of chaos.) And to accomplish this, the council would "need" to violate people's religious rights/freedom. It simply wouldn't have "any" other choice.

For example, birth control (including court-ordered sterilization and abortion), would almost certainly become mandatory — which would be a violation of people's religious rights/freedom. But that's simply the way it'd have to be since, in the council's new society, population control would be enforced — would "need to be enforced.

At the United Nations in 1967, thirty nations agreed that: "The Universal Declaration of Human Rights describes the family as the natural and fundamental unit of society. It follows that any choice and decision with regard to the size of the family must irrevocably rest with the family itself, and cannot be made by anyone else."

This might've been fine back then (although inaccurate; the individual, not the family, is the "fundamental" unit of society). In the council's new society, however, this declaration would be discarded — would "need" to be discarded — because the world's population simply can't be allowed to continue growing at its present rate. Just look at the numbers: In 1950, the world's population was about 2,500,000,000. In 1988, just 38 years later, it had doubled, whereas the previous doubling took almost a hundred years, and the doubling previous to that took almost two hundred years. And before that, almost 1,700 years!

There are those who say that population growth will eventually "level out," and everything will be fine. But that's simply not true because by the time it "levels out" — if it indeed does — it might very well be too late. Irreparable damage might've been done. The ozone layer, for instance, might be beyond repair, and if that happens...well, let's just say that conditions on Earth won't be very pleasant.

Then there are those who say that population growth isn't the "real" problem. The "real" problem, they insist, is that the world's wealth is unequally shared; a few have a lot and a lot have a little. And if it were more equally shared, population growth wouldn't be a "problem."

This might indeed be true. A "big" problem, however, is how to divide the world's wealth "equally," since it's not equally distributed over the planet. Plus, from a quick examination of history, it's quite clear that there'll "always" be those who'll claim that they're not getting their fair share, no matter how equally everything is shared. And it's also quite clear that drastic changes need to be made regarding the use of the world's wealth. And one of those changes is that humans simply "have" to use "less" — of "everything" — and one "sure" way to accomplish this is by strict population control — and people will simply "have" to accept it — just like they'll also "have" to accept losses of other "rights/freedoms."

In America, for example, many believe that one of their greatest rights/freedoms (many believe it's "the" greatest right/freedom) is the right/freedom to possess firearms. And if anyone questions that right/freedom, fingers will immediately point to the Second Amendent of the Constitution: "A well regulated Militia, being necessary to the security of a free State, the right of the people to keep and bear Arms, shall not be infringed."

In the council's new society, however, that amendment would be removed from the Constitution, since the council has decided, after "much" debate, that citizens of its new society won't have the right/freedom to own firearms. It'll become a "privilege." And that privilege will be "severely" restricted — as will firearms themselves. For example, "all" repeating firearms will be prohibited, and will have to be surrendered to the government — as will all single-shot firearms over .22 caliber and .410 gauge (and maybe even those won't be allowed).

This, of course, will enrage most gun owners (especially since there probably won't be much — if any — compensation for surrendered firearms — except perhaps for good citizen merit certificates from the government). But again, it's something that those in the council's new society will just have to accept, since it's simply far too dangerous for society to allow ordinary citizens to be heavily armed — despite anything the Constitution says.

And should the Second Amendment be removed from the Constitution, anyone — such as "militias" — who try fighting its removal with violence will be dealt with "severely."

These people like to think of themselves as "patriots" — "saviors" of America — but they're not. They're misguided souls who, among other things, aren't very intelligent. Not long ago, for example, a number of these camouflage-clad "patriots" actually appeared in a popular military/mercenary-type magazine, posing with their weapons (all military-style firearms that'll be first to be prohibited when the Second Amendment is removed from the Constitution). And, proving their lack of intelligence, most of them didn't even make an attempt at concealing their faces.

This is beyond stupid (and thinking that they stand "any" chance against the American government/military is beyond that — "far" beyond; they've simply lost "all" touch with reality).

Of course, it wouldn't matter if they had covered their faces, or never appeared in the magazine at all. The council has been keeping track of such individuals and groups for many years now (since 1955, to be precise), and has "completely" infiltrated this "movement." For example, all these people read the same magazines — gun/survival/military/mercenary magazines — and many, being economically-minded, have subscriptions, and the council has subscription lists for "all" these magazines, as well as mailing lists from "all" book publishing companies who publish books on weapons, combat, survival, etc. And the council even actually owns (very "indirectly," of course) publishing companies and magazines, as well as companies/stores that sell firearms, ammunition, and various other equipment/supplies to these people. And, of course, the council also has agents "directly" inside all the major groups that make up this "movement" (and some of them are "high profile," especially in a "crazy" sense; they say and do outrageous things that attract a lot of attention and create a negative image, such as posing with guns and raving about hating government/politicians and using violence against them/it).

Consequently, the council knows what, where, and when. So, should it decide to raise *Operation Tranquility* to Level One (it's at Level Eight at the moment), and formally announce that it's assuming total control of the world and repealing the Second Amendment and enacting strict gun control laws, and be met with violence from these individuals/groups, they won't stand a chance. The council —

or more accurately, the American military — will hit them "hard" (particularly the more racist groups/individuals; racism/racists simply won't be tolerated — in "any" manner — in the council's new society), using "anything" needed to get the job done, including "heavy" weapons, such as helicopter gunships and jet fighter-bombers.

Actually, they're already starting to get hit "hard," since *Operation Spring* (an operation inside *Operation Tranquility*) was raised to Level Five.

It began in February 1993, when federal agents raided the Branch Davidian (a religious cult) compound near Waco, Texas, to search for illegal weapons. The Davidians, led by David Koresh (who claimed to be Jesus Christ), opened fire on the agents, killing four of them. This led to a 51-day siege. Then, on April 19 (keep this date in mind), agents attacked the compound, using armored vehicles to smash holes in the walls. The Davidians again fought back. A fire started inside the compound and quickly engulfed the woodframe structure, killing 82 of the Davidians, including twenty-four children.

It was a horrifying spectacle viewed by millions on TV, and many immediately began blaming the agents for the deaths, claiming that tear gas projectiles fired by them had ignited the buildings.

It was quickly revealed, however, from examining videotapes (and no, the tapes weren't "doctored"), that tear gas projectiles hadn't been fired into the buildings. Tear gas had been "pumped" — not "shot" — into the buildings. Therefore, the Davidians — especially Koresh — were blamed for the inferno. They were the ones who started the fire. It was a mass suicide, similar to the one at Jonestown, Guyana, in late 1978 (in which over 900 died).

Many didn't accept that, of course — and still don't. They insist that the agents were/are to blame, at least in the sense that, while the Davidians might have indeed started the holocaust — while it indeed might've been a mass suicide — it was "caused" by the agents because, if they hadn't attacked the compound, the Davidians wouldn't have been "forced" to start the fire — if they did indeed really start it; if it wasn't really started by agent-fired tear gas projectiles.

Well, to set the record straight: The fire wasn't started by tear gas projectiles fired by the attacking agents — nor was it started by the Davidians.

Yes...the council is responsible for the horrendous blaze (four radio-controlled incendiary devices that were planted in the compound by council agents almost a month before the February raid). The council, in fact, is responsible for the "entire" affair. "Everything" — Koresh stockpiling weapons, his increasing "craziness" (we were controlling his mind in exactly the same manner we controlled Hitler's mind), the inept raid in February..."everything" — was orchestrated by the council (and, after putting together such events as World War Two, the *Cold War*, the *Cuban Missile Crisis*, the Vietnam conflict, etc., etc., it wasn't difficult at all).

And why?

So that two years later — "exactly" (April 19) — a huge truck bomb would go off in front of the Alfred P. Murrah Federal Building in Oklahoma City, killing and maiming as many "innocent" people as possible (the death toll, at last count, is 168, with many more injured, to one degree or another).

Yes...the council is responsible for the horrific Oklahoma City bombing. And why?

Simple...to make it appear that the bombing was done in retaliation for what happened at the Branch Davidian compound, and that those responsible are part of the "new patriotic movement." (That's why the Oklahoma City bombing happened when it did. The holocaust at the Branch Davidian compound occurred on April 19 and the Battle of Lexington, which began the American Revolutionary War, took place in 1775 on April 19 — all very symbolic; the "new patriotic movement" was declaring war on the American government on the 200th anniversary of the Battle of Lexington, and the second anniversary of the attack on the Branch Davidian compound.)

Or, put another way: The Oklahoma City bombing is — should the need arise — a "Pearl Harbor" of all these groups/individuals (although other actions are planned, such as more bombing of government buildings, sabotaging planes and trains, and political assassinations), in exactly the same way the bombing of the World Trade Center (which killed 6) in New York City on 26 February 1993 (yes, the council is also responsible for that) is a "Pearl Harbor" for the world's fundamentalist Moslems (although should the council undertake a "major" action against these groups, it'd probably stage a much larger "Pearl Harbor," such as a plane filled with 5 or 6 tons of explosives being inserted into the White House by a suicide-pilot or remote-control).

Yes, yes...it all sounds terrible — "beyond" terrible. But, one way or another, "the people" of the world are eventually going to "have" to change. And it appears that there simply isn't any easy way of making that change happen.

For example, even if the council takes overt global control without first collapsing the world's economic/social system and stepping back for a number of years and letting the world go through a lengthy period of great upheaval — and even if "all" the world's people accept that control and cooperate with the council — there'll still be, to one degree or another, a "collapse" of the world's economic/social system as it's presently known. And that collapse will be "extremely" difficult for "many."

It seems it simply can't be avoided.

~

The council has spent innumerable hours studying and discussing the impact of the council taking overt global control without first collapsing the world's economic/social system and stepping back for a number of years.

And we've concluded that it's simply "impossible" to conduct such an action without "major" damage being done to the existing global economic/social system — especially in the highly-developed countries, such as America, Canada, Great Britain, France, Germany, Japan, etc. — even if "everyone" accepts our control and cooperates with us (which is so highly unlikely that it's not really worth even considering — not even for a moment; there's simply too much stupidity in existence).

Consider the global armaments industry, for example. Since there wouldn't be "any" major conflicts and /or arms race in the council's new society, the world's armaments industry would be slashed by at least 90% — which, of course, would mean a "major" job loss — more major than most realize, since most don't seem to understand much about economics/employment. Many, for instance, will scream at government to cut spending, then, when government does cut spending, they scream because they suddenly find themselves unemployed — even though they weren't employed by government. They didn't understand the "ripple effect" of unemployment.

Take government spending on military, for example. Many who don't work in the military/armaments industry will insist that government should cut military spending because, as previously mentioned, they feel it's a "waste" of money. However, as also previously mentioned, spending on military/armaments "isn't" a waste of money because it creates jobs — and taxpayers/consumers — which, in turn, creates more jobs, taxpayers/consumers, and so on and so on...

Or examine it from a "tighter" perspective. There's a small city somewhere in America — let's call it "Boomtown" — with a population of twenty thousand. The main employer of Boomtown is "Boom Inc.", a factory that manufactures artillery shells, bombs, and various other high explosive military ordnance. Boom Inc. employs three thousand Boomtowners, and Boomtown's unemployment rate is 2%, five points lower than the national rate of 7%.

Suddenly, it's announced that the world is now under council control and, effective immediately, the global armaments industry is being cut by 90%. Overnight, employees at Boom Inc. drop from three thousand to three hundred — a loss of 2,700 jobs — and Boomtown's unemployment rate promptly jumps from 2% to a staggering 29%.

But it doesn't end there. The unemployment begins spreading, or "rippling," like when a stone is thrown into a pond. Other businesses in Boomtown — food stores, department stores, furniture stores, appliance stores, hardware stores, restaurants, clothing stores, car dealerships, etc., etc. — begin experiencing a sharp drop in revenue and are forced to issue layoffs as former Boom Inc. workers are forced to cut their spending. Within six months, 600 more workers are unemployed and the unemployment rate has risen to 35%. And because Boom Inc. has to cut its tax payments to Boomtown by 90%, the city has to issue layoffs to many of its workers — let's say 300 — bringing the unemployment rate to an unbelievable 38%.

And the unemployment ripples spread from Boomtown to other parts of the country. Boom Inc., for instance, imports various metals and explosives/propellants in the manufacture of its products. But, since it now only needs 10% of what it previously needed, companies supplying Boom Inc. with those metals and explosives/propellants find themselves having to lay workers off. And companies supplying raw materials to the metal and explosive/propellant companies also find themselves having to lay workers off as a direct result of the 90% cutback at Boom Inc. And companies supplying the metal, wood, and cardboard that Boom Inc. uses in the packaging of its products also find themselves sending workers to the unemployment ranks. And transport companies that ship Boom Inc. products around the world — as well as shipping the raw materials and processed raw materials used in Boom Inc. products — have to lay workers off. And on and on and on...according to Seat Four, within just one year of the 2,700 workers losing their jobs at Boom Inc., about 5,400 more workers will lose jobs as a direct result of that action — a total of 8,100 jobs lost.

And, using Seat Four's calculations, on a global scale, that number is multiplied by three thousand, which means that approximately 24,300,000 world-wide will lose jobs within one year following a 90% cut in the global armaments industry (although Seat Four says it could be closer to thirty million). And in the year following, the number could go as high as 50 million — and by the end of the third year, one hundred million could be unemployed.

There are those who'll glibly say that the solution to the problem is simple, simple, simple...just switch from manufacturing armaments to manufacturing non-armament goods. Instead of manufacturing military aircraft, for instance, manufacture non-military aircraft. Simple, simple, simple... But it just isn't that simple. Certainly, some armament manufacturing can be replaced by non-armament manufacturing. However, those who believe it's simple to switch from manufacturing armaments to manufacturing non-armament products and, at the same time, keeping the same number of people employed, don't seem to realize (or don't "want" to realize; or don't want to "admit" they realize — perhaps for "image" reasons; they don't want to appear as though they endorse the making of weapons) that there are some "major" differences between armaments and non-armament products.

Non-military aircraft, for example — or "non-combat" military aircraft, to be precise — don't need the high-performance engines and handling capabilities needed by combat aircraft. Nor do they need the sophisticated avionics required by combat aircraft (such as radar guidance systems for air-to-air missiles and radar to detect enemy radar lock-on). Nor, of course, do they need the weapons needed by combat aircraft — and equipping a combat aircraft with a complete array of weapons — and keeping it well-equipped — can "easily" be more expensive than the cost of the basic aircraft.

Consider a modern multirole combat aircraft, for instance. It's designed to function as both an air-to-air fighter and a ground-attack fighter. Consequently, it needs a large assortment of weapons.

First, it needs a cannon, or cannons, that can be used for both air-to-air combat and attacking ground targets (which means that at least two different types of ammunition will be needed). Then it needs at least two varieties of air-to-air missiles — short and medium-range — but to be "really" complete, it should also have long-range missiles. Then it needs air-to-surface guided missiles of various sizes and ranges, as well as unguided air-to-surface rockets of various sizes and ranges (although most unguided rockets are classified as "short-range"). It then needs bombs... high explosive general purpose bombs, "retarded" bombs, "smart" bombs, incendiary bombs, cluster bombs, anti-concrete bombs, fuel-air bombs, napalm bombs...bombs for every conceivable problem.

Therefore, after all the necessary weapons have been purchased, the cost of the aircraft might have "easily" tripled, say, from $30 million to $90 million. This might sound highly exaggerated, but consider that just one short-range air-to-air missile might cost $500,000 or more, a medium-range might be a $1,000,000 or more, and a long-range might be $1,500,000 or more (much depends on the quantity being purchased). As well, there are spare parts to consider. Combat aircraft need a good supply of spare parts — especially "complete" units, such as complete engines — because under combat conditions there simply isn't the time to order parts or do lengthy repairs.

There's an even bigger problem, however, as concerns switching from manufacturing armaments to manufacturing non-armament products: The world simply doesn't need anymore manufactured goods of "any" kind. Humans need them (or, more accurately in most cases, "want" them). But Earth doesn't "need," or "want," them. In fact, not only doesn't Earth need/want anymore machines, tools, buildings, bridges, dams, power lines, power plants, rail lines, highways, etc., etc., it also doesn't need/want anymore humans — in fact, it doesn't need/want humans at all.

Many humans, however, don't seem to realize this. They believe Earth "needs" them — that they're actually "essential" to Earth's survival — like those who arrogantly say things like: "The world was nothing before humans came along."

It boggles the mind (at least those of the council) how anyone (except for the very young and those with severe mental disorders, of course) can "think" like this — especially those who've gone to schools and are supposedly "educated/intelligent" — because it's obvious that Earth wasn't a "nothing" before humans arrived. It was very much a "something," and the notion that humans have "improved" Earth — in "any" way — is ludicrous beyond belief. It's like saying fleas or cockroaches or rats have improved the human species.

Even more ludicrous, however (if that's really possible) — and arrogant beyond belief — is when these people say: "All human life is priceless." This is perhaps the most foul-smelling piece of crap in the cesspool of human stupidity since, in saying that "all" human life is priceless, one is actually saying that no one is worth anything. Someone who's devoting his/her life to helping people, for example, isn't worth "any" more than someone who's devoting his/her life to hurting and/or destroying people. Or, put another way: When one says that "all" human life is priceless, one is also saying that "good" and "bad" have equal value. And, ironically, all those who utter such garbage as, "all human life is priceless," are often the same ones who are constantly complaining about "moral degeneration." It's no wonder there's "moral degeneration" with so much stupidity clogging the brains of so many.

Some might argue that I'm taking the statement, "all human life is priceless," too literally. But I'm not, since the statement is an "absolute." There isn't "any" room for "interpretation." It'd be different if it was, "some human life

67

is priceless," or, "most human life is priceless." But it's "all" human life is priceless.

Although, even if it was that "most," or just "some," human life is priceless, it still wouldn't be correct because no single human life is "priceless." Human life — "every" human life — has some kind of value. A doctor, for instance — let's say, just a general practitioner — has a higher value than a professional athlete. Or a medical researcher who's trying to find a cure for a deadly disease is worth more than a fashion designer, or fashion model.

And if people would only realize this, and/or, more importantly, "accept" it, as well as realizing/accepting the "fact" that humans need Earth, but not vice versa, things would be so much better. Or perhaps "easier" is the more appropriate word since, no matter how it's done, and even if there's a "high" level of realization/acceptance, as I've already said, the formation of the council's new society will be an "enormous" shock to "many," especially those in the world's highly-developed countries, such as America, Canada, Great Britain, France, Germany, Japan, etc., because the council will be "deindustrializing" the world.

I previously mentioned how the world's armaments industry will be cut by at least 90% — well, that's just the beginning. "All" industry will be severely slashed (with the exception of the food and medical industries, of course). For example, "all" aircraft production — not just military combat aircraft — will be cut by 90%, as will production of "all" types of motorized transportation, and fossil fuel production will also be cut by 90%. And the manufacture of most other goods — especially "luxury" items, such as hair dryers, CD players, video games, etc. — will also be cut by about 90%, and in some cases — video games, for example — the cut will be 100%.

As well, there'll also be "drastic" cuts in electricity production. We don't know exactly how drastic, but electricity produced by fossil fuels and nuclear powerplants will be cut by about 90%. And there'll also be "strict" regulations regarding the use of electricity and fossil fuels. It'll be illegal, for example, to use gas or electric lawnmowers.

"But you can't do all this! You simply can't "deindustrialize" the world and put hundreds of millions out of work just like that! You just can't do it!"

Yes...we can hear all the outraged people — billions of them — yelling and screaming that the council can't do this or that. The "fact," however, is that the council "can" indeed do this or that. The council can do "anything" it desires — even destroy the entire human species — and there isn't "anyone" or "anything" in the world that can stop us.

Many, simply unable to comprehend and/or accept that such absolute power exists — or they haven't been listening carefully — will undoubtedly say things like: "But the American military — even if it is the only military with nuclear weapons — can't possibly defeat all the other armed forces in the world if they all joined together into one huge army." Or: "But the American military — even if it is the only military with nuclear weapons — can't possibly defeat all the world's non-American armed forces "and" all "the people" of the world if they all joined together into one huge army."

Consequently, I'll say it again: The council doesn't just control the American military. It controls "all" the world's armed forces. One command from the council can put "every" country in the world under "martial law" — and "the people" of the world wouldn't be able to do anything about it.

Oh, certainly, they can take to the streets in great numbers and demonstrate and riot — throw rocks, break

69

windows, overturn cars, throw gas bombs, burn buildings and cars — and they can even pick up guns and stage an armed revolt. But, no matter their numbers, they simply won't win. It's an "impossibility." The days of revolutions of "the people"— at least, "successful" revolutions — are over. In fact, they have been for many years — ever since the council took control of the world following World War Two.

Some might argue that this simply isn't true, that since the end of the war there have indeed been "successful" revolutions of "the people," such as the revolutions in Iran and Nicaragua in the late seventies, and the revolutions in the Philippines and Romania in the late eighties.

And yes indeed, those revolutions certainly were successful. No question about it, "the people" definitely did triumph. Their success, however, wasn't due to their revolutionary fervor and/or sacrifice and/or numbers. They won because the council wanted them to win, just like it wanted Castro to win in Cuba in the late fifties. Had the council desired, "all" these revolutions would've failed. In fact, they wouldn't have even started.

Therefore, the quicker "the people" of the world abandon "any" thought of a revolution of "the people" against those in power, the better. Or, put another way: The sooner "the people" face reality — and accept it — the better. The only ones who'll lose in a revolution of "the people" will be them, "the people." And no amount of revolutionary "POWER TO THE PEOPLE!" "DOWN WITH THE ESTABLISHMENT!" rhetoric and razzmatazz is going to change that. And perhaps they'll lose a "lot." Maybe they'll end up with another butcher like Hitler or Stalin or Mao. Or Pol Pot...yes, he mustn't be forgotten. He was, after all, actually a worse tyrant — taking into account the population of the country he ruled — than Hitler, Stalin, or Mao.

70

In April 1975, a communist guerrilla group called "Khmer Rouge" took over the Southeast Asian country of Cambodia.

They were led by Pol Pot, a man who had a vision of Cambodia becoming a great country based solely on the growing of huge amounts of rice (not a good idea, since basing a country's whole economy on just one agricultural crop is very dangerous; a disease, for example, could attack the crop and leave the country in a "terrible" mess).

Now, the council could've intervened. It knew of Pol Pot's crackpot idea, and could've stopped him — and we seriously considered it. We decided, however, to give him free reign and let him do "whatever" he wanted. It was a council "experiment," so to speak.

Pot began his great plan by having the towns and cities of Cambodia forcibly emptied, forcing the "New People" (those who'd been living in the towns and cities, and were therefore "contaminated" by "capitalism") into the country, where they had to work ("slave") eighteen or more hours a day, seven days a week, under the supervision of the "Old People" (those who'd been living in the country, and were therefore uncontaminated by capitalism).

Of course, many of the New People didn't even make it to the country because they were executed after being judged as being "undesirable"; they were too old and/or feeble; they'd been employed in a "capitalistic" profession, such as teacher, doctor, dentist, lawyer, etc.; they were too well-educated (a university degree of "any" kind — even one in agriculture — could be enough reason for execution); they'd been a former enemy soldier or government worker of "any" kind; they were the "offspring" of an undesirable, and were therefore too "tainted" for "reeducation"...

As well, many also didn't stay in the country for long

because they just couldn't take the hard labor (Pot believed that modern farming equipment — even if it was built in "communist" countries — was part of the "evils of capitalism") and/or the merciless treatment of the Old People, many of whom were, ironically, "young" people of 12-18, and were often the most vicious of the "Angka" (the Khmer Rouge command group).

They kept the New People under "strict" control, brutally executing many (usually after hideous torture) with bayonet and club for a wide variety of "serious" offences, such as not working hard enough; falling asleep during the day; asking too many questions; not answering questions quickly and/or "honestly" enough; playing "non-communist" music and singing or humming "non-communist" songs; eating "unauthorized" food (they were forced to live on a diet of rice gruel, and trying to supplement it, even with ants or worms, was forbidden — and punishable by death); having "forbidden" items, such as eyeglasses or false teeth (they were objects of "capitalism"); religious worship ("every" religion was illegal); having "unauthorized" sex (men and women, even if married, were kept separated, and permission was needed for any kind of sexual contact; a kiss could mean instant death)...it was a living hell that many view as having been "much" worse than Hitler's Germany or Stalin's Russia or Mao's China.

Consider the death toll. Between April 1975 and January 1979, more than a third of Cambodia's population of 8 million perished — about 2,700,000 people of all ages. (If the same thing happened in America, the death toll would be about 87 million; if it were to happen world-wide, the death toll would be about 1,850,000,000.)

Then, in early 1979, the council decided to end Pol Pot's "vision." It pulled the necessary strings and fighting erupted between the Khmer Rouge and their neighbors (and former allies) the communist Vietnamese, and the Vietnamese, having a much stronger military (courtesy of the council, who made sure America left huge amounts of weapons and ammunition behind when it withdrew its forces), invaded Cambodia and occupied it...but the Khmer Rouge nightmare didn't totally end for the Cambodian people because for many years the council allowed the Khmer Rouge (aided by China) to wage a guerrilla war against the Vietnamese, and any of their fellow Cambodians they felt were aiding the Vietnamese (and simply talking to a Vietnamese could be interpreted as "aiding").

And the nightmare still hasn't "really"ended because, even though Vietnam has pulled its troops out of Cambodia, and the United Nations (or the council, to be precise) has provided much stability in Cambodia, and the Khmer Rouge is only a pale ghost of its former self (especially after the recent death of Pol Pot), the many years of war and horror (especially Pol Pot's reign of terror) will affect, to one degree or another, many future generations of Cambodians (land mines, for instance, which were planted in the millions, will probably be crippling and/or killing people fifty or more years from now).

Of course, because of all the war and horror that has occurred globally during the past few thousand years, the same could be said regarding many future generations of all the world's people — and yes, it can definitely be argued that the council is every bit as "bad/evil" as any Pol Pot, Hitler, Stalin, Mao, etc — but it isn't. The council and its new society of the future can't, in "any" way, be compared to "any" of these monsters and their "new orders." As well, were it not for the council, the world would've been taken over by "the organization" — which would've been just as bad —

probably even worse — than the "new orders" of any of these butchers — even Pol Pot.

Fortunately, the council discovered the organization in time and was able to destroy it before it could destroy us and enslave the people of the world who, of course, never knew about the organization and its plans — although they did experience a part of the action.

It occurred on 22 November 1963 in Dallas, Texas, when the 35th President of the United States, John Fitzgerald Kennedy — or "JFK" as he was more popularly known — was assassinated.

~

Yes...the council was responsible for JFK's death —
even though he wasn't part of the organization.

There have been many theories about who killed
Kennedy, and why: it was the Soviets, because of the way
they were humiliated by America — by JFK, in particular —
during the *Cuban Missile Crisis*; it was Fidel Castro, because
of the American-backed — JFK-backed — *Bay of Pigs
Invasion*; it was a combined effort by Castro and the Soviets;
it was the Mafia, because of a Kennedy administration
crackdown on organized crime (especially since it was
strongly rumored that the Mafia had helped get Kennedy
elected in the first place); it was Cuban anti-communists,
because they believed JFK abandoned them during the *Bay of
Pigs Invasion*; it was a combined effort by Cuban anti-
communists and the Mafia; it was the Pentagon, because it
was feared Kennedy was going to end American involvement
in Vietnam, and since war was (and is) the Pentagon's
business, no Vietnam conflict (with America as a combatant,
not just a supplier of arms) would mean a "major" loss of
business; it was American arms manufacturers, for the same
reason as the Pentagon; it was a team effort by American arms
manufacturers and the Pentagon; it was the CIA, because it
was afraid that JFK was going to disband the agency after the
disastrous *Bay of Pigs Invasion* (the invaders, after all, had
been trained and supplied by the CIA); it was a group effort
by the CIA, the Pentagon, and the arms manufacturers; it was
a group effort by the CIA, the Pentagon, the arms

manufacturers, and the Mafia; it was a team effort by the CIA, the Pentagon, the arms manufacturers, the Mafia, and Cuban anti-communists; it was an American right- wing anti-Communist group, or groups, like the John Birch Society, the Minutemen, the Ku Klux Klan, etc., because they believed JFK was being too soft with communists — and doing far too much for black Americans; it was a group effort by American right- wing anti-communist groups, the CIA, the Pentagon, the arms manufacturers, the Mafia, and Cuban anti-communists; it was Lyndon B. Johnson (LBJ), JFK's vice-president, because he wanted to be president; it was some individual, or group, who wanted LBJ to be president; it was Richard Nixon, because he was mad about Kennedy beating him in the 1960 presidential election (by only a little over 100,000 votes); it was done, as the *Warren Commission* stated in its *Warren Report*, the "official" report on the assassination, by one Lee Harvy Oswald who had been "acting alone and without advice or assistance"...but none of these theories are even close to the truth.

And the truth is: About a year before the *Cuban Missile Crisis*, a number of people in high places — some in "very" high places (no names can be mentioned for security reasons) — accidentally gained "extremely" intimate knowledge of the council.

Consequently, they decided to overthrow the council and take control of the world — or, to be more precise, "enslave" the world, since their *New Global Order* was based on the belief that the white race is the superior race, with the "God-given right" to rule over "all" non-white races.

Their plan, like all good plans, was simple. They'd strike when the council was having a full-member meeting and kill us all, then simply take our place (which would've been quite easy, since no one on the council was known to the general public; we were — and are — generally speaking, "invisible").

They were then going to start a war — a nuclear war — between Russia and America (making it appear that Russia started it, of course). After nuking the Soviets into submission, the Chinese were going to be next (with the organization, of course, making it appear that China started it). Then, using the threat of nuclear annihilation, the organization was going to turn the world into a huge totalitarian state (and they were prepared to keep using nuclear weapons until they achieved their goal, no matter how many were killed — including Americans; they were fully prepared to nuke fellow Americans should they resist).

They, of course, would be at the top of the pyramid. Below them would be the rest of the white race (except for "undesirables," of course, such as anyone who didn't believe in the supremacy of the white race and/or wasn't Christian), then the yellow and red races (except for "undesirables," of course, such as those who weren't Christian, or wouldn't become Christian) — with the black race and the Jews...well, the organization intended to fulfill Hitler's dream of a world without Jews and blacks.

And this all could've easily become reality — it was a solid plan — except a member of the organization made a big mistake. He fell victim to one of the seven deadly sins: lust.

Yes, he met a beautiful — an "extremely" beautiful — woman, and fell madly in love with her — or at least he called it "love." As I've said, it was "lust," not "love." It was her voluptuous body and sexual skills he was in "love" with (her vaginal, oral, and anal skills were legendary; just one night with her — even just one hour — could turn a man's mind into mush).

77

Unfortunately for him, however — and fortunately for us — she was working for the council as a "troller" (someone who circulates in certain areas of society and trolls for information that might be valuable to the council, using beauty as bait and sex as the hook). (Of course, she didn't know she was working for the council; she thought she was simply working for the CIA — but it, of course, is controlled by us; although most CIA employees don't know "anything" about the council.)

And also unfortunately for him (and fortunately for us), he was also a victim of another of the seven deadly sins: pride.

Actually, it was really pride more than lust that sank him — and the organization. He simply couldn't refrain from boasting about the organization, and what it was going to do — although, to his credit, he didn't reveal everything he knew (which was also fortunate for our troller because the council would've had to eliminate her if she'd learned too much — which would've been a great loss, since her talents were extremely valuable). He didn't, for instance, reveal any of our names. Or that the *Cold War* and nuclear arms race were illusions. Or that the council was in total control of not just America, but the entire world. All he said was that there was a secret group controlling America, and that another group, of which he was part (a "big" part, naturally), was going to overthrow that group and take control of America, and he was going to be "unbelievably" rich and he'd be able to buy her anything she wanted — furs, diamonds, cars, mansions...anything!

After a few nights with her it was obvious that, despite her beauty and sexual skills, he wasn't going to reveal anything more. The council then decided it was time for him to spend a night or two with them.

To get some idea of what a night or two with the council might be like under such circumstances, imagine a visit to a dentist when one doesn't need any dental work and, after being securely strapped into the chair, the dentist begins using those wicked-looking instruments (particularly the "hand excavator" and the "explorer") and that horrible-sounding drill — without first administering any anesthetic...oh, yes, it's a horrifying experience, to say the least.

But dental instruments aren't the only tools used by Seat Thirteen, the council's interrogation expert (and a "master" when it comes to inflicting pain/discomfort; he knows "every" nerve in the body). He also uses electricity; sleep and food/water deprivation; ultra-bright lights; temperature extremes; fire (he often doesn't even have to light the blowtorch); water (a shower of boiling water — or even just the threat of one — can "dramatically" change a person's attitude); unpleasant noises (such as someone shrieking in pain as he/she is being burned or boiled or skinned alive) amplified to ear-splitting volume; drugs of all kinds — sleep inhibitors, sleep inducers, mind-scramblers, opiates, truth serums...whatever is needed; insects and reptiles (someone who's terrified of spiders and/or snakes, for example, is tied naked in a room and some spiders and/or snakes are released into the room); threatening loved ones — including children — including "babies" — with pain and/or mutilation and/or death...oh, yes, the council can get extremely nasty if it has to.

And I don't make any apologies for it. Sometimes we "need" to do "bad" things — especially when the very existence of the council is being threatened. Or, put another way: sometimes the ends "do" justify the means. It might be "wrong" — sometimes "very" wrong. But sometimes "wrong" things — "very"wrong things — "need" to be done in order to survive.

Seat Thirteen, however, usually doesn't have to do anything more than show some film footage to convince someone to cooperate with the council — and such was the case with this man from the organization.

First, Seat Thirteen questioned him — "politely" — about the group he belonged to. The man denied any knowledge of any such group. Seat Thirteen played him a portion of tape the council had recorded at the troller's apartment. The man claimed he was just trying to impress her, just trying to be a big shot.

Seat Thirteen then had the man connected to a polygraph machine. He failed miserably — but continued to insist that he didn't know anything about any group that was going to take control of America, that he was just talking big to impress the woman. Seat Thirteen then told him it was showtime.

The film, shot in Cuba in the late fifties, stars four members of Batista's secret police, four male Cuban citizens suspected of anti-government activity, and a number of surprise guest stars. It's a film of exceptional quality — excellent lighting, focus, and angles — and sound. The screams, shrieks, and moans of absolute agony are chilling beyond belief. It's been almost 40 years since I first (and last) heard them, but they're still reverberating in my brain with an appalling clarity. And the visual images are still as vivid — and terrible — as they were when I first saw them.

The 40- minute film is divided into four equal parts. In the first part, a naked man is stretched out on a large table, and is being given electric shocks through alligator clips attached to various parts of his body (ear/penis, nose/penis, lip/penis, tongue/penis).

In the second part, a naked man is tied on a vertical

rack made of steel bars, and is having his most sensitive areas worked over with an icepick and a blowtorch. In part three, a naked man is strapped to a metal chair that's bolted to the concrete floor. The seat of the chair has a large opening in it. Beneath the chair is an adjustable metal stand with a large vise mounted on it. The man's scrotum is clamped between the steel jaws of the vise. The secret police take turns working the vise handle, slowly bringing the jaws of the vise together until the scrotum — and everything in it — is totally destroyed.

And the fourth part of the film...well, it's in a class all its own. A naked man is stretched out horizontally in a wire mesh cage that resembles a large coffin. His body is slashed in a number of places — toes, legs, penis, stomach, fingers, arms, lips, nose, and ears — with a straight razor. The wounds are superficial, but produce quite a lot of blood.

The door of the cage is then lowered and locked. In the middle of the door — above the man's bleeding stomach — is an opening, about six inches by six inches.

Two secret police enter the room, carrying what looks like a stretcher with a large box on it. It's quickly revealed that the box is actually a cage constructed of fine wire mesh and the poles are carrying handles. The cage is set on the wire mesh coffin, directly over the square opening. The floor of the cage is a sliding plate that's held in place by a locking pin. One of the secret police removes the pin and pulls the handle attached to the sliding floor. As the floor slides out of the cage, the occupants of the cage — the surprise guest stars — three large ferocious rats that haven't eaten for a few days and are in a frenzy at the smell of fresh blood — tumble through the opening into the wire mesh coffin and...well, I don't really think I have to continue. It's obvious what's next going to happen is probably one of the most disgusting things a person

81

could ever witness. I vomited so hard after only watching for about a minute I thought I was going to have a heart attack, or, at the very least, rupture something — and I've got an "extremely" strong stomach.

The man from the organization only lasted about two minutes into the fourth part of the film before he started spewing — which was actually pretty good. Some haven't even been able to make it through the first part of the film without puking.

After being allowed to clean up and compose himself, the man happily confessed. He babbled everything: how it all began (the accidental discovery of some documents that shouldn't have been where they were); who first conceived the idea (a very famous American who, for security reasons, can't be named); the names of everyone in the organization and everything he knew about them (such as that a few of them loved traveling to certain foreign countries where one could find brothels that featured children, both female and male, as young as ten-years-old; and that another loved dressing up as a woman and taking it in the rear from the young men who were constantly around him);where they met; what they planned to do after killing the council...we actually had trouble shutting him up. He just didn't want to stop talking because he was certain that as soon as he ran out of things to tell us, we were going to feed him to a bunch of hungry rats. He actually even begged us to shoot him, or hang him, or club him to death, or poison him...anything but the rats!

The council, of course, wasn't interested in killing him. We wanted him alive. He'd become an agent working for us. Or, more accurately, he'd become our "slave" (the council isn't against slavery if someone "deserves" to become a slave) — and we made it clear that there wasn't "anywhere" in the world he could escape from us. And should he think about trying to escape from us by committing suicide...well, he had a mother, father, two brothers, a sister, a nephew, and two nieces; they could all become the main course at some future rat feast should he try, in "any" way, to escape from us (although we'd never take such a threat past the verbal stage — unless, of course, it was "absolutely" necessary; if a council member's life was in jeopardy, for instance, such a threat might indeed be carried out if it was the "only" way to save his life).

The council then went after the rest of the organization and, in a few months, it was completely neutralized — and not "one" person was killed, and very few were physically harmed. They were all "mentally" harmed, however. They were all forced, for instance, to watch Seat Thirteen's film. (Actually, they were forced to watch a number of films; Seat Thirteen had — and has — quite a large collection of films showing people dying the most hideous deaths imaginable — being eaten alive by rats, dogs, crocodiles, and alligators; being boiled, burned, and skinned alive...it's "totally" disgusting, but they've certainly proved to be a useful tool.) But what mentally harmed them more than anything was their sudden loss of power — and pride.

For the first time in their lives they found themselves being treated like lowly servants...no, like "slaves" — which the council felt was appropriate, since they'd intended to turn most of the world's people into slaves (not to mention what they'd planned for the world's Jews and blacks). They were, for example, forced to use toothbrushes to scrub shit-encrusted toilets, floors, and garbage cans in 90-degree heat (the stench was unbelievable!) — an "extremely" humiliating experience for people who'd never even had to do simple menial tasks, like taking out garbage, their entire lives. Yes, it was quite an education for them — especially for those who were given "special" education.

Those who had satisfied their cravings for child sex in foreign countries were, after going through the toothbrush ordeal, given the opportunity to experience what it felt like to be sexually exploited.

They were stripped naked and leather hoods with openings for eyes, nose, and mouth were locked over their heads. The hoods were for security reasons, not punishment. We didn't want them recognized, since they were, like the others in the organization, high-ranking — "very" high-ranking — government officials who, after being taught their lesson, would be resuming their governmental duties.

They were then locked in rooms and the keys were given to six men who'd been procured from the darkest corners of the criminal underworld. They were told that they could use the hooded men as sex slaves, but they couldn't kill them, or break any bones or teeth, or slash or puncture their flesh, or burn them — or remove the hoods — or try to find out their identities. Then, after the time limit expired (twelve hours), they'd each receive five thousand dollars — providing they'd kept their part of the deal, of course, and hadn't seriously hurt the two (except for their pride — and anuses, of course).

The two members of the organization then went through the most hellish twelve hours of their lives as they were repeatedly sodomized and forced to perform oral/genital and oral/anal sex (plus, one of them was defecated and urinated on, since he loved doing that to his child sex toys at the end of his sessions with them). After that, simply the word "children" would cause them to have painful flashbacks of those nightmarish twelve hours.

But what the hell does all this have to do with the

assassination of JFK? Where does it — if he wasn't part of the organization — fit into all this?

Simple...the council assassinated JFK to prove to those who'd been in the organization (and certain others in the world) just how powerful the council "really" was; it could assassinate the President of the United States in broad daylight in front of thousands — billions, if TV coverage (especially "reruns") is included — and get away with it.

Even more important, however — the council could do it in such a manner that "all" investigations into the assassination would point, in one way or another, to all those who'd been part of the organization. It would be the council's final punishment, so to speak. (And it would also be an important "experiment," in that valuable information regarding human behavior would be obtained by observing how "the people" of America — and the rest of the world — reacted to the assassination — especially if it was done in a way that would indicate that people in high places — "very" high places — were, to one degree or another, involved in either the assassination, or a cover-up conspiracy, or both. How many of "the people," for instance, would accept the *Warren Report* without any argument?)

And it worked perfectly (or "almost" perfectly; both JFK and his wife, Jackie, were supposed to die — it would've made the assassination "much" more shocking and tragic — but a faulty cartridge primer saved her; the crosshairs were on her, the trigger was squeezed, and the firing pin slammed into a dud primer — and there wasn't time for a second shot).

Consider the *Warren Report*, for instance. It, as stated earlier, was the "official" report on the assassination that was issued in 1964 by the *Warren Commission*, which was created a week following the assassination by Lyndon B. Johnson, who went from vice president to president following

Kennedy's death. It was headed by Earl Warren, the highly respected Chief Justice of the United States, and its other members were: Richard B. Russell; John Sherman Cooper; Hale Boggs; Gerald R. Ford; Allen W. Dulles; John J. McCloy.

Now, I'm not saying that LBJ or Earl Warren, or any member of the commission was, in "any" way, part of the organization. The "fact," however — as anyone who's studied the Kennedy assassination even a "little" will attest to (if they're being honest, that is) — is that the *Warren Report* emits a stench that could wake the dead.

Take, for example, the firearm that was supposedly used by Lee Harvey Oswald, the alleged assassin (I use the terms, "supposedly" and "alleged" because, despite the findings of the commission that Oswald, "acting alone and without advice or assistance," killed Kennedy, it's "never" been "proven").

It's an Italian-made Mannlicher-Carcano bolt-action 6.5 mm carbine of pre-World War One vintage (it's often referred to — as in the *Warren Report*, for instance — as a "rifle," but its short barrel — 18.75 inches — puts it into the "carbine" category), and it's definitely not the firearm one would want for the fast, precision shooting needed for hitting a target in a moving car.

For one thing, its bolt-action — even when clean and well-lubricated — is "slow." And for another, its recoil — because of its short barrel — is "harsh." It's totally absurd to believe that Oswald used the weapon to fire 3 accurate shots in 5.6 seconds at a moving target about 280 feet away...but, for the sake of argument, let's say the *Warren Report* is correct, and Lee Harvey Oswald did indeed, "acting alone and without advice or assistance," kill Kennedy. Let's, for a few moments, step into the shoes of Lee Harvey Oswald. And let's forget about Oswald's early history — except for the fact that, at one point in his life, he was a United States Marine — and get right to the assassination.

Alright, Lee Harvey Oswald, you've decided to kill the President of the United States because...oh, let's just say, you hate his guts.

You now need two things: a firearm and somewhere to shoot from. Now, the firearm isn't "any" problem because it's America 1963 and almost everyone in the country is within a few minutes from a well-stocked gun store, and there isn't "any" problem in purchasing one — especially long arms. Just pick one, pay for it, and walk away. Easy.

Finding somewhere to shoot from isn't nearly as easy, however. Even if you know that the president is coming to town on a certain date and will be traveling through town in a motorcade, you won't know the exact route because, to protect the president from people like you, the route is a "well-protected" secret. It's only revealed a short time before the president arrives, and by that time, the route has undergone an "extensive" security check, with any dangerous areas — such as open windows, or windows that can be opened — having been secured.

But you're "extremely" lucky Lee (that's what you should be called: "Lucky Lee") — or else you're psychic — because you don't have "any" trouble finding a spot. In fact, you don't even have to "find" one, since you've already got one. A month before Kennedy arrives in Dallas, you get a job at the Texas School Book Depository, which just happens to be on the route that Kennedy's motorcade will be taking — a remarkable "coincidence," to say the least — especially since there's a sixth-floor window in the building that's "perfect" for what you need. You couldn't get a better position. Amazing!

87

Now the weapon. You could simply go to a gun store in Dallas and buy an excellent rifle...but no, you're smarter than that. You get an address from a gun magazine and mail-order one from a company in Chicago. And you, a former-U.S. Marine, a man who is more than a little familiar with firearms, chooses to buy the cheapest piece of crap on the market ($18.95 — and that even includes a telescopic sight!). But perhaps you simply can't afford anything better (after all, you're only making $1.25 and hour at the depository, and you've got a wife to support) — or maybe you're just being economical?

Anyhow, it's time. The president lands in Dallas and you go to the sixth-floor of the depository. You slide up the window (the one that was somehow overlooked during the security check), then take the weapon from its hiding place, load it, and wait...and before long, the president's motorcade appears.

You work the bolt (sure, it's slow — but look at all the money you saved!) and chamber a round. You make sure the safety is off. The motorcade is coming closer, directly towards you.

You raise the weapon, using the windowsill as a rest, and look through the telescopic sight — and there he is! John Fitzgerald Kennedy, the 35th President of the United States of America, sitting in the open rear seat of a 1961 Lincoln Continental Limousine (and isn't that just perfect!?!; he decided at the last moment — with a little "advice" from a certain someone "very" close to him — to travel without using the clear, bullet-resistant bubbletop because, as the "advisor" so kindly pointed out, it would show the American people that their president isn't a coward). He's smiling and waving at the crowds lining the street. It's perfect beyond belief! He's moving directly towards you! You can't miss —

not even with that piece of junk! But you don't squeeze the trigger. Instead, you wait until his car has turned the corner under your position, then you train the scope at the back of his head, which is now moving away from you at a sharp angle. It's a terrible target compared to when he was moving up the street directly towards you...but, of course, you're Lucky Lee.

You squeeze the trigger — Bang! — the weapon's recoil is harsh. It slams back into your shoulder with the kick of an angry mule, throwing you off-balance as the barrel jumps into the air, taking it off-target. You work the bolt (the "slow" bolt), eject the spent casing, chamber another round, get your finger back on the trigger, get the barrel back on target, and — Bang! — the weapon slams back into your shoulder as the barrel again goes skyward and off-target. You again work the bolt (the "slow" bolt), eject the spent casing, chamber another round, get your finger back on the trigger, get the barrel back on target, and — Bang! — you fire the third and last round. You then leave the weapon right there by the window (with enough fingerprint evidence on it to "prove" that you were the shooter, of course) and leave the book depository, bursting with pride. You've done it! You've killed the President of the United States of America! And without "any" advice or assistance from "anyone"!

Yes, Lee, you did it! You're one hell of a shot! In fact, you're the best in the world because, in tests following the assassination — using a six-story shooting platform and a target in a car moving at the same speed the president's Lincoln was moving — no one could duplicate what you did — not even after they fixed the telescopic sight.

Yes, they needed to fix the sight because it was loose and therefore, "useless." A number of "official" reports have stated that this was indeed true. It was "officially" concluded, however, that it must have become that way "after" the shooting. You must have banged it or dropped it after you killed Kennedy. Or maybe a policeman dropped it or banged it on something? Anyhow, it was alright when you were using it.

It wasn't alright, however. The sight wasn't just "loose." It was actually improperly mounted (the council made certain of that). And...I could go on and on and on about this, but I've said enough. I'll just add that Lee Harvey Oswald was a poor peckerhead who believed that he was part of a plot to frame someone for the attempted assassination of Kennedy. And the members of the organization were all unlucky peckerheads who made a "major" mistake — although, they did bring up a very interesting — and disturbing — point.

When questioned about their idea of the white race being the superior race, they replied: "If the white race isn't the superior race, then why does it have all the power? Why is it at the top of the social/economic/military pyramid? Isn't it only fair to assume that the white race is, because it's at the top of that pyramid, the superior race? And isn't it also only fair to assume that, since God created everything, it's all part of God's plan that the white race be superior?"

~

It's been over thirty-five years since the council first heard those questions — and I must sadly admit that, despite countless hours of debate, we still haven't been able to come up with any "conclusive" answers.

This might make the council sound racist, but, even though it (including the sub-councils) is composed solely of white people, it isn't, in "any" way, racist. The reason there aren't any non-whites in the council is...well, because that's simply the way things have happened. There isn't "anything" racist about it.

Now, it'd be great if the council could give "nice," or "pleasing," answers to the questions: "No, it's not part of God's plan that the white race be superior; God created everyone equal."; "No, it isn't fair to assume that the white race is the superior race just because it's at the top of the social/economic/military pyramid, since no one race is superior to another race."; "The white race is at the top of the social/economic/military pyramid, not because it's "superior," but because it's more aggressive — and greedy — and luckier — than other races."

Unfortunately, however, we simply can't give such answers because it's just not that simple. We can say, for a "fact," that we know there are individuals who are "superior" — but that applies to "all" races, not just the white race.

And while everyone in the council would like to believe that no one race is superior to another, and that it's not part of God's plan (if there even is a "God" with any kind of "plan") that the white race be superior, the "fact" is: The white race is indeed at the top of the pyramid. There's absolutely "no" argument about that. And since it is, it definitely can be argued that the white race is indeed the superior race.

Many, of course, will argue that, yes, the white race is indeed at the top of the pyramid, but it got there by huge amounts of treachery, brutality, exploitation, oppression, etc., etc. — and yes, I've already admitted the truth of that. The white race is, in many ways, "terrible" — "beyond" terrible. It, however, is still at the top of the pyramid. It's still in a "superior" position — or, more accurately, "the" superior position. And, from a certain perspective, it doesn't matter how it got there. All that matters is that it's there — and that it stays there.

I know this might not sound "good." But before anyone condemns me, or the council, or the white race, in general, it should be clearly understood that those who originally created the council (of which I'm one) didn't have "any" thoughts, or dreams, or desires, of totally controlling the world. As I've said before, we were "forced" into it. And, as I've pointed out a number of times, had we not done what we did, the world would be "much" different today. For one thing, it wouldn't have as many races as it currently does, since the black race would've been "completely" eliminated — which brings up an interesting point.

The white race has treated the black race "terribly" at times — slavery is an excellent example — and it still does, to one degree or another, depending on the location. However, were it not for millions of the white race — those, for example, who fought against Hitler (including the council, of course) — there wouldn't be a black race today. Consequently, it's a "fact" that today's black race actually

92

owes it very existence to the white race.

Many blacks will undoubtedly be outraged by this because they've been brought up believing that white people — "all" white people — are "bad/evil." Or, more accurately, they've been "manipulated" into believing this by certain black "leaders." And these "leaders" have also been manipulated...no, not by the council — at least not "directly."

Shortly after World War Two, the council realized it had a major problem concerning black Americans: because whites had once enslaved blacks in America (an abomination that'll probably never be "totally" healed by any amount of time), black Americans, generally speaking, would never "totally" trust — or "forgive" — white Americans. They would "always" harbor, to one degree or another, a resentment — a "hatred" — for white Americans. And this would, of course, make dealing with them "extremely" difficult.

So what do we do? How was an all-white council going to control black Americans without it (or its figurehead government, to be precise) appearing to be racist?

The answer was: It couldn't. It was impossible. No matter what the council did, or didn't do, black Americans would still, in one way or another, be able to point at government (even if it contained a representative number of blacks) — and white Americans, in general — and scream, "Racial Discrimination!" There simply wasn't any way of avoiding it.

The council, however, had to do something...and what it finally decided was to establish a council (a "secret" council, of course) of black Americans who, following council orders, would assist it in controlling (yes, "manipulating" would probably be more accurate) "the people" of black America.

93

A big problem, however, was that, since none of the council was black and none of us had ever "really" personally known a black person (and talking to a black railway porter, shoeshiner, maid, etc., for a few minutes simply didn't count), we didn't "really" know what it was "really" like to be a black American — or, more precisely, an "average" black American; one of "the people" — although we felt that we had a pretty good idea of what it was like.

But we were...yes, I admit it...naive. We foolishly believed, for instance, that black Americans were, because of the way they'd suffered (and we suffering) at the hands of white Americans, a "united" people — in the sense that they had a common bond — a "togetherness" — that white Americans, for the most part, didn't have. More of a "family" togetherness, so to speak; for example, they often referred to each other — simply because they were black — as "brother" and "sister."

It was deceiving, however, as we soon discovered from the first members of the black council, BSSC ("Black Sub-Sub Council"). Yes, black Americans did have a "togetherness" because of skin pigmentation and the racial discrimination from whites that resulted from it. But as a race, however, they were "exactly" like all other races, in that they brutalized each other as much — even more, in some cases — as they were brutalized by other races.

They, for example, had been oppressed — and enslaved — and slaughtered — by white people. At the same time, however, they had also oppressed, enslaved (including selling fellow blacks to white slave traders), and slaughtered one another. For example, Chaka (often spelled, "Shaka"), the black man who founded the Zulu Empire in southern Africa in the early 1800s, ruled his fellow blacks "harshly," often instantly killing anyone who went — in "any" way — against his will. He didn't have any mercy and sometimes made people suffer — including members of his own tribe — for bizarre reasons. In 1827, for instance, when his mother died, his grief was so great that he had about 5,000 fellow Zulus, including "all" pregnant women and their husbands, slaughtered. He then ordered that no crops be planted for a year, and that all cows with calves be killed, so that the calves would experience the loss of a mother. Crazy? No doubt...but that doesn't alter the fact that he was a black person who treated fellow black "brothers" and "sisters" terribly. (And, of course, in more modern times, two excellent examples of blacks treating fellow blacks terribly can be found in Idi Amin's Uganda and the recent horror in Rwanda.)

Now, I'm not suggesting — in "any" way — that because blacks abuse fellow blacks, it justifies whites abusing blacks. There's absolutely "no" excuse for racism. Of course, it must be remembered that many blacks — but especially men — actually like, even love — racial discrimination because it allows them to blame all their problems on that discrimination. For example, a black man gets fired from a job, but it isn't his fault; he isn't lazy — he's the victim of racial discrimination. A black man steals, but it isn't his fault; racial discrimination is making him do it. Every problem in Negro society — poverty, alcoholism, illiteracy etc., etc. — is blamed on racial discrimination. And if whites argue that blacks are also responsible for their problems — or criticize blacks in "any" way — they'll be labeled as "racist."

And it was this attitude — plus the fact that there was indeed a lot of racial discrimination in America — that made the council's observation correct: No matter what the council did, or didn't do, black Americans would still be able to point at government (even if it contained a representative number of blacks) — and white Americans, in general — and scream,

95

"Racial Discrimination!" It was simply a no-win situation. The best we could do was form BSSC and hope for the best.

And, generally speaking, it's worked out quite well. Certain things have happened that we didn't approve of, such as the assassinations of Malcolm X and Martin Luther King Jr. (who were both killed by the BSSC — without first consulting the council — for political" reasons; much the same as we killed JFK for "political" reasons). For the most part, however, black Americans are "much" better off today than they were fifty years ago. Many will no doubt vehemently deny this, of course, but, as I've already said a number of times, there wouldn't even be any black Americans — or black people, in general — if it weren't for the council. We saved the race from "certain" extermination/extinction.

And if the council took overt control of the world, we could explain this to them — or at least "try"to. As early members of BSSC told us: There'll "always" be a large percentage of blacks who'll "never" believe "anything" whites say, as well as "never" accepting whites, no matter how "good" they might be, in a position of power over them — just the same as a large percentage of whites will "never" accept blacks, no matter how "good" they might be, in a position of power over them.

"Were positions reversed — if Negroes had the power — how would you white people feel?" early members of BSSC asked us (or, more accurately, asked members of the various sub-councils who were dealing with them since, for security reasons, no one on the main council has ever had any direct contact with any members of BSSC).

And, to be honest, we definitely wouldn't feel good about it. In fact, the thought horrifies us. But not because of their skin pigmentation per se. We simply don't believe that the white race, because of the way it's treated the black race (even though it also saved the black race from extinction), would fare very well if it was under the control of blacks who had the world's only nuclear arsenal — no matter how "good" the black leadership was. We'd simply "never" be able to trust them. Things might be alright for awhile, but chances are that someone would eventually start preaching against the "white devils," and before long, the white race would be heading for extinction....

Consider South Africa, for example. How many white South Africans would feel safe if Nelson Mandela was in control of South Africa's formidable arsenal?

Many in the world (of all races) believe that Mandela is some kind of saint, or messiah — and perhaps he's indeed both...I don't know. I do know, however, that he's a remarkable person — even if just for simply having survived over twenty-five years as a black man (a black "terrorist," to be precise) in a South African prison (although the council played a large role in his survival; his white jailers wanted to kill him — making it look like a suicide, or a "natural" death — but the council prevented it because we felt he might one day prove useful to us). But what if he had "real" power?

Many will undoubtedly argue that he does have "real" power. He is, after all, the President of South Africa. Which is true. He is indeed the President of South Africa. But (forgetting for a moment that he's being controlled by the council), despite being president, he doesn't have "real" power because he doesn't control the South African arsenal. And without military power, one simply doesn't have "real," or "maximum," power. (I'm not saying — or even trying to suggest — that Mandela would start slaughtering white South Africans if he had control of South Africa's arsenal. But if I was a white South African, and Mandela controlled the arsenal, I know I'd be "extremely" nervous; in fact, I'd get out of South Africa as quickly as possible.)

Many believe money is the maximum power. That's an illusion, however. Consider Japan, for instance. It's considered to be a powerful country because of its economic strength. But, while it is indeed economically powerful, it lacks military strength (and its mineral resources are still negligible, and it's still a small island nation that can easily be isolated). It has the military strength necessary to keep internal control. But if it's threatened by another country, it could be in "serious" trouble. For example, should America (forgetting for a moment that the council controls Japan's government/military/economics, and that there are already about 50,000 American troops stationed there) decide to invade and occupy Japan — or simply seize all its foreign assets and isolate it with a naval/air/communications blockade — all Japan's monetary wealth would be useless. Or should China decide to pay Japan back for all the atrocities Japan committed in China before and during World War Two — and America refused to aid Japan in any way — again, all Japan's monetary wealth would be useless.

There are many who believe that military forces — especially now that the *Cold War* is over (or so they think) — should be drastically cut back. Or even eliminated altogether, or turned into "environmental," or "green," forces, doing such things as planting trees and cleaning up oil spills, etc., instead of training for combat. And that people world-wide should all learn to "love and understand" one another and live together in peace.

These are wonderful notions...however, since humans are still basically the same emotionally and instinctually as they were thousands of years ago, they still need weapons and people skilled in their use to defend themselves from one another. And also for "control."

The idealistic belief that "all" people can learn to "love and understand" one another and live together in peace without any kind of police/military control is, well...idiotic (there's often a very fine line between idealism and idiocy) because, in "understanding" people, one will quickly learn — or "should" quickly learn (remember, humans, generally speaking, can't stand much reality — and many are just plain "stupid") — that many simply aren't interested in a "peaceful" world. They aren't interested in "loving" others (except in a sexual sense — which often doesn't have anything to do with "love"), or in being "loved" themselves (except, again, in a sexual sense). They're only interested in getting — and keeping — "power." And they'll do "anything" to get — and keep — that power.

Yes...I know many will say this sounds exactly like the council. Nothing could be further from the truth, however, since, as previously stated, those who started the council didn't have "any" desire to rule the world. We were "forced" into taking control of the world. And we're being "forced" to keep that control because, as I've said before, without us in control, the world will collapse into the bloodiest chaos in history. And once it begins, it'll be "extremely" difficult to stop — maybe even "impossible." It'd probably simply have to run its course, like an earthquake, or any other natural disaster.

Of course, this could happen even with the council in control. This might sound contradictory (how can such a thing happen if we're in "control"?). But it isn't because, while I use the term "control," I don't mean "total" control, since "total" control is "impossible." The council simply can't control "everything." It can't, for instance, control natural occurrences, such as natural disasters, or health problems, like unexpected heart attacks and strokes, or sudden attacks of mental illness. And sometimes the council loses control of something it's controlling — which can sometimes result in disaster.

AIDS, for instance, is one example — the best example (or "worst," depending on how one looks at it) — of such a loss of council control.

~

That's right...the council is responsible for the AIDS epidemic.

It accidentally occurred during — ironically — research into improving the human species.

Yes, I admit it...the council is involved in scientific research (and has been for many years; forty-five, to be precise) that uses humans in "exactly" the same way laboratory animals are used in scientific research. It simply can't be avoided because, as I earlier pointed out, in order to "really" study the human species — and improve it — humans "need" to be used in "exactly" the same way laboratory animals are used in research, since animals, no matter how humanlike they might be, are still only human "like"; they aren't "human."

I know "many" will "vehemently" condemn the council for this, screaming that it's "wrong," "evil," etc., etc. But before anyone lets their intellect be totally consumed by their emotions, they should first note that the great majority of the research subjects weren't even going to be born in the first place, since they were going to be aborted. And the rest have been those who've proven, to one degree or another, to be detrimental to society, such a rapists, killers, etc., etc.

And it should also be noted that this research is for the benefit of "all" humans, since the council isn't trying to create a super "race," such as Hitler dreamt of. It's working towards creating a super "species"; it wants "all" humans to be "super," in both mind and body.

Certainly, many have died during this research (over five hundred thousand, not counting all those who've succumbed to AIDS), and there's been much suffering, since some of the experiments have proven to be very painful. However, as terrible — "beyond" terrible — as it may sound, the knowledge gained from this research more than makes up for these deaths and suffering.

Scientists, for example, are working at creating a virus that'll make humans less aggressive. I don't know exactly how it's supposed to work because the scientific explanations of those doing the research is beyond me. But the basic idea is that the virus will somehow affect the part of the brain that's responsible for aggressive behavior (especially in an "offensive" sense) and act as a damper.

It's hoped that this "peace" virus — if it can indeed be produced — can one day be introduced into the general public — perhaps hidden in something like a measles vaccine, and perhaps also with the ability to be transmitted through the exchange of body fluids, such as blood, semen, and saliva. And that, as it spreads throughout the world, the human race will become much more peaceful — perhaps even "totally" peaceful. The council believes it's a long shot. But if it is indeed possible...just think of the benefits to the world!

Unfortunately, however, an accident early in this research is what caused the AIDS epidemic — which, of course, is beyond terrible. The good news, though, is that it appears that a drug has been discovered that'll prove to be effective against AIDS. It's the same drug — or, more accurately, a variation of the same drug — that was developed to cure cancer...yes, that's correct. A cure for cancer has been discovered!

It took council-financed scientists almost thirty years, over 170 million hours of work (not counting all the work done by computer), and over five hundred billion dollars — but they did it! (And yes, it should also be mentioned that over 300,000 people sacrificed their lives in the development of this miracle drug.)

And its effectiveness is unbelievable! Someone suffering from terminal cancer — say with just a few months to live — begins receiving injections of the drug, and within a few months the cancer has completely disappeared. And without any harmful side effects! It's amazing! And I'm speaking from personal experience, since the drug saved me from pancreatic cancer — "terminal" cancer — over eight years ago.

Sadly, however, there are a few problems with this drug. For one thing, it's "extremely" complicated to make and the current cost of just one dose is $1.2 million. And it can take as many as twenty doses for a complete treatment (mine took sixteen, costing almost $20 million).

But even if the cost was to drop dramatically, there still exists a "huge" moral/ethical problem, since one of the drug's key ingredients can only be found (so far) in human fetuses between the ages of twelve and twenty-four weeks. And it takes between six and fifteen fetuses (it depends on the age and size of the fetuses) to make just one dose.

Scientists are working hard to reduce the number of fetuses needed (as well as working hard to find a non-human fetus alternative).But even if the number can be significantly reduced — say, to even just one-quarter of a fetus per dose — or even just one-sixteenth or less — I'm certain that "many" ("most" would probably be more accurate) would still find it morally wrong (to the "extreme") to use fetuses (even if abortion is the alternative) in such a manner, no matter how many lives can be saved and/or how much suffering can be prevented.

And I can't say I blame them because there's definitely something abhorrent about using fetuses in such a manner — even if they are destined for abortion. And there's also definitely something abhorrent about abortion per se, since it does go, without question, against the "life force."

At the same time, however, when I was dying from cancer, I wanted so much to keep living that had one dose required a hundred — or a thousand — or ten thousand — or a hundred thousand — or a million — to die for its manufacture, I wouldn't have hesitated. I would've chosen my life over all theirs.

Yes, I know this sounds beyond terrible. But I'm simply being honest (and not even mentioning the fact that I was also a "guinea pig," risking what life I had left — perhaps a year — since the drug was still in an experimental stage and was by no means a "sure thing").

Of course, while many praise and encourage honesty — calling it a "virtue" — they'll quickly turn around and condemn someone for being honest if that honesty doesn't conform to their beliefs. For example, a man being honest, says he hates certain people because of their skin pigmentation. He'll be quickly condemned, and won't be praised, not even for a fraction of a second, for his honesty.

But, of course, this isn't surprising, since honesty is a "reality" and, as stated a few times before, humans, generally speaking, can't bear much reality — although, that's probably for the best, since it makes controlling them "much" easier, which, in turn, makes it easier for us to improve the human species — if it can indeed really be improved.

The council knows that it might prove impossible to improve the human species — or at least, improve it to any great degree — no matter what it does, or doesn't do.

But, being human, we won't quit trying — even if

104

some of our research does take a few tragic turns, such as what happened with the peace virus — and even if some of it does seem a little far-fetched and/or "bizarre," like our "alien" experiment.

It unofficially began on 3 July 1947, a few years before the council officially (but "unofficially" in a "public" sense, of course) began its research into improving the human species, when a top-secret council-financed aircraft crashed near Roswell, New Mexico, and rumors began circulating that it was an alien spacecraft.

The council began talking about the possible existence of beings from other planets, and what those beings — if they actually existed — would think about the human species.

The question intrigued us, and became a frequent topic of conversation over the next few years. Then shortly after the council officially began its research program, Seat Three suggested that the council create some "aliens," who'd be sent to Earth to study the human species and report their findings back to their home planet.

This would, Seat Three explained, give the council a whole new perspective on the human species, which could prove to be invaluable. He was quick to point out, however, that no matter how the council did it — no matter how successful the council was at creating the "aliens" — the experiment would, to one degree or another, be "tainted," since, no matter what was done, the "aliens" would still be humans with human brains. And those brains, no matter how much they were "conditioned," would still retain the human "life force," and would naturally — "instinctually" — be inclined to present some kind of favorable impression of the human species — even though they might find it repugnant as a whole.

An "alien," for example, might find the human species

to be, generally speaking, a "worthless" life-form, yet, at the same time, also find that certain humans were much less worthless than others — therefore concluding that, while many humans should be eliminated, the entire human species shouldn't be eliminated. Or, put another way: While the human brain is capable of creating/committing horrendous acts, such as huge wars and the genocide of millions, it's highly unlikely (although Seat Three was certain that there were probably a few exceptions) that it's capable of putting into effect a plan that would intentionally destroy the entire human species.

However, as long as this knowledge was factored into the experiment, the experiment could prove very useful in providing the council with some — maybe "many" — answers to the many problems confronting the human species.

The idea interested everyone in the council. There was, however, much skepticism — especially as concerned the "creation" of "aliens." Exactly how could "aliens" be "created"?

Seat Three explained that the council would establish ultra-secret laboratories in remote regions in various parts of the world. These facilities would "officially" be for the study of infectious diseases (although they wouldn't, of course, really be "official" since, because they'd be ultra-secret, they wouldn't even exist in any kind of "official" sense), and would be placed under the tightest possible security (which, of course, because the council was in "total" control of the world, would be "tight").

The council would then acquire — or "buy" — babies of different races from women who were planning on giving them up for adoption after birth, or who were planning on having abortions. These babies would then be taken to the facilities where they'd be raised as "aliens."

They'd grow up in underground chambers in the facilities, believing they were traveling to Earth on a spacecraft to study that planet, of which little was known — except that it appeared to be very similar to their home planet and that its most important inhabitants appeared to be very similar to themselves.

They'd be told that, for their safety, and the safety of their mission (which, it would be "strongly" emphasized, was "much" more important than they were), they weren't being taught their own language. Instead, they were being schooled in the most important Earth language: English. (This would also eliminate the problem of having to create a new language.)

They would, however, be extensively educated about their home planet — "Nevaeh" — which, by human standards, would be "perfect." It'd be composed of one country with one language and culture, and one religion — or "spiritual force" — DOG (short for "Directions Of God") — which would be an unwritten code of life/living orally passed from generation to generation (and would also make political parties unnecessary).

It would be the nucleus of the society — and the reason for its perfection. There wouldn't, for instance, be "any" violence, hatred, racism, greed, dishonesty, poverty, or environmental destruction. Nor any problem of overpopulation, since reproduction would be "strictly" controlled, taking place only through artificial insemination (which would also eliminate all sexually transmitted diseases) — and only those with the proper genetic qualities would be allowed to take part in the process, with those not allowed to reproduce being sterilized and given a drug — a "vaccination" — that would kill all sexual urges. They'd "never" have "any" lustful thoughts.

And there also wouldn't be any problems of alcoholism or drug addiction, since alcohol and drugs would be banned (except, of course, for "official" drugs, which would be extensively used to not only curb lustful thoughts, but too also help keep the population emotionally and "spiritually" stable; but, of course, they'd be called "vaccines," or "vitamins," in order to keep away from the negativity of the word "drugs" that they'd find on Earth).

Nor would there be "any" crime, since no one would have "any" desire or need (partially because of drugs — but mainly because of *DOG*) to do anything anti-social — and there also wouldn't be any anti-social behavior recorded in history books.

Of course, there wouldn't be "any" history books; there'd only be *DOG*, in which the past would be "exactly" the same as the "perfect" present. And there also wouldn't be books of "any" kind — or art, film, music, etc. — containing "any" kind of anti-social behavior, such as violence, hate, racism, sexism, lust, lying, cheating, stealing, cruelty, anger, greed, jealousy, drinking alcohol, taking "non-official" drugs, smoking anything...yes, Nevaeh would definitely be a totalitarian world of the strictest sort — and many might wonder how I can call such a society "perfect."

Well, it isn't totalitarian in a "bad" sense, since there isn't any "oppression." No one is "forced" to do anything. Everyone does what they do because it's the "right" thing to do. It's what makes the society "good." It's what makes the society "perfect." And besides, they don't know anything else, since their past is "perfect."

Also, compared to our present global society, such a society is, beyond a doubt, "perfect." Certainly, it's a system that denies personal freedom, and many believe such a system is "bad" — that only a "democratic" system, with much personal freedom, is "good." This thinking is seriously flawed, however. (And it should also be noted that the "good" and "bad" of a governmental system depends on "perspective." People being oppressed, for instance, will say that the system oppressing them is "bad," yet, should they overthrow that system and establish their own government, they'll insist that their system is "good," no matter how cruel/unjust/oppressive it becomes.)

The truth is — the "reality" is — that a democratic system isn't really "good" because "the people," generally speaking, aren't competent enough — or "smart" enough, if you will — to "properly" manage their lives in a "collective" sense. Hell, many can't even properly manage their lives in a "family" and/or "individual" sense.

Or, put another way: It's foolish to believe democracy is "good"simply because it's the rule of the majority since, because intelligence isn't necessarily cumulative, the majority can have the collective intelligence, or simple "common sense," of a maggot. A million people, for example, each with an IQ of 100, won't have a collective IQ of a hundred million. In fact, because of the number of people involved, chances are they won't even have a collective IQ of 100; it'll probably be more like 90, or 80 or 70, or 60, or even lower — maybe "much" lower.

They could also, of course, have a very high collective IQ — but "all" evidence "clearly" indicates this to be an "extreme" rarity. For instance, simply that fact that so many believe that democracy "really" exists "clearly" shows a "huge" lack of collective intelligence since, after all, democracy doesn't "really" exist.

It's an "illusion" since, as I earlier pointed out, as Orwell wrote in *1984*, there have only been three kinds of people in the world — High, Middle, Low — and no matter what's happened (wars, revolutions, etc.), that basic social structure has "never" changed — and it "never" will. There'll "always" be a High, Middle, Low — even in a totalitarian system — in the sense that the lower half of the High are the Middle.

And if people — "the people" — would only accept this "fact" and let the High — yes, us, the council — run the world without trying to oppose us, they — and Earth itself — would, generally speaking, be "much" better off...yes, it could become "perfect" on Earth — or, at least, "much" better than it is. (As I've said before, concerning Earth and humans, Earth can't ever "really" be "perfect," since humans aren't — and probably never will be — "perfect.")

Although, of course, as previously mentioned, the problem, or "danger," of the council openly running the world is that someone like a Hitler might somehow overthrow the council, get control of the nuclear arsenal, and turn Earth into a hell for billions. Or perhaps it'd be more accurate to say, a "bigger" hell, since Earth is already, to one degree or another, a "hell" for " many" — which, of course, "greatly" distresses the council. It simply can't be helped, however, as long as the council is forced to operate covertly — or, more accurately, "chooses" to operate covertly, since if it wanted it could begin operating overtly.

Of course, even if it did begin operating overtly, it still wouldn't "really" be overtly, since it wouldn't "directly" expose itself to "the people." It'd simply be too dangerous. It'd have to operate through others, just as it does now — except "the people" would be told about its existence and it's plans for the future — to a certain degree, anyhow. The council simply wouldn't be able to reveal "everything" to "the people."

They wouldn't, for example, be given "any" details

about the council's activities during the past sixty years —
which, in a way, is a shame, because it's definitely one of the
most — if not "the" most — interesting periods in history.

And the most interesting single part of that period has
been, in my opinion, the "alien" experiment, or, as it became
known: *Operation Nevaeh.*

And it's also one of the most difficult
experiments/operations ever conducted by the council. In fact,
at times it's been so difficult we almost terminated it,
reasoning that it wasn't really an "essential"
experiment/operation — such as being the first to get the
atomic bomb — so it wouldn't really matter if we went ahead
with it or not. Fortunately, however, we decided that, while it
indeed might not be "essential," *Operation Nevaeh* was
"extremely" important — therefore we kept it alive.

At first there weren't any problems — or, at least,
"major" problems (every operation has "problems" of one sort
or another; weather, for instance — especially bad weather —
can prove to be a huge problem, as can natural disasters and
diseases).

Building the facilities and turning them into
"spacecraft" went quite smoothly. Seat Two was in charge of
creating the "spacecraft," which, generally speaking, were
nothing more than simple illusions created by Hollywood-
type sets and props, including "cockpits," where one could
view the "space" the "spacecraft" was hurtling through. The
"space," of course, was simply film taken by a high-flying jet
fighter during a night flight and "doctored" a little, and was
only run when the "aliens" made their single visit to the
"cockpit" of the "spacecraft" they were on.

It was all very impressive — and "extremely"
convincing — especially to the "aliens." But, of course, Seat
Two was — and is — an expert at "convincing." He's a

master illusionist (or "magician," as many would call him). He's the one who created the facilities to manufacture all the fake nuclear weapons that've been — and are still being — "manufactured." And he did it so skillfully the people working on the "weapons" believed — and believe — they're actually making "real" weapons.

Of course, in a sense, they are making "real" weapons, in that the components are indeed "real." They just never get "totally" put together — although it " appears" they do. Seat Two devised an ingenious scheme of switching workers from position to position, and shift to shift, and facility to facility, so no one (except for the council, of course) ever really knows "exactly" what's going on. For example, today worker A installs a switch, and tomorrow worker B removes it, and the following day worker C installs it again — and so on and so on and so on...in reality, the workers aren't really doing anything except putting on a performance — except, of course, they don't realize it (or if some do — or have some suspicion — they've kept silent about it because, after all, they're subject to the "highest" security; one wrong word and a person can suddenly find themselves in...well, let's just say, "beyond" trouble).

And staffing the facilities also went quite smoothly, as did acquiring babies. In fact, they were as easy to get as bread in a bakery. There was, however, a problem getting "quality" babies — ones that were in "perfect" health.

As well, there was the problem of perfect babies becoming flawed as they grew. One female, for instance, was a perfect baby who grew into a perfect child, but shortly before her sixth birthday she developed an inoperable brain tumor and was dead three months later. It was heartbreaking, putting all that energy into raising her (and she showed such "enormous" potential), only to have her suddenly die like that.

Even more heart-breaking, though, were those who became flawed in their teens, after "much" energy had been put into their development. One male, for example, was a perfect baby, grew into a perfect child, then into a perfect teenager — showing "tremendous" potential — but in his eighteenth year, a blood vessel burst in his brain, resulting in major — and permanent — brain damage.

Then there were the accidents. One sixteen-year-old male, for instance, tripped and fell down a flight of stairs — only six damn stairs! — and broke his neck and died. Hell, I've fallen down flights of twenty, thirty stairs — and been thrown off horses a few dozen times — and been in two serious car accidents — and one serious plane crash — and I've never been seriously hurt. Lots of bruises and a few broken bones — but nothing serious. He falls down six stairs and dies!

However, "the" major problem was in "creating" the "aliens." At first it sounded quite simple, like creating soldiers, or football players, or politicians...but it wasn't simple. It proved to be an "extremely" difficult task.

~

$\mathfrak{T}$he first major difficulty was creating *DOG*, the spiritual force and nucleus of Nevaehen society.

The council quickly decided that *DOG* should be as short as possible, since it felt that one of the main problems with Earth religions was that their scriptures were "much" too long. The Bible, for instance, was about 750,000 mindnumbing words. The council wanted something that was...say, maybe a few hundred words, or less.

As well, the council felt that *DOG* should be as simple as possible, since it also believed that another big problem with Earth religions was that they were "much" too complicated for "average" humans to "really" understand — although it also realized that humans, generally speaking, were superstitious beings (including many who were "well-educated") who were greatly impressed by things — especially of a religious/spiritual nature — that were complicated and filled with mystery and ceremony (especially ceremony; humans, generally speaking, love "ceremony" — and "tradition").

Of course, the "aliens" weren't "human." They were "aliens" from Nevaeh, a planet many light-years from Earth. Therefore, not having anything to compare with, their religion/spiritual force could (and "should") be short and sweet, like, for instance, Einstein's simple equation, "E=mc2" (which, of course, is the basis for nuclear power).

We did discuss having Nevaeh and its people being completely secular, but quickly realized that such a state is impossible for the human mind (and the "aliens" were, after all — no matter how much they were conditioned — still "human"). It "needs" some kind of "religion," or "spiritual force" — some "reason" for "being" — some reason for continued existence — and no human mind is exempt (except perhaps for those suffering serious brain damage of one kind or another).

But "exactly" what would *DOG* say? And, even more importantly, "exactly" how could the council say it? What words could it use?

How could the "aliens," or "cadets," as they quickly became known, be taught about *DOG* — and Nevaehen society, in general — using the English language — or any other Earth language? Or, put another way: How could the council teach the cadets about a perfect society by using a language from a flawed society?

Take the word "peace," for example. How did one explain "peace" without also explaining the opposite of peace? Remember, Nevaeh was "totally" peaceful, and "always" had been. Its past was the same as its present. There wasn't anything to compare with.

A teacher, for instance, says, "Nevaeh is, and always has been, a peaceful planet." A student then asks, "What does "peaceful" mean?"

Now, what does the teacher say? How can the concept of peace be explained without using words such as war, violence, killing, aggression, hatred, etc.? Or how can the idea of a crimeless society be explained without also exposing students to "crime"? Or how can "love" be talked about without also talking about "hate"? Or how can the notion of "good" be presented without also introducing "bad/evil"? Or how can "right" be defined without also defining "wrong"? It was the double-edged sword of knowledge.

If the council used Earth as a comparison when teaching the cadets, it would taint them; they'd know too much about Earth before they got there — and the experiment would be seriously compromised.

On the other hand, however, if the cadets were kept pure, or too pure, there was the danger that what they found on Earth — all the hate, violence, greed, poverty, misery, etc., etc. — would overwhelm them and they'd have serious — maybe even "fatal" — nervous breakdowns. They could, of course, be supplied with drugs that would, to a great degree, counter such breakdowns. At the same time, however, drugs — especially overuse — could cause serious damage to the experiment. We didn't want the cadets turning into zombies. We wanted cadets who'd be able to write intelligent, perceptive reports...it drove us crazy and, as previously mentioned, we nearly terminated the operation a number of times.

But, of course, we didn't. We persevered. And one thing we finally realized was, since their education of Earth society would have to be limited to keep them from becoming too tainted, "cold" insertion of the cadets into Earth society just wouldn't be a good idea. We'd have to do more than simply give them identification papers, bank accounts, and install them in apartments or houses. We'd also have to give them "guards"; people who'd constantly shadow them — such as living next door to them — and come to their aid should it be needed. If they got into some kind of trouble with police, for example, someone would instantly be there to insure their safety — no matter how serious the situation (the guards would have authority over government officials and police on "all" levels — including the "highest" levels).

And the great thing was that we wouldn't have to create these guards, since we already had a small army of them around the world. Or, more accurately, a "big" army of them, since the council also controlled all of the world's "official" police/military/government organizations, such as the FBI, CIA, KGB, etc.,

The council quickly realized, however, that it'd need much more than just these guards. It'd also need some kind of "nests" — staffed with "families" — for the cadets to drop into after they left their "spacecraft," where they could be sheltered while they received the second part of their "education," since it was decided that their education would definitely need to be a two-stage process.

The first stage would take place in the secret facilities — the "spacecrafts" — and would consist of teaching the cadets about their home planet, Nevaeh, and its spiritual force, *DOG* — and, of course, their important mission to Earth. But not much would be taught about Earth in the first stage. They'd simply be taught that the physical qualities of Earth were very similar to Nevaeh, and that it was inhabited by beings who were physically very similar to themselves. But they wouldn't be given any details about humans and their society. Nor would they be taught any English words that might influence their opinions of the human species before being inserted into Earth society.

They wouldn't, for instance, hear or see words such as hate, violence, war, revolt, revolution, kill, weapons, offensive, defensive, maim, destroy, bomb, annihilate, murder, crucify, torture, rape, genocide, carnage, patriotism, greed, jealousy, lust, conquer, defeat, crime, punishment, prison, execute, battle, fight, conflict, good, bad, evil, misery, poverty, hopelessness, despair, guilt, aggression, riot, crazy, insane, bloodbath, assault, peace, lie, cheat, honest, steal, racism...they'd be exposed to all these words/ideas, and many more, after they "arrived on Earth," and were safely

117

established in their "nests," with their "families," who'd assist/teach/guide them — with the aid of comprehensive libraries of books/magazines/newspapers/ audio tape/film — in a "non-judgmental" manner. The cadets wouldn't, for example, be told that something, such as violence, was "good" or "bad," or "right" or "wrong." It'd be up to them to come to their own conclusions. And the council would do its best to keep from influencing those conclusions in "any" way. The council, for instance, abhorred racism, but it wouldn't, in "any" manner, attempt to pass that feeling to the cadets. They'd simply have to come to their own conclusions about racism, and everything else. That, after all, was what the experiment was all about.

Of course, before the cadets got to their nests/families on Earth, they had to be taught about Nevaeh and *DOG*...but, how could we teach them about Nevaeh and *DOG* using an English vocabulary that was so limited?

We finally decided to use film, not words, as our primary teaching tool. We wouldn't start by trying to "tell" them about their home planet, its people, and *DOG*. We'd start by "showing" them Nevaeh, a world of eternal tranquility where people of different skin pigmentation lived without hate, violence, crime, etc. And they'd be exposed to the film right from the moment they arrived at the facilities at two or three weeks of age. It'd become an integral part of their lives, being constantly shown on screens in every room throughout the facilities.

Then, as they got older, the words would begin: food, water, air, light, dark, sleep, hot, cold, rough, smooth, wet, walk, talk, hand, fingers, plant, grow...all the "positive" words we could think of. The words would then lead to lessons — "non-human" lessons — in mathematics, biology, astronomy, agriculture, geophysics, physics...everything except the human species — except, of course, to say that humans appeared to be very similar in appearance to Nevaehens.

And, of course, they'd also be taught about *DOG*, the Nevaehen spiritual force — the exact wording of which confounded the council for a long time. What words — "exactly" — could we and/or should we use? Remember, our vocabulary was "severely" limited.

One of the first words we all agreed on was "share," since it didn't have any antonyms of any great strength. Another was "respect," which also didn't have any strong antonyms. (I'm sure there are many "educated" people — such as "academics/intellectuals" with university degrees, for example — who'd hotly argue about our reasoning regarding word usage and/or non-usage — especially when it comes to semantics — particularly concerning the fine details — the "hair-splitting," if you will — of word usage.

However, we simply didn't have the time to indulge in the endless discussion/debate that's so loved by these people. We had to "act"; we had to make "concrete" decisions and go with them — even if they were a little flawed at times. Had we not, nothing would've got accomplished — except, of course, for the expulsion of much hot air.)

One of the words we argued most about was "love." Some felt that "love," despite having such powerful antonyms as "hate" and "abhor," could prove to be useful — such as in, "Love thy neighbour." Others, however — including myself — felt, besides having such strong antonyms, "love" was far too nebulous a word (what "exactly" did it mean?), as well as being a word that'd been severely weakened by many years of indiscriminate use (I love that car...I love that color...I love that movie...I love that chair...I love those shoes...I love that song...I love that toilet paper...one could "love" virtually everything — yet not really be able to explain what they "really" meant by "love").

And it was also decided, after much debate, that *DOG* also wouldn't contain the word "honest," or any of its derivatives (too many strong antonyms; plus "honest" and its derivatives had been corrupted by too much dishonest use — especially by politicians); "truth," or any of its derivatives (same reasons as honest and its derivatives); "honor," or any of its derivatives (same reasons as the preceding two); "freedom/liberty" (same reason as the preceding three); "equal," or any of its derivatives (as I've said before, people simply aren't "equal")...the council kept hacking away until it was left with the following:

DOG
God created everything and directed that:
 * All shall share with one, and one shall
  share with all.
 * The land shall share with all, and all
  shall share with the land.
 * All shall respect the land, and the land
  shall respect all.
 * All shall respect one, and one shall
  respect all.

Fifty words, not counting the title. Short and sweet. Just like we wanted. Of course, we knew it wasn't "perfect" because, despite the zealous ravings of many, there simply isn't "anything" of a spiritual/religious nature that's "perfect." It was, however, a hell of a lot more perfect than many — or maybe "all" — of the religious/spiritual writings/ideas that existed on Earth — even if only for its brevity.

And, of course, if the council felt something should be added, we had plenty of time to do so, since it was going to be a long experiment. The first cadets, after all, wouldn't be "landing" on Earth until they were 16, 17, 18, 19, 20...much would depend on individual personal growth. Some might be ready at sixteen, or even earlier. Others might not be ready until twenty, or later. And some might never be ready, and might have to be eliminated from the experiment...but, fortunately, those who didn't make the grade in *Operation Nevaeh* could be used in other experiments/operations, such as the one that resulted in the discovery of a cure for cancer. Or they could be put to sleep and various body parts could be harvested from them for use in council members who might need them.

Seat Eight, for example, has a heart obtained from a cadet who didn't make the grade in *Operation Nevaeh* (he had superb physical qualities, but, unfortunately, his mental qualities simply couldn't — not even by using drugs — be brought up to an acceptable level). And Seat Eleven has eyes from another cadet whose mental qualities also couldn't be brought up to grade. (Yes, yes, I know...using humans in such a manner is beyond terrible — "far" beyond — a million light- years beyond — but, it must be remembered that they were — and are — being used in "exactly" the same manner as laboratory research animals; and it also must be remembered that many of them were going to be aborted before the council acquired them; at least they had a chance at some life.)

But not all *Operation Nevaeh* rejects have been used for body parts or as research subjects in other experiments (although, it can definitely be argued that "everything" the council does is, to one degree or another, an "experiment," since it analyzes — in "great" detail — "everything" it does).

Many males were rejected early enough to be transferred to the army of "guards" I mentioned earlier. In fact, these rejects were actually the beginning of a whole new

121

breed of guards.

The first guards were men recruited from the ranks of various militaries, but mainly the American military...no, that's not quite accurate. The first guards actually came from the criminal world, or "underworld," since the founding members of the council (of which I'm one) were criminals — or, more accurately, legitimate businessmen who were involved in various criminal activities (the illegal manufacture and sale of alcohol and other drugs, gambling, prostitution, pornography..."anything" to make a buck). (Or, perhaps even more accurately, we were involved in the crime/punishment "industry," since we were also heavily involved in politics and law-making — and law-enforcing — and "everything" else connected to the "industry"; we had laws made and had police enforce those laws, making certain that they'd catch plenty of criminals to fill the prisons we'd constructed — after they were convicted by "our" judges and juries, of course...hell, we made — and make — money, no matter what. We simply never lose. We simply can't afford to lose!)

Then, when we got together to get control of the atomic bomb and save America — and the rest of the world — from an atomic bomb-armed Hitler, or someone like him — we began recruiting guards from the military and ex-military — as well as continuing to recruit from the criminal world. (We had no intention of stopping our involvement in crime. In fact, we intended to expand — on a "big" scale — in that area; it would've been "extremely" stupid to have done otherwise since, after all, the crime/punishment industry is such an integral part of the global economic system. Win the "war" against crime and millions will become unemployed — police, judges, lawyers, prison guards, people who build prisons, etc., etc. Or, in other words: Crime really does "pay.")

We then began taking rejected cadets and training them from as early an age as possible to be guards — which quickly led into a new program. We began establishing orphanages around the world and, like we did with *Operation Nevaeh*, actively sought out pregnant women who, for one reason or another, didn't want to, or couldn't, keep their babies, and wanted to either have them adopted or aborted. We encouraged adoption and discouraged abortion (not difficult to do with handfuls of $100 bills). These unwanted babies were then taken into the orphanages, where they were "adopted" to "special" parents who took them to very nice homes and trained them to be guards — except for females, that is.

The council has a strict policy: No females can be members of the council (or sub-councils), or guards. This isn't because the council is misogynic. It's because, as experience has taught, females, for the most part (there are exceptions), lack the ruthlessness — the "killer instinct" — that's necessary to be a guard.

And the reason for this is simply that females are "much" closer to the "life force" than males, since they play a "much" bigger role in reproduction than do males. After all, a male only has to squirt some semen — a few seconds of intercourse is sufficient (or he can simply squirt into a jar and a doctor can later artificially inseminate the female). But the female has to carry the fetus for nine months (and then, of course, give birth, which is an experience unique to females — one that can be "extremely" painful; a comparable experience for a male might be trying to shit out a turd the size of a bowling ball). Therefore, because of their more intimate relationship with the "life force," females tend to hesitate when it comes to hurting and/or killing fellow humans — which simply isn't adequate, since guards have to

123

be ready to inflict pain and/or death without "any" hesitation.

Females, however, can be "agents" of one kind or another and, in fact, in many cases — particularly those involving heterosexual males — they make the best agents. Take, for instance, the agent — the "troller" — who netted the man who belonged to the organization that was planning to overthrow the council. No heterosexual male — or at least, very few — could resist her charms...hell, even today, over thirty years later, in her mid-sixties, she's still "extremely" beautiful (she looks at least twenty years younger than she is), and even more talented than ever in the sexual department — or so I've been told.

I wouldn't personally know for sure, since I haven't had sexual relations with another human for many years — and neither has anyone else on the council (and sub-councils). In fact, it's "strictly" forbidden for council and sub-council members — and guards — to be sexually active (except for masturbation, of course). It's been a council law for many years. Everyone "must" be asexual — or nonsexual.

And the reason for this is simple: It's just too easy for security to be compromised when people are sexually active (except for masturbation, of course). The man who was part of the organization planning to overthrow the council is a good example. Had he been asexual, or nonsexual — and had everyone in the group been the same — they very likely would've succeeded in overthrowing us. Their downfall was lust, pure and simple.

Or take Hitler. Lust was a major factor in his downfall since, using her sexual skills, Eva Braun, his long-time mistress — and also a council agent (and a hero of the "highest" magnitude, since she willingly sacrificed her life to make certain Hitler was defeated) — was able to "greatly" influence him. It was truly remarkable how only one act of fellatio could alter his thinking — or, more accurately, turn his brain into mush. For example, he was uncertain about attacking Russia, but after a major performance of "mouth music" (as Eva called it) — as well as a few words of extravagant praise for his huge ego (and a number of mind-altering drugs he believed were "vitamins") — he was ready to single-handedly conquer Russia.

Actually, it was Eva's sexual manipulations of Hitler that led the council to make its decision regarding the sexual conduct of its members — and guards. Everyone — and that meant "everyone" — would have to refrain from having sex with other people. It was simply too dangerous. And if someone — "anyone" — in the council, sub-councils, and guards was discovered breaking this rule, it'd mean immediate execution — as well, in order to prevent any possible breaches of security, the death of his partner/s.

And since this rule was implemented, only two people — a guard and the woman he had relations with — have had to be terminated — which was a shame. He'd been an exemplary guard and only had relations with her a few times, and she wasn't guilty of anything. She certainly didn't deserve to die — but rules were rules, and there simply couldn't be "any" exceptions — not even for a famous, beautiful movie actress...yes, the council is responsible for the death of Marilyn Monroe. Or, more accurately, the guard who had relations with her is the one who's "really" responsible since, had he not broken the rules, she wouldn't have had to be terminated.

I know this sounds like I'm trying to shift the blame — that the council could've spared her life — but that's simply not the case. We hated having to end her life, but, as I've already said, rules were rules — and there just couldn't be "any" exceptions because, once exceptions begin,

125

corruption also begins. And the council "must," at "any" cost, avoid corruption.

Of course, many will no doubt argue that the council is already corrupt — "beyond" corrupt. But that simply isn't true because if it was, the council wouldn't be so concerned about making the world a better place.

Certainly, the council has done — and is doing — many things that, on the surface, may appear to be "corrupt," "bad," "evil," etc. — such as creating wars and using people in "exactly" the same way laboratory research animals are used. But "everything" we've done — and are doing — is, as I've already said a number of times, for the benefit of "all" humans — or, more accurately, the human "species."

Operation Nevaeh, for instance, wasn't created just for the council's benefit. It was created for the benefit of "everyone" — but especially those of future generations. And while many might condemn us as being "evil" for using humans in such a manner, there simply wasn't "any" other way for us to get a "totally" different perspective of the human species.

Many might argue, of course, that we "really" didn't "need" a "totally" different perspective of the human species — that we knew enough about it already — and should have simply taken overt control of the world following the atom-bombing of Japan.

This, at first, might sound like a legitimate argument. At the time, however, we felt that we definitely didn't know as much about the human species as we needed to know. And, because of that, even if we'd taken overt control of the world following the atom-bombing of Japan, we still would've used humans in "exactly" the same way research animals are used, including using them in *Operation Nevaeh* because we still would've wanted — "needed" — a totally different perspective of the human species. It was, we decided, something that was "necessary" — "absolutely" necessary for the future good of the human species.

And today, twenty years after the first cadet "landed" on Earth — and after tens of thousands of pages of reports by them — we know we made the right decision.

~

$\mathfrak{T}$he first cadets entered various "spacecraft" in 1957 (March 17, to be precise), and the first cadets (three males: one white, one black, one yellow; and three females: one white, one black, one yellow) "landed" on Earth in 1975 (July 23, to be precise).

They were immediately installed in "nests" — large, secluded, palatial, top-security estates (all over fifty acres) near major American cities (Los Angeles, New York, Dallas) — that were staffed with female cooks and maids ("agents"), male servants, chauffeurs, gardeners, and handymen ("guards"), and fathers and mothers ("special" agents). The latter would help guide the cadets in the second phase of their education, as well as making certain the cadets ate properly and got plenty of exercise. (The cadets were led to believe that their "parents", and the rest of the staff, were Nevaehens who'd arrived on an earlier craft, in order to make things ready for the cadets. But the cadets were instructed to only talk to their "parents" about Nevaeh. Under "no" circumstance were they to talk to "any" of the other staff about Nevaeh — for "security" reasons; which was the truth because the other staff members didn't know any details of the experiment. They only knew it was a Level Red, Class 1A operation — the most top-secret of the top-secret.) As well, they'd make certain that the cadets took their medication — which was "extremely" important, since it was "needed" to keep the cadets emotionally stable; it'd act as a cushion between them and Earth's reality.

128

Just try to imagine spending your first eighteen years or so inside a sealed "spacecraft" — a "strictly" controlled environment, with no wars, crime, pollution, poverty, traffic jams, natural disasters, etc., etc. — then suddenly landing in Los Angeles, or New York, or any other heavily-populated area...it'd be an "extremely" traumatic experience, to say the least.

Remember, you've "never" experienced "outside" in your life. You've never actually felt "real," or " natural," sun, wind, rain, etc. Or actually seen the "real" sun, moon, sky, etc. Everything you've experienced of the "natural" Earth has been presented in still pictures and film, or has been artificially created (you've learned about rain, for instance, from being doused with water from huge shower heads, and you've learned about the sun from being exposed to gigantic heat lamps). Nor do you know "anything" about war, crime, poverty, hate, greed, etc., etc.

Consequently, because of the "tremendous" shock they'd experience on "landing" on Earth, the cadets would definitely "need" secure nests "and" medication (hell, many "regular" — or "normal" — humans can't take Earth's reality without medication of one kind or another).

As well, they'd also have to take medication to suppress — or, more accurately, "kill" — any sexual feelings (and both males and females would also need to be sterilized, and females would also need to be given clitoridectomies), since "any" kind of sexual feeling/contact could seriously jeopardize the experiment.

Also, "desexualizing" the cadets would help make them feel "nonhuman" (though not necessarily "inhuman"), which would be "extremely" important, since the council "needed" the cadets to observe the human species as objectively — with as little "human" emotion/empathy — as possible. They were to consider the human species to be no more important than any other Earth species — and that "truly" meant "every/any" species. For instance, humans and cockroaches were to be considered as being on the same level of importance...and, in fact, the first report the council received from the cadets contained some interesting observations on cockroaches and humans. It was from Cadets One and Two, the white male and female who landed on 23 July 1975. (It was decided to nest the cadets in male/female pairs and, later, doubling, tripling, and quadrupling the pairs, including "mixed" grouping, such as one pair of white male/female, and one pair of black male/female.

This was done because we felt people, generally speaking, tend to think/work better when they're part of a team — and we also wanted to see how groups of interracial "aliens" would act/react together in a racist world; remember, while the cadets were observing humans, the council was also observing the cadets.)

It's dated 3 March 1980, and the section concerning cockroaches reads:

"Most humans consider themselves to be the most superior of Earth's creatures. It definitely appears, however, that the most superior of Earth's creatures — at least in the sense of "natural" survivability — is the insect called the "cockroach."

There are about 3,500 species of cockroaches world-wide and, by current estimates, they appeared on Earth at least 300 million years ago — making them much older inhabitants of Earth than modern humans, or "Homo sapiens," who, by current estimates, first appeared only about 300,000 years ago — with their predecessors perhaps having first appeared as much as four million years previous — which isn't even close to the 300 million years of the cockroach.

Cockroaches can — and do — live virtually anywhere on Earth without needing any external help, such as that needed by humans (clothing, shelter, heating, etc.) — except for polar, or "frigid" regions — although one species is reported to be able to survive freezing for as much as 48 hours.

As well, cockroaches can live on virtually anything, including glue, paper, and soap — and one species, the "American" cockroach, can live without "any" food for three months, and without water for one month. (The longest recorded case of a human surviving without food and water is only 18 days.)

And cockroaches can also tolerate much more nuclear radiation than humans, as well as also having the ability to become resistant to poisons and other toxins (the reason for this isn't yet known by humans — which is one definite proof that humans aren't nearly as intelligent/ superior as they believe they are; they can't even discover the inner-working of an insect!).

Humans, generally speaking, hate cockroaches because they carry viruses and bacteria that cause diseases, such as hepatitis, polio, typhoid fever, plague, and salmonella (but they aren't incubators of infection, like mosquitoes, for example — and they've never been conclusively linked to epidemics of disease) — although we strongly suspect that much of that hate is really because humans are jealous of cockroaches — especially since, no matter how hard they try, humans just can't get rid of them — they just can't "conquer" them. (And humans, generally speaking, seem to have a strong "need" to "conquer" — especially "nature"; human history books are filled with references to "conquering" and "taming" wilderness, rivers, oceans, jungles, swamps, animals, etc.; in some humans this desire to conquer and tame can definitely be classified as a "sickness.") For example, in the United States alone, about $500 million is spent yearly on cockroach extermination — but cockroaches still survive — and, in fact, "thrive" — which leads us to conclude that, as previously stated, cockroaches definitely appear to be the most superior of Earth's creatures."

Every cadet team wrote similar pieces about cockroaches and humans — and they all strove to keep to what it said in *DOG* about, "All shall respect one, and one shall respect all."

It quickly became apparent, however, that they were having great difficulty in respecting humans. In fact, at the end of their first report, Cadets One/Two wrote:

"We know *DOG* says, "All shall respect one, and one shall respect all," but we're having a problem respecting humans because, generally speaking, they show very little respect for anyone or anything — including themselves.

Certainly, there are exceptions, but as far as we've been able to determine, they're quite rare. In fact, it appears that perhaps only about 10% of 1% of the world's adult population (which is about 60% of the world's total population of about 4,400,000,000) has — taking "all" levels/definitions of "respect" into consideration — an acceptable level of respect — meaning therefore that only about 2,640,000 adult humans out of 2,640,000,000 have an acceptable level of respect.

Consequently, this being the case, it's very difficult respecting those who don't have acceptable levels of respect with as much respect as we accord those who do —and in some cases — actually "many" cases —

we're having great difficulty
giving "any" respect at all."

The council — or "Control," as it was (and is) known by the cadets — instructed Cadets One/Two to endeavor to maintain as high a level of respect for humans as possible, and enlarge their report's 105-page section that was titled, *Detrimental Human Behavior: Past and Present.* (It should also be noted that all the other cadet teams also had problems respecting "all" — or "most" — humans; and the council gave them the same instructions as Cadets One/Two received.)

Eighteen months later, Cadets One/Two sent an enlarged version (1,311 pages) of *Detrimental Human Behavior: Past and Present.* And in the years following, it was joined by 83 similar cadet-team reports of varying length (273 - 1,934 pages), with a total page count of 39,063, and a total word count of 11,718,396 — which, because of duplication (all the major wars, for instance, were included in every report), the council subsequently edited to an 822,563 word, 2,357 page, 3-volume report (bearing the title Cadets One/Two first coined).

And it's...well...the council believes the great majority (let's say 99%) of adults (anyone over 18) would find *Detrimental Human Behavior: Past and Present; Volumes 1-3,* to be "extremely" shocking — "beyond" extremely shocking. This is because the council requested that the cadets also supply ideas that might/could stop, or at least "control," the detrimental behavior of humans and, if it meant keeping humans — as a species — from destroying themselves, they could ignore *DOG* — at least, to a "great" degree. Anything they suggested had to be tempered with at least some respect — and compassion. They weren't to "punish" humans, no matter how "bad" they'd been, or were being. They were

135

simply to evaluate detrimental human behavior, past and present, and "suggest" ideas that might/could stop, or "control," this behaviour.

The council's request puzzled the cadets at first, since they'd been brought up believing *DOG* to be sacred. They questioned the council about this, worried that, by going against *DOG*, they'd be doing something "wrong" — which, of course, was a concept they'd only learned on Earth, since on Nevaeh — and the "spacecraft" — "wrong" didn't exist.

The council, of course, was prepared for their questions since, as previously mentioned, the cadets were under constant surveillance. They couldn't escape our cameras and listening devices — which were (and are)the most sophisticated in existence. We have cameras, for example, that can "clearly" photograph a golf ball from a distance of ten miles — in "total" darkness (although, technically speaking, "total" darkness is extremely rare; there's usually "some" light present in "darkness"). And we have listening devices that can capture the slightest sounds at incredible distances (one device, for instance, can "clearly" hear "one" mosquito flying around in a 10,000 square foot room — or a 100,000 cubic foot room, if the ten foot ceiling is taken into consideration), as well as having the ability to filter out background noise (loud music, for example, can be playing in the room the mosquito is in, but can be completely filtered out, leaving only the sound of the mosquito).

Oh yes...*Big Brother* is watching and listening! He isn't, however, like the *Big Brother* of *1984*. The council isn't keeping "everyone" under constant surveillance — except in the most general sense; reading "letters-to-the-editor" in newspapers and magazines, and listening to radio and TV talk shows and phone-in shows — because "average" people aren't worth such an effort since, generally speaking, they're wholly predictable, unimaginative, and uninteresting.

The cadets, however, aren't "average" people. They're subjects in an experiment and "need" to be "constantly," and "closely," observed — even when sleeping — even when going to the toilet. They're "never" out of council sight/hearing.

Yes, I know to many this sounds beyond terrible. But it must be remembered the cadets don't have "any" idea they're under constant surveillance. And it also must be remembered they're living in luxury very few will ever know...hell, most don't even have enough imagination to imagine it.

But they don't have any freedom — they're prisoners — many will no doubt argue. And, yes, there's definitely some truth in that — but only "some" — a "little" — "very" little. They actually have a "lot" more freedom than " many" in the world. Certainly, they don't have the freedom to just get up and go somewhere by themselves. But they have freedom of speech — "complete" freedom of speech — which "many" in the world don't have (including "many" in the so-called "free" world). And they also have "complete" freedom of worship — which "many" in the world don't have (including "many" in the so-called "free" world). (Yes, they've been brought up to believe in *DOG*, but no one is forcing them to keep believing in it. They have the freedom to believe in any religion they might want to believe in — and, in fact, it would add a very interesting facet to the experiment if some of them began believing in other religions. So far, however, not one cadet has shown the "slightest" interest in following "any" Earth religion, since they all consider *DOG* to be "far" superior to "all" Earth faiths.)

And they also have the freedom to read or look at "anything" — which is a freedom "many" in the world don't have (including "many" in the so-called "free" world)...hell, they even have the freedom to leave their nests and families because after they've been on Earth for a number of years — and know about "freedom" — it's made clear that if they ever feel they're being mistreated or oppressed and want their "freedom," they're free to leave.

And it's a legitimate offer. It isn't any kind of game. The council isn't the least bit worried about a cadet leaving a nest, then going to the media and telling about coming to Earth from the planet Nevaeh on a spacecraft and being put in a " nest" (hell, the world is already full of people like that). In fact, we welcome it. We'd like to see what would happen if a cadet, or cadets, left. Would they be able to survive on their own? Or, perhaps more accurately, how "long" would they be able to survive on their own?

Of course, if a cadet, or cadets, wanted to leave, the council wouldn't be cruel. It'd give them identification papers and a big bundle of hundred dollar bills — say, twenty or thirty thousand dollars worth — as well as a six month supply of "vitamins." But, at the same time, the council doesn't have any "emotional" ties to the cadets. They're research subjects, not "family," or even "friends" — and like I've already said: They don't have "any" human/civil "rights." (Actually, we do have some idea of what would happen if cadets left their nests because we once conducted an experiment. We had a number of cadets — six, to be precise; three male/female teams — taken to different locations. Each team was left with identification papers, a month supply of vitamins, and five thousand dollars in cash — but no knowledge of where their nests were — and no reason given for why this was being done. All they were told was that they were "totally" on their own for one month.

The experiment's purpose was simply to see how

they'd make out on their own — without "any" help from us — for that month. And it didn't turn out very well for them.

They could've simply got hotel rooms and stayed safely inside for the month, watching TV and having food, etc., delivered by room service. But they didn't. They had to go exploring — which, of course, was only natural. But it was also disastrous. They didn't fare too well in the strange new world — even though they'd received "extensive" education about it.

Inside of ten days, two had been killed after stumbling into traffic; one was raped and killed; two were robbed and killed; and one committed suicide — or fell — or thought he could fly out of an eighth-story window — or maybe he was pushed? It really wasn't clear...but it was clear that it was "extremely" hazardous for the cadets to leave their nests on their own.)

However, not even one has ever shown "any" interest in leaving a nest — at least, not in a "permanent" sense — or unaccompanied. They've all requested to visit certain places — but never without someone, like a mother or father, or both, to accompany them. (The most popular destinations are art galleries, museums, music concerts, sports events, and amusement parks — especially Disneyland and Disneyworld; "every" cadet loves the whole Disney experience.) In fact, generally speaking, the outside world scares the hell out of them. It must be remembered, after all, that they know more about the world — and all its many horrors — than most (especially those fortunate enough to live with the kind of security the cadets have) because, while they haven't experienced the horrors "personally," they've studied history and humans, past and present, "extensively" — "much" more extensively than "most" — including "many" who are well-educated/well-traveled (or "supposedly" well-educated/well-traveled).

No, I doubt if you'll ever hear any cadet complain about not having enough "freedom." In fact, they all believe "the" biggest problem in the world today — aside from the human species per se — is that there's simply "far" too much "freedom" — especially since people, generally speaking, don't recognize the dualistic nature of their very existence.

As they've written:

> "Humans, generally speaking, don't recognize the dualistic nature of their existence. For example, most think of many things in simplistic terms of bad "or" good. For instance, "hate" is regarded by most as being "only" bad — but that simply isn't true. Hate is "both" bad and good. For example, hate can be extremely valuable in fighting disease, in that, if a person with a disease — especially a "serious" one, such as cancer — can focus hate against it, the disease can often be defeated, or at least be prevented from getting worse — or at least, be considerably slowed down."

This is followed by thirty-nine pages containing seventeen examples of hate being successfully used, to one degree or another, to combat serious illness. This is then followed by:

"On the other hand, however, hate can be terrible. For example, racial hatred — people hating people simply because of their skin pigmentation — is "extremely" detrimental to the human species."

This is followed by two hundred and thirty-seven pages containing three hundred and sixty-two of the worst — or best — examples of racial hatred the cadets could find. This is then followed by:

"Another example of thinking in terms of bad "or" good is "freedom." Most regard freedom as being only "good" — but that simply isn't true. It's "both" good and bad. Consider, for instance, one of the most popular freedoms — the freedom of speech. To suggest that it should be severely controlled — even if it's for the "good" of "all" — will produce screams of outrage from the "great" majority. And the most outraged will be those who use this freedom to their advantage — or, more accurately, "abuse" this freedom to their advantage, such as those who constantly

use — or "abuse" — their
"freedom of speech" to spread
messages of hatred —
"negative" hatred, that is."

This is followed by fifty-three pages containing forty-three examples of freedom of speech being used to spread racial hatred. Following that are sixty-eight pages containing forty-nine examples of freedom of speech being used to spread religious hatred. And following that, forty-seven pages containing twenty-eight examples of freedom of speech being used to spread ethnic hatred. This is followed by:

"Let us now examine
another popular freedom —
the freedom of worship. To
suggest that this freedom
should be strictly controlled —
even if it's for the "benefit" of
"all" — will bring forth cries
of "extreme" anger from the
"great" majority. And the most
angered will be those who use
— or, more accurately,
"abuse" — this freedom to
their advantage, such as those
who, in one way or another,
use/abuse their "freedom of
worship" to control others,
including controlling — or
attempting to control — the
freedom of worship of others."

This is followed by one hundred and forty-seven pages containing eighty-three examples of people using their freedom of religion to control — and attempting to control —

others — including controlling/attempting to control the freedom of religion of others — including persecuting others because of their religious beliefs. This is followed by:

"On 6 January 1941, United States of America President Franklin D. Roosevelt stated that any settlements made after World War Two should be based on four freedoms. He defined these freedoms as: freedom of speech; freedom of worship; freedom from want; freedom from fear. His speech was as follows:

"In the future days, which we seek to make secure, we look forward to a world founded upon four essential human freedoms.

The first is freedom of speech and expression — everywhere in the world.

The second is freedom of every person to worship God in his own way — everywhere in the world.

The third is freedom from want — which, translated into world terms, means economic understandings which will secure to every nation a healthy peaceful life

143

for its inhabitants —
everywhere in the world.

The fourth is freedom
from fear — which, translated
into world terms, means a
worldwide reduction of
armaments to such a point and
in such a thorough fashion that
no nation will be in a position
to commit an act of physical
aggression against any
neighbor — anywhere in the
world."

Now, Roosevelt's
speech sounds "good" — but,
in reality, it's "seriously"
flawed. For example, the
fourth freedom: freedom from
fear — in which there is to be
a worldwide reduction of
armaments to such a point and
in such a thorough fashion that
no nation will be in a position
to commit an act of physical
aggression against any
neighbor, anywhere in the
world — is saying that every
country in the world will
become military equals —
which is "absolutely"
ridiculous.

In fact, because of
what we know of human

behaviour (such as the strong dominating the weak), it's so ridiculous that we wonder if Roosevelt wasn't suffering from some form of mental impairment when he wrote it — if he indeed "really" did write it? Perhaps it was written for him, and he was forced to read it? He was, after all, despite being the President of the United States of America, severely physically disabled because of the disease poliomyelitis. Take away his wheelchair, leg braces, crutches, canes, drugs, etc., and he was "totally" helpless on his own. It's "highly" doubtful that a person in such a condition can "truly" be a powerful political/military figure.

However — going to his third freedom: freedom from want — which, translated into world terms, meant economic understandings which would secure to every nation a healthy peaceful life for its inhabitants, everywhere in the world — is saying that all countries would also be economically equal — which is (again from what we know of human behavior, such as the strong dominating the weak; and the strong being greedy) also "absolutely" ridiculous.

And his second freedom — the freedom of every person to worship God in his own way, everywhere in the world — is also "totally" absurd, since such a freedom can only result in disunity — including violence — i n c l u d i n g l a r g e conflicts/wars."

This is followed by one hundred and fifty-two pages containing eighty-seven examples of violence/wars caused by various religious beliefs. This is followed by:

"And Roosevelt's first freedom — the freedom of speech and expression, everywhere in the world — also is "totally" ridiculous because, as has clearly already been illustrated, such a freedom is a "major" factor — or, perhaps more accurately, "the" major factor — behind global disunity. The world needs "much" less freedom of speech — and "much" less freedom, in general.

Take the freedom of reproduction, for instance. In most places in the world, people are free to reproduce as often as they choose, without any regard for the subsequent impact it'll have on society — including the Earth itself — such as the extra strain it puts on the Earth's fresh water supply.

Certainly, one child doesn't affect the Earth's fresh water supply to any noticeable degree — but multiply that one child by millions, tens of millions, hundreds of millions, billions...and a "huge" problem emerges — especially since no attempt is made to control the quality of the children being produced, which results in the creation of an extraordinary number of substandard children who, in turn, grow up and produce more substandard children, and so on and so on — which, of course, is "extremely" detrimental to the human species as a whole — and the Earth itself. (Note: We use the term "substandard," not in any kind of "derogatory" manner, but simply as a generalized category for all those born with "any" kind of physical and/or mental defects — but particularly the latter, since mental defects are "much" more serious than physical defects — in that the former are the cause of "all" detrimental human behavior.)

Perhaps even more detrimental, however, is that "many" humans consider all forms of birth control, and any kind of selective breeding (including artificial insemination), and such things as genetic engineering/re-engineering — or "eugenics" — to be "wrong/bad/evil" — even though it's a "fact" that all of these things could be used — and, in our opinion, "should" be used — to help make the human species "much" better, so it can "greatly" improve conditions on Earth.

Of course, there'd still be the problem of existing substandard humans — of which there are billions (about three billion adults alone). One solution would be to exterminate them — but we simply can't bring ourselves to advocate this. We can, however, definitely support — and even encourage — that those who control Earth — who "really" control Earth — take overt control and establish the strict kind of authority that's needed for a "better" world — especially as regards the future.

We don't know the identity of these people — those who "really" control Earth — but we're quite certain that "none" of them are "recognized" world leaders, such as presidents, premiers, prime ministers, etc.

We are quite certain, however, that they're Americans because, after "much" study, it simply can't be anyone else."

~

 es...the cadets discovered the council — or, more precisely, they discovered names they strongly "suspected" were names of some, or all, of those who were "really" controlling the world.

Many will no doubt say: Certainly, they discovered the names because they were manipulated by the council into discovering them — just like they were manipulated by the council to arrive at certain conclusions, such as those regarding freedom of speech and religion.

And, yes, that is indeed a legitimate argument. Unfortunately, however, there simply isn't "any" truth in it. It wasn't council manipulation. It was simply superior brainpower producing brilliant deductive reasoning — although, it really shouldn't take "superior" brainpower to figure out something that simple. And it is "simple." For example, in *Who Controls The World? World Power, Past and Present; Real and Imagined,* a selection of cadet writing (1,972 pages; edited by the council from an original manuscript of 16,921 pages), is the following:

> "It's unarguable that when America produced the world's first atomic bomb in 1945, it also became the first country in history to possess the power necessary to "totally" dominate the world — especially since it also

150

possessed the biggest military in history.

It was a "huge" (with about 15,000,000 personnel) global military (the "only" military that "truly" was "global"), with an air force of about 80,000 aircraft (including over 3,000 B-29 *Superfortress* strategic bombers; the biggest, longest-ranged bombers ever built to that time; it was the B-29 that delivered the atomic bombs to Japan), and a navy with 102 aircraft carriers, 21 battleships, 26 heavy cruisers, 45 light cruisers, and 745 destroyers. And this massive force was also made stronger by the fact that both the militaries of Germany and Japan were destroyed, and none of the Allied militaries were anywhere close to the strength — even when combined — of the American military.

The world's history books, however, claim that America failed to capitalize on this "golden" opportunity when it allowed another nation, the Soviet Union —

"definitely" a potential enemy — to also get the atomic bomb.

Some might argue that America couldn't have prevented the Soviets from getting the bomb because the Soviet Union was huge, and the Soviets could've secretly built atomic bombs in remote regions of the country.

This might, at first, sound reasonable. The Soviet Union, or Russia, was indeed a huge country (8,647,250 square miles, to be precise). However, there weren't many in the world, let alone Russia, who possessed the skill/knowledge that was necessary to build atomic weapons. These people, therefore, were easy to monitor and, as a consequence, easy to control — especially since it's quite obvious that America had "many" monitors, or "spies," in Russia long before 1945.

In fact, it's also quite obvious that America was actually "controlling" Russia — and every other country in

the world — long before 1945
— and was, in fact, actually
responsible for the creation of
World War Two."

This is followed by one hundred and fifty-six pages
detailing why they believe what they do.

This is followed by:

"Therefore, because of all this,
it's also quite obvious that
America did, in fact, gain
"total" control of the world
following World War Two,
and that the *Cold War* that
followed was nothing more
than an illusion of "gigantic"
proportions.

This is followed by one hundred and seven pages
detailing why they believe what they do.

This is followed by:

"We can't, of course, "prove"
any of this, since we're simply
not in the position to do so —
and can't see when we'll ever
be in such a position."

Well, the council just might one day put them in such
a position. Yes, indeed...we just might give them that proof.
We just might arrange a meeting between them and us, where
they'll be informed (after the council warmly welcomes them
to Earth, of course) that they're now in total control of the
world, and that we are now their humble servants — except
they will, of course, still have to take orders from their
superiors back on Nevaeh. Or, put another way: The Earth
just might one day be invaded — and conquered — by

"aliens" from Nevaeh, or some other fictitious planet.

To explain this fully I must first go back to 3 July 1947, when the top-secret, council-financed aircraft crashed near Roswell, New Mexico, and rumors began that it was an alien spacecraft.

Not only did the council talk about the possible existence of beings from other planets, and what those beings — if they actually existed — would think about humans, we also talked about the possibility of beings from other planets invading and conquering Earth.

We then took the subject a little further, and began discussing the possibility of the council taking control of the world under the guise of beings from another planet.

This, at first, might sound absolutely ridiculous — like children fantasizing. But we weren't indulging in mere fantasy. We were 100% serious. We outlined a plan to take control of the world — or, more accurately, "switch" our control — by fooling everyone into believing that Earth was being invaded by beings from outer space. And we knew, beyond any doubt, that we could successfully pull if off because, not only were we in a position of ultimate power and had the resources for such an illusion, but the people of Earth — or at least many Americans — had already been fooled into believing that aliens had invaded Earth.

It happened on 30 October 1938, when Orson Welles, a radio broadcaster working for Columbia Broadcasting, produced H.G. Wells' science-fiction classic, *The War of the Worlds.*

At the beginning of the broadcast Welles announced that it was a radio adaptation of *The War of the Worlds,* and repeated this three more times during the hour-long show, and newspaper program guides had also printed this information.

Many Americans, however, for one reason or another,

didn't get the message that it was only a radio play, and believed the broadcast was for "real." And they, to say the least, panicked. There were unbelievable traffic jams as people tried to flee from the "invading" — and "murderous" — "aliens" (who were killing "everyone" in their path, it was reported on the show). And phone lines were clogged as people phoned police stations and radio stations to find out about the "alien invasion." And, tragically, a few even committed suicide rather than face the "invaders." It was, without a doubt, the most brilliant illusion ever created — at least, until the council came along with World War Two and the *Cold War* — except, of course, World War Two and the *Cold War* weren't illusions created for "entertainment." Nor, of course, were there any kind of warnings about World War Two and the *Cold War* being "fake," or "illusional," as there were with Welles' radio broadcast.

And the reason for the council thinking about creating the illusion of aliens taking control of Earth was simple. As I've previously said, the reason the council didn't take overt control of the world after World War Two was because it didn't want to make it obvious that the world's nuclear arsenal was under the control of just one group since this would be too tempting a target for a would-be Hitler. So the council created the *Cold War*; the "communist" world versus the "free" world. The "good" against the "bad."

And it worked perfectly — and it's still working because, as I've also previously said, communism hasn't really collapsed — it's only in a state of suspension. A "new" communism could emerge tomorrow and be stronger than the "old" communism. (Remembering, of course, that communism — "true" communism; that based on the writings of Marx and Engels — simply can't exist because in "true" communism there aren't any "classes" of people — except at the very beginning when, after the owners/rulers have been overthrown, a "ruling class" of "the people" is needed for a short period until conditions stabilize. Then the "ruling class" of "the people"is supposed to be absorbed into the main body of "the people," or "proletariat," and the state becomes a "classless," or "one-class," society. But that simply doesn't happen. Take the Russian Revolution of 1917, for example. Following the defeat of the ruling class, those in the "temporary" ruling class of "the people" wouldn't let go of the power they'd obtained (and who can really blame them?) — and the same has happened in "every" country that's become "communist."

Therefore, in reality, "communism" is nothing more than "totalitarianism" — which is "far" different than "true" communism." But the word "communism" has a better "sound" to it than "totalitarianism" — it's more "ominous," like the word "cancer" ("totalitarianism" sounds more like a fancy word for "constipation" than a word for a governmental system). Plus "communism" is also easier to spell and pronounce than "totalitarianism"— which is "extremely" important when dealing with large numbers of people who aren't overly bright.)

Instead of a new communism emerging, however, what might appear might be a force of aliens from another planet — the planet Nevaeh, for example — who'll quickly get control of the global nuclear arsenal and take overt control of Earth...yes, indeed, we just might put our old idea into motion.

Or, more accurately, put it into a "higher" level of motion, since we've actually been actively working on this plan ever since we first started talking about it in 1947, in that, not only have we created "aliens" from the planet Nevaeh, we've also — using weather balloons, remotely piloted vehicles (such as the *Canadair* CL-227 RPV), aircraft(including "experimental" aircraft), faked pictures, computer graphics, and false testimony — created the illusion that aliens are exploring Earth and its people.

Yes...we're responsible for "all" the "alien", or "UFO" (Unidentified Flying Object), activity that's taken place since the end of World War Two (including alien "abductions" and experimental operations/testing that've taken place during these abductions) because we decided that, while we wouldn't, at that time, take overt control of Earth in the guise of aliens, we'd create an obvious "alien" presence so that sometime in the future we could, should we desire — or the "need"arose — take overt control under the guise of aliens.

No, that's not quite accurate. Since the council would be hiding behind those "aliens," it wouldn't "really" be "overt" control. It would, however, be a control that'd "appear" to be "nonhuman," which would therefore mean that humans would "appear" to be powerless against it. And it'd be fairly easy to do because, after all, it'd be nothing more than a simple illusion — exactly like World War Two and the *Cold War*.

And I do mean "simple" in the most literal sense because "all" illusions — including "elaborate" ones, such as World War Two and the *Cold War* — are "simple," in that they all rely on one "simple" thing: altering the viewer's "perception." And, generally speaking, doing that is "extremely" easy.

Take weapons, for example. All weapons possess, to one degree or another, an "illusionary" facet. (As Sun Tzu wrote in *The Art of War*: "All warfare is based on deception.") A knife, for instance, "looks" dangerous from a distance of ten feet; up close, however, it's revealed that it's only a "prop" knife with a rubber blade. Or, from fifty feet, that rifle "seems" a serious threat; up close, however, it turns out to be a harmless prop that can't fire real bullets. Or, from a few hundred feet, that tank "appears" to be an awesome weapon; up close, however, it's nothing more than a plywood mock-up — and so is that artillery piece, and that jet fighter, and that helicopter gunship...and even huge weapons, or weapon "platforms," can be faked — especially when using cameras; that huge aircraft carrier you see on your TV screen, for example, might only be a small model floating in a small pool.

With some weapons, however, it's "impossible" to tell whether or not they're real or fake, no matter how close-up one gets — and this applies to the three most dangerous weapons in existence: the lethal chemical, or "nerve gas," weapon (or "LCW," or "Lethchemwep"); the nuclear weapon; and the most dangerous of all — the lethal biological, or "germ," weapon (or "LBW," or "Lethbiowep"), a small one of which can, theoretically, destroy the entire human race.

Consequently, one doesn't need to actually possess any of these weapons in order to have an arsenal of them — or, more accurately, to "appear" to have an arsenal of them. One can simply have empty containers of various sizes — everything from small aerosol cans to cylinders the size of large missiles — and claim that they're "real." And no one — at least no one in their right mind — is going to want proof that they're real" because, unlike with other weapons, it's simply "far" too dangerous to "live-fire" these weapons (that is, in "combat" live-firing tests where it's "impossible" for conditions to be "totally" controlled).

Of course, it wouldn't be wise to rely completely on a totally illusional arsenal of chemical/nuclear/biological weapons, since there might be times when "real" nuclear/chemical/biological weapons are "needed."

Yes, I know this sounds beyond terrible — but that's "reality." For instance, say it's discovered that someone like Iraq's Saddam Hussein is secretly building lethal biological weapons that could kill millions, tens of millions, hundreds of millions, billions — maybe the entire human race! The council, in order to prevent these weapons from being completed, might have to use (or, more accurately, let the American military, or some other military, use) nuclear and/or lethal chemical and/or lethal biological weapons that, yes, might indeed result in the deaths of thousands, tens of thousands, hundreds of thousands — maybe even millions — maybe even tens of millions (especially if LBWs are used; the council has a number of LBWs that use viruses that've been designed to have short life-spans and therefore, not travel far — but, under the right conditions, they could travel a lot farther than anticipated — especially if they "mutate"; and no matter how carefully a virus has been engineered, under the right conditions, it can suddenly mutate and go from a short life-span virus to a long life-span virus).

Of course, the chance of someone like a Saddam Hussein successfully creating a "secret" weapon of any kind is "extremely" slim because, as previously mentioned, "every" world leader — or "so-called" leader — is controlled by the council and kept under "constant" — and "close" — "extremely" close — scrutiny (if they say something in their sleep, for example, the council will hear about it; hell, if they burp or fart, the council will hear about it). And so are scientists and chemists — and "potential" chemists and scientists (the council, for instance, keeps track of high-school students around the world who show excellence in chemistry and/or biology — and continues to follow them after they leave high-school...and wherever they go for the rest of their lives; and, in fact, the council also helps many of them get jobs).

And the same also applies to those gifted in other fields — especially electronics, computers, and television (particularly in the area of "special effects," or "FX") since, should the council take overt control of the world — or take control in the guise of aliens — its main weapons won't be weapons of violence...they'll be non-killing/non-maiming "tools" of manipulation (although these tools of manipulation will, of course, be backed-up by tools of violence).

To illustrate, let's go back to Welles' 1938 radio dramatization of *The War of the Worlds,* then jump forward seventy years, and try to imagine a television dramatization of a similar story done by the council — but not for "entertainment." And don't forget that the council controls the world's communications systems and electricity — and "everything" else; we have the "power" — "the" power.

Now...let's say you're living in America and it's the year 2008. It's Superbowl Sunday and you're settling down in front of your TV/computer to watch Superbowl XLI.

Suddenly, Superbowl disappears, and a notice appears that says something like: EMERGENCY ANNOUNCEMENT! STAY TUNED! The sense of urgency is heightened by a chilling beeping sound.

You're transfixed. Something big — "really" big — is happening! Maybe there's been some kind of colossal natural disaster somewhere in the world!?! Or maybe another American president has been assassinated!?! Or maybe that new communist regime in the new Russia has fired nuclear missiles at America like it's been threatening!?! Maybe you're just a few minutes away from nuclear annihilation!?!

Then the beeping stops, the notice disappears, and a worried-looking — "extremely" worried-looking — newscaster appears. In a stunned, shaky voice, he announces that three huge circular spacecraft have just materialized in front of a naval carrier battle group conducting a training exercise two hundred miles southwest of Hawaii. And by radio the as yet unseen occupants of the craft have demanded that all humans must submit to them!

At first you think it's some kind of joke — an April Fool's Day joke, maybe — except it isn't April — and the newscaster doesn't really seem to be joking. Then you remember a story your grandfather once told you, about how some guy — an Oscar Wills, or something — put on this radio show way back — sixty or seventy or eighty years ago or something — about Earth being invaded by aliens from Mars or someplace, and everyone believed him, and there was this big freak-out...but, Christ, the newscaster really looks — and sounds — "really" worried...no, that's not quite right...the newscaster looks and sounds "terrified" — "totally" terrified.

Suddenly, the newscaster transfers the broadcast to another newscaster who — just coincidentally — happens to be covering the battle group's training exercise. He's aboard the battle group's flagship, the missile cruiser *Ticonderoga*. In the distance, perhaps half a mile away, and about half a mile apart, are two huge nuclear powered *Nimitz*-class carriers, the *Carl Vinson* and *Theodore Roosevelt,* surrounded by sixteen other warships; seven destroyers and nine frigates — a very impressive little battle group. No country in the world would want to tangle with it...but, about two miles in front of the group — in a three-point configuration, about a mile apart — are — incredibly! — three huge circular craft that "definitely" aren't of this world!

In a faltering voice, the bug-eyed newscaster says that the silver craft appear to be at least two thousand feet in diameter — about twice the length of the gigantic carriers — and at least a hundred feet from top to bottom — the equivalent of a ten-story building. They don't have any discernible markings or windows, and are hovering motionless about half a mile above the water.

Suddenly, the camera pans to the *Roosevelt* and *Vinson*, and from both, shriek 24 F-14 *Tomcats*, one of the world's best fighter planes; almost forty-years-old, but constant updating has kept them first-rate. They're followed by 24 F-18 *Hornets* from each carrier; almost thirty-years-old, but constant updating has also kept them first-rate.

Ninety-six of the world's best fighter planes, armed with the world's most sophisticated — and deadly — air-to-air missiles; the new *Super Sidewinder*, *Super Sparrow*, *Super Phoenix* — and even two of the new *Super Genie* nuclear missiles...nothing can withstand this awesome firepower — "nothing!"

The 96 warplanes quickly get into strike formation and begin launching their missiles at the three spacecraft and, in about thirty minutes, every missile has been fired — and all have scored direct hits! Then, after the planes are safely out of the way, the spacecraft are hit by another barrage of missiles as all nineteen warships launch a variety of surface-to-air missiles. And it's spectacular — "beyond" spectacular! A total of 1,028 of the world's most powerful air-to-air and surface-to-air missiles have hit the spacecraft!

But after the smoke clears, it appears — horrifyingly! — that the spacecraft haven't even suffered the slightest scratch!

The newscaster aboard the *Ticonderoga* is stunned speechless. He looks like he's going to faint. About five seconds pass — perhaps the longest five seconds in history — then beams of eerie green light begin blasting from the spacecraft with ear-splitting screeches and, in less than five minutes, all 96 planes have been blown out of the sky!

Then the green beams begin striking the warships and, in just a few minutes, only the *Ticonderoga* is left. The other 18 ships have all been ripped apart by huge explosions and have sank, or are sinking.

The newscaster is on his knees sobbing uncontrollably. It's quite clear that his mind has completely snapped. The cameraman, however, has remained unbelievably calm, capturing all the horrific action with unshaking clarity (but, of course, you don't notice this; it doesn't occur to you — not even for a fraction of a second — that this all could have simply been an illusion, using computer graphics and a few actors). Then there's a blinding flash and your screen goes black. Obviously the *Ticonderoga* has gone to join the rest of the battle group at the bottom of the Pacific.

Then the President of the United States is on the screen, live from the Oval Office. To say that he looks stunned would be an understatement of the greatest magnitude. He looks like he's aged at least fifteen or twenty years overnight.

In a voice crackling on the edge of insanity, he announces that Earth has been invaded — no, it's being "expropriated" — by beings from another planet — the planet Nevaeh — and all humans must submit to these beings — "immediately!" Resistance is "totally" futile. After all, in just one hour, Nevaehen forces have sank 19 of America's best warships, including two *Nimitz*-class carriers, and destroyed 96 of America's best combat planes — with a total loss of over 18,000 lives! And American forces haven't been able to do "any" harm to the Nevaehen forces! (And perhaps this is partially true; perhaps the battle group has indeed "really" been destroyed; perhaps, in order to add realism to the event, the council has "really" destroyed the battle group.)

He then begins sobbing uncontrollably...then disappears as the screen suddenly turns bright pink, filled with black words announcing:

"People of Earth — greetings! We are from the planet Nevaeh, which is many light-years from Earth.

We have come here because, for our survival, we must expropriate Earth.

We have come in peace — and apologize with deepest regrets for the damage we've inflicted upon you — but we did issue adequate warnings, which you failed to heed.

Please do not panic. We do not want to inflict further harm to you."

An emotionless, mechanical voice then begins reciting the message, and you think, God, this just can't be happening! It just can't! You switch to other channels, but they're exactly the same. You switch to computer mode to see what's happening on the Internet, and there's the same message — and it stays on the screen, no matter what keys you press.

You pick up your phone and dial a friend. A familiar voice answers with: "People of Earth — greetings! We are..." You slam down the receiver and turn on your radio. Sure enough. The same voice. The same message.

You go outside. Many on your street are already there. Everyone, to one degree or another, is in a state of shock. Everyone stares at the sky. Someone suddenly begins pointing and screaming, "Look! Look!"

Everyone's attention focuses on where the finger is pointing — and there it is! A spacecraft! Two spacecraft! Three spacecraft! It's difficult to estimate their size because they're so high — at least thirty thousand feet — but they certainly look big...hell, they look huge!

People begin fainting. Some drop to their knees, sobbing and babbling prayers. Some run wildly down the street, screaming insanely. Some just stand still, screaming insanely. Some just stand still, open-mouthed, too shocked to emit any kind of sound. You feel faint. You go and sit on your front steps. You can't believe it...yet, at the same time, you do. This is the day aliens from outer space invaded Earth! This could easily — despite what the words on the screen and the voice say — be the last day of your life! You saw what those things did to the battle group! They can't be stopped! You're doomed! You're all doomed!

You think about committing suicide...it'd be much better than letting the aliens get their hands, or claws, or whatever, on you...and millions — tens of millions — hundreds of millions — around the world are also thinking the same as news of the invasion spreads; in just a few hours, about 95% of the world's people have seen the tape of the destruction of the battle group, and about 50% have personally seen at least one alien spacecraft — and no one believes — at least not any longer — that this is any kind of hoax.

Of course, not everyone's perception has been altered in the same way. Many believe, for instance, that what's really happening is the *Second Coming of Jesus Christ*! Nevaeh, after all, is actually Heaven spelled backward.

And, yes...Nevaeh is indeed Heaven spelled backward — and maybe it is the *Second Coming of Jesus Christ*...oh, yes, that can indeed be arranged...of course, there'd first have to be *Armageddon*, the last great battle between good and evil that, according to the Bible, takes place at Megiddo, in the Plain of Esdraelon, which is about ten miles southwest of the town of Nazareth, in northern Israel.

But, should *Amageddon* and the *Second Coming of*

Christ take place, the country of Israel would...well...cease to exist....

~

But would the council actually orchestrate the destruction of Israel — killing millions, maybe tens of millions, in the process — just to fool the world's people into believing that Christ has returned?

Well...because of Biblical prophecy, we simply wouldn't have any other choice. Remember, we're not talking about "entertainment" here — something to amuse and thrill and chill people for a little while, like the Welles' radio show. We're talking about making it appear as though Christ has "really" returned — and this simply can't be done without there first being an *Armageddon* — and there can't be an *Armageddon* without the destruction of Israel. It's impossible.

And the council does indeed have the plans for such an operation. It's called *Operation Return*. It's an "extremely" complicated plan, with "many" variations; the whole thing fills over fifty thousand pages. But, "basically," it goes something like this: A charismatic leader — a "fundamentalist" leader — emerges in the Moslem world and, over a number of years, gains a "huge" following in "all" Moslem countries. And eventually, "every" Moslem country in the world falls under the control of this leader and his *Warriors of Allah,* and the Moslem world becomes united into a confederation called...let's say, "World Islamic Confederation," or "WIC," for short. (Many might argue that, because of the huge theological split in the Moslem world regarding the interpretation of the Koran, such a union simply isn't possible. This split, however, is really only an illusion,

167

in that it's being kept alive by the council — so all we have to do is adopt a new plan, and the Moslem world becomes united like never before.)

And WIC's main goal, despite any peace treaties that've been signed in the past, is to conduct a Holy war — or "jihad" — against the world's Jews — but especially the Jews of Israel.

Many countries, of course, strongly condemn this. WIC, however, with all its oil money, simply shrugs off the condemnation, and begins forming a huge military force to destroy Israel.

This force begins assembling in the four Moslem countries bordering Israel — Syria, Egypt, Jordan, Lebanon — and includes personnel from every WIC country, as well as personnel from non-Moslem countries, such as America, as the call goes out to every young, loyal, healthy Moslem male in the world: It's your sacred duty to join the Holiest of jihads!

And in the following years, WIC puts together the most awesome force Israel has ever faced: over 12,000,000 troops with 12,000 tanks, 36,000 pieces of artillery, and 3,000 combat aircraft (compared to Israel's 1,000,000 troops — 2,500,000, counting Jews who travel from other countries to help defend Israel — 5,000 tanks, 10,000 pieces of artillery, and 800 combat aircraft).But, of course, Israel has the "defensive" advantage (and because it's a small country — only about 8,000 square miles — this advantage is even greater — "much" greater). The enemy is coming to them — and to greet that enemy, Israel fortifies itself like never before.

Along its borders, for example, almost one billion additional anti-tank and anti-personnel mines are planted, with some of the minefields being over fifteen miles wide (and in some places containing as many as two million mines

168

per square mile, with many of the mines containing lethal chemicals). And hundreds of thousands of additional concrete and steel anti-tank obstacles are erected; hundreds of extra miles of deep anti-tank ditches are dug (and mined); hundreds of additional miles of thick tangles of heavy razor wire are laid down; and, of course, every square inch of these defensive zones is targeted by a maximum number of carefully emplaced artillery pieces, rocket launchers, mortars, automatic grenade launchers, chemical dispensers, and machine guns (including multi-barreled, electrically fired weapons capable of firing as many as 10,000 rounds per minute)...in the history of warfare — not just Israel's history — there have never been defensive zones any deadlier.

Of course, WIC forces aren't just going to blindly charge into these areas without first softening them up. They're not stupid. Before they attack they'll fire millions of artillery and rocket rounds into these zones to explode mines, cut razor wire, and destroy anti-tank obstacles and ditches and artillery, mortar, and machine gun emplacements, etc., etc. But, while this pre-invasion barrage will indeed destroy much of Israel's border defenses, it'll also badly crater these zones which, in turn, will "severely" hinder the attacking WIC forces — especially since, in anticipation of the pre-invasion barrage, Israel has buried hundreds of thousands of barrels of lethal chemicals in these zones; and if the pre-invasion barrage doesn't rupture them, Israeli soldiers can detonate them by remote control, releasing their contents and turning the craters into pools of deadly toxic sludge, and filling the air with thick clouds of lethal gas...but, of course, "the people" of the world will never know the dirty little details of this battle, since it's going to be the "last" battle/war, and all such violent history will vanish as Christ returns and takes control of the world.

All "the people" of the world will see is the creation of WIC, the formation of the huge WIC force on Israel's borders, some of Israel's preparations for the coming invasion, and some of the invasion itself — which, of course, will succeed because WIC forces will eventually get through Israel's horrific defenses (the council will make certain of that; but WIC forces will lose five or six or seven million in the process) and will gradually push the Israelies back, back, back...towards Megiddo.....

Before this final battle begins, however, there'll first have to be "much" more conflict in the world to... let's say, "heighten" the tension.

Take North and South Korea, for example. They're two of the world's largest militaries, with North Korea being fifth and South Korea being seventh. (Israel, by comparison, is thirtieth; Egypt is thirteenth; Syria is fourteenth.) And they've been on the brink of war for many years (or so it "appears"; in reality, of course, this conflict was created — and is being maintained — by the council).

All that's needed is one brief command (just one word followed by three numbers and a certain symbol) from the council and, a few hours later, the two countries will be engaged in a full-scale war...but maybe we'll create an entirely different situation — such as the reunification of North and South Korea (just like we did with East and West Berlin; most believe that the power of "the people" did that, but, make no mistake about it, the power of the council is what reunited those two countries).

Yes...perhaps a new leader — a "charismatic" leader; let's call him "Sung Dark" — will emerge in either North or South Korea and reunite the two countries. And, during this reunification, he'll begin blaming America and Japan for dividing Korea in the first place — and for causing the

170

Korean War (1950 - 1953), which killed and maimed millions of Koreans. But the main heat of the blame will be concentrated on Japan, since it annexed Korea from 1910 to 1945, during which it committed many "unspeakable atrocities" against the Korean people, such as rape, murder (including "mass" murder), turning people into slaves, forcing women into prostitution, etc., etc.

Japan doesn't deny these charges, because they're true, and have been well-documented. But it's apologized "many" times for its actions during that time and, besides, it all happened many years ago — and the past should be forgotten. Forgive and forget. Look towards the future!

And Sung Dark agrees...yes, look towards the future. But Koreans will "never" forget what Japan did to them — "Never!" Nor will they "ever" forgive the Japanese for what they did — "Never!" Their barbaric crimes can simply "never" be forgiven — "Never!"

And the Korean people, reunited after so many years of being split apart, cheer Sung Dark with a patriotism that's chilling in its intensity. News cameras show millions of Koreans — tens of millions — faces twisted in patriotic — and "spiritual" — ecstasy, waving the new Korean flag (a garish amalgamation of the old flags of North and South Korea), and chanting the name of their new God-like leader — their "savior" — with a patriotic thunder never before heard in Korea, North or South.

And news cameras also show the militaries of the old North and South Korea uniting into a mighty force of over two million troops — giving the new Korea the world's third largest military — which grows even larger as reserves are called to active duty, and young men, their patriotic blood pumping hot, rush to enlist. In just a few months following reunification, the new Korea has a military of over 4,000,000 troops, with the great majority concentrated around Pusan in southern Korea — just a little over a hundred miles from southern Japan. And news cameras also show the Korean arms industry doubling — then tripling — then quadrupling — as it churns out huge quantities of weapons and ordnance of all kinds, including thousands of landing craft and assault craft equipped with multiple rocket launchers — making it quite clear that the new Korea is planning to invade Japan.

Japan, of course, strongly condemns Korea for its hostile attitude and military build-up. But it isn't really worried because, after all, it has America for an ally. Should Korea attempt an invasion, America will intervene. Therefore, smug with this knowledge, Japan begins insulting Sung Dark, calling him "crazy," "demented," "warped," "insane," etc., etc.

But America, who's withdrawn all its forces from the former South Korea (and left behind "many" weapons and "much" ammunition — to help pay for any pain it caused during the Korean War), suddenly decides that it shouldn't get involved in a dispute between Japan and the new Korea because it's a ...well...it's kind of a "family" dispute — an "Asian" dispute — and America really shouldn't be meddling in it.

And "the people" of America agree (except for Japanese-Americans, of course — and a small number of "white" Americans who sympathize with the Japanese and/or dislike/hate the American government for one reason or another). It simply isn't America's problem — and besides, Japan did insult Sung Dark and the Korean people. It shouldn't have done that — just like it shouldn't have attacked Pearl Harbor back in 1941...oh, yes, sixty, seventy, eighty, etc., years later, Americans (speaking of non-Japanese-Americans, that is) still remember the Japanese

172

attack on Pearl Harbor.

They might not have even been born when it happened... hell, their parents might not have even been born when it happened, but the memory has been kept alive in books and on film, as well as being orally passed from generation to generation. And "many" believe that Japan, despite its humiliating defeat and being hit with two atomic bombs, didn't really suffer enough for what it did at Pearl Harbor. They believe, for instance, that America shouldn't have helped rebuild it into an economic giant after the war but, instead, should've let Korea and China divide it up and give the Japanese a taste of their own medicine. Consequently, the great majority of "the people" of America aren't at all concerned when America begins withdrawing its forces from Japan. They, in fact, cheer the move.

Nor are they concerned when China suddenly sides with Korea, because it also suffered "unspeakable atrocities" at the hands of the Japanese before and during World War Two. It — also under the leadership of a new "charismatic" leader; let's call him "Wung Hung" — pledges a force of at least two million troops, with 500 combat aircraft, 2,000 tanks, 5,000 pieces of artillery, and 30 warships (not counting a few thousand landing craft), to assist Korea in "administering justice" to Japan for its past crimes.

Japan insists that America must keep its forces in Japan — must, in fact, increase their strength — to help defend it from Korea and China. America responds by quickening its withdrawal from Japan which, of course, enrages Japan, and Japanese businessmen threaten to shut down "all" Japanese-owned businesses in America if America doesn't help protect Japan from Korean and Chinese aggression.

America replies to this threat by informing the

businessmen that, should they attempt any kind of shutdown, or slowdown, of Japanese-owned businesses in America, America will nationalize all those businesses and not pay "any" compensation for them. And it'll also impose a naval and air quarantine on Japan to prevent it from receiving "anything" from "anywhere" — which, of course, will mean "serious" problems for Japan, since it doesn't have any mineral resources and has to import all its oil, coal, iron ore, etc., etc.

Of course, even without an American quarantine, Japan has "serious" problems — more serious than ever before. But the situation isn't "hopeless." For example, even though its military is small (it ranks 24th in the world), it can, because of it's large population (almost 150 million), quickly be enlarged. As well, it still has the economic power to purchase tens of billions — hundreds of billions — of dollars worth of arms — as well as everything else, such as food, fuel, raw materials, etc., etc. — for a prolonged war. (And America announces that, while it won't protect Japan from Korean and Chinese aggression, it will sell arms to it — "conventional" arms, that is. Under no circumstance will it sell Japan nuclear, biological, or chemical weapons; although it will — "covertly," of course — sell Japan plenty of ingredients for chemical weapons.)

And, because it's an island nation, Japan is also in an excellent defensive position — especially since it has enough air and naval power (taking into consideration that it spends many extra billions for additional arms) to prevent itself from being isolated by Korea and China. But even if it does become isolated, it'll still be able to avoid being conquered by Korea and China for many years — providing, of course, that it has enough time to properly prepare — and also providing that it's prepared "properly" (it takes "much" more than a lot of heavy firepower to make an effective military; brawn without brains doesn't last very long against brains with brawn) — and also, of course, providing that the council doesn't want it conquered.

If we want Japan conquered — and enslaved — by Korea and China, we can have that occur within a year or two. And, of course, on the other hand, we can also make it "impossible" for Korea and China to conquer and enslave Japan. As well, naturally, we can also make it possible for Japan to go from a defensive position to an offensive position and conquer Korea and China — or at least a large part of China (we'd let other countries — such as Russia and Taiwan — also have sections of China).

It must, after all, be remembered that we're in "total" control of the world — or, at least, "almost" total control, since, as previously mentioned, there are some things we simply can't control, such as natural disasters and "natural" illnesses. A key figure like Sung Dark, for instance, might suddenly have a fatal heart attack or stroke, and we can't do anything about it — but we can use such an incident to our advantage.

For example, let's say Sung Dark has a "natural" and fatal heart attack or stroke. We can easily manipulate people into believing that an enemy of Sung Dark's and/or an enemy of Korea's — like Japan, for instance — was behind the death. All we have to do is start a rumor that it wasn't a "natural" death. It was actually an assassination! A Japanese agent slipped him a lethal drug!

Or maybe it's an attempted assassination. For example, let's say Wung Hung has a heart attack or stroke, but lives. We can easily make it appear as though his condition was caused by a drug given him by an agent of the Taiwanese government. This, of course, enrages "the people"

175

of China and, following the emergence of a new charismatic leader, it's decided that it's time for Taiwan to again become part of mainland China. For many years, China has threatened to invade Taiwan and "liberate" it — and now it's time for that to happen.

Over the next few years, in China's Fukien province, opposite Taiwan, an invasion force is assembled (5,000,000 troops, 2,000 combat aircraft, 2,500 tanks, 10,000 pieces of artillery, 50 warships, 3,500 landing craft, and 1,500 assault craft equipped with multiple rocket launchers), making things appear "extremely" grim for Taiwan — especially since China's population exceeds Taiwan's by at least 1.45 billion so, should it need to, it can "easily" send an additional five or ten or fifteen million troops against Taiwan. And, making things even worse for Taiwan, its longtime ally, America, decides that it shouldn't get involved in a dispute between China and Taiwan because it's a "family" quarrel. So it abandons Taiwan — except for selling it arms (for cash and/or goods, of course; Taiwan's precarious position makes it an "extremely" poor credit risk).

Taiwan's situation isn't as hopeless as it appears, however. Calling its reserves into action — plus doing some extra recruiting — Taiwan can easily field a military of 2,500,000 personnel, with 600 combat aircraft, 1,750 tanks, 12,000 pieces of artillery, and 40 warships. And, of course, it also has the advantage of being in the defensive position — and it's a great defensive position because it's an island nation. China has to cross 125 -175 miles of water to get to Taiwan, and the Taiwanese, of course, will turn their coastline into a series of killing zones as deadly as those being created by Japan and Israel. For every attacker who makes it through these zones of death in all three countries, there'll be 30, 40, 50, 100, etc., who won't make it — and it could take many months — or even many years — for these zones to be penetrated.

Or they might never be penetrated — except for Israel's, of course, since the *Second Coming* does require that final battle at Megiddo.

And there also "needs" to be "much" more conflict in the world than just WIC versus Israel, Korea and China versus Japan, and China versus Taiwan. This might sound beyond terrible, but it must be remembered that this is the lead-up to *Armageddon* and the *Second Coming.* The world "must" be brought to the "abyss"(or, more accurately, "appear" to be brought to the abyss).

Consequently, other conflicts erupt. India and Pakistan, for instance, who've fought a number of wars in the past, begin fighting again — on a "large" scale (maybe even using nuclear weapons). Then China, who's fought with India in the past, joins the fray when it attacks northern India with a couple million troops. And it also renews its hostilities with Vietnam — only this time, instead of simply trading artillery fire with Vietnam, China invades Vietnam with four or five million troops, while its ally, Cambodia, begins attacking southern Vietnam. Thailand and Myanmar then begin fighting each other, with China aiding Myanmar, including sending a million troops into Thailand.

Meanwhile, civil strife greatly escalates in Malaysia and the Philippines, as well as in many African countries, especially in southern Africa, where a "charismatic" black leader emerges and unites the aboriginal peoples of that region into a huge force dedicated to ridding the area of "all" whites. (Nelson Mandela, Desmond Tutu, and all other black leaders who worked towards peaceful coexistence between blacks and whites, have long since disappeared from the region; in fact, blacks in the region now consider Mandela,

177

Tutu, etc., to be "traitors" who conspired with whites to keep blacks in a subservient position.) And they do get rid of many — most of whom simply flee the area because they're too scared to stand and fight. A small number, however, declare they'll "never" — under "any" circumstance — leave southern Africa, or, more precisely, South Africa. God, after all, gave them South Africa, and they'll "fight to the death" to keep what God gave them. And no one who knows these people have any doubts about their determination, since most of them are *Afrikaner* (descendants of South Africa's first white settlers, the Dutch, who first came to South Africa in the 17th century), and have a reputation for being "extremely" stubborn and closed-minded — especially concerning black people. (They consider black people to be on the same level as animals — cattle, for example — and would sooner see South Africa "totally" destroyed — every animal, every plant, every human; including themselves — rather than it being controlled by blacks.)

And even though they're "greatly" outnumbered — at least 25 to 1 — they control South Africa's small, but formidable, military, which has, along with modern combat aircraft, warships, artillery, and armored vehicles, a large arsenal of lethal chemical and biological weapons, as well as some small nuclear weapons — or so it's been rumored.

They, of course, deny having any such weapons, insisting that they've "never" had "any" lethal chemical or biological weapons, and what few nuclear weapons they had were destroyed long ago.

But rumors of their existence are "extremely" strong — as are rumors that they've already actually used air-dropped biological weapons to start epidemics of typhoid and cholera among blacks in South Africa and neighboring countries.

And there are also strong rumors that the country who supplied them — or at least "assisted" in supplying them — with these three types of weapons is Germany who, of course, "emphatically" denies "any" such involvement. Certainly, German-owned chemical companies — including some that manufacture pesticides — have factories in South Africa. But "none" are involved, in "any" way, in manufacturing lethal chemical weapons; some tear gas and other crowd control gases, yes...but not lethal gases, such as Sarin. And, yes, there are indeed a number of German-owned companies in South Africa that are engaged in medical research involving communicable diseases, such as typhoid and cholera. But "none" are involved, in "any" way, in the manufacture of biological weapons.

And, yes, German-owned companies have helped South Africa build a few nuclear power plants. But they haven't, in "any" way, been involved in manufacturing nuclear weapons. And, yes, German-owned companies are involved in the mining — and refining — of uranium in South Africa. But "all" of what's being mined and processed — "all" of it! — is being used for peaceful purposes, such as nuclear power.

Of course, the great majority of the world's population isn't really too concerned about what's happening in South Africa. It isn't necessarily that they don't care what happens to the black people (although, of course, many don't, because they don't have much — if any — use for black people), or that they don't care what happens to the white people of South Africa (although, of course, many don't, because they don't have much — if any — use for racists). It's simply that there are "much" bigger problems in the world. There are, for example, the problems of WIC versus Israel; Korea and China versus Japan; China versus Taiwan, Vietnam, and India; India versus Pakistan...and, of course, the "new" Russia, with its new leader, a man called...let's say, "Ivan."

Ivan is in his early forties, and is "extremely" charismatic. He reminds many of John F. Kennedy. In a few short years, he's transformed Russia, or the "Russian Federation" as it was known when he took power (in a "democratic" election), into one of the most dynamic countries in the world.

In doing so, however, he's also turned it into one of the most dangerous — if not "the" most dangerous — countries in the world. In fact, Russia has become so dangerous that another *Cold War* has started. And it's "much" worse than the first one because that one didn't have someone like Ivan as Russia's leader.

Never in Russia's history has there been a leader as loved — as "worshiped" — as Ivan. For that matter, never in world history has there been "any" leader more loved than Ivan...hell, even people — millions of them — in other parts of the world (including America, Germany, France, Italy, and Great Britain, who Ivan has declared as Russia's greatest enemies — particularly America) have fallen under Ivan's hypnotic spell. It's unbelievable!

But most Americans, Germans, French, Italians, British, and their allies, haven't fallen under Ivan's spell. They see him as the greatest threat they've ever faced — "far" greater than any of the Russian leaders in the first *Cold War* — and even "far" greater than Hitler, Mussolini, and the Japanese leaders of World War Two.

They see him as...well, rumor has it that he's got a birthmark somewhere on him that looks like three sixes — which, of course, according to the Bible, is the "mark of the Beast" — which means, if the rumor is true, Ivan is the *Antichrist*!

And rumor quickly turns to "fact" for many (the *Second Coming* does, after all, "need" the *Antichrist*) when Ivan bans "all" religious faiths in the new Russia. Marx wrote: "Religion is the opium of the people." Ivan, however, isn't as gentle as Marx. (In fact, Ivan is contemptuous of Marx, calling him, among other things, "one of history's biggest idiots.") He states (as "fact," not "belief/opinion") that religion — at least "all" religion to date — has been "the worst disease to have ever afflicted the human race." What the world needs, Ivan asserts, is "spirituality," not "religion." And the kind of spirituality it needs is his kind of spirituality, which is one that celebrates the Earth and its creatures (especially the Russian people), and doesn't have "the people" cowering before a "God" that's been fabricated by evil people who use that "God" — or, more accurately, the "fear" of that "God" — to control "the people" as they exploit them and get richer and richer from them.

Naturally, many around the world — especially religious leaders — "strongly" condemn his words and actions. But criticizing Ivan is like throwing gas on a fire. He poses the question: "If what I say isn't true — if all religion to date hasn't been the worst disease to ever afflict the human race — then why is the human race in such a terrible condition? Why is there so much poverty, hunger, starvation, misery, and unnecessary sickness and death?" He then answers it with: "Because of religion, that's why!"

He then begins singling out individual religious leaders and condemning them. He calls the Pope, for instance, an "evil bloodsucking leech who's the head of the most evil criminal organization in the world," and claims that he can "prove" it. He says he possesses "tons" of documentation that "proves beyond any doubt" that the Pope and Vatican are "heavily involved in the world's illegal drug trade, as well as the worldwide pornography trade." He then declares that the Pope and "every" other high-ranking Vatican official should be "burned at the stake — after first being skinned alive — for all the misery the Catholic Church has inflicted on the world's people — especially poor people — over the centuries." He then tells the world's Catholics that, if they'll publicly renounce their evil faith and burn their Bibles, they'll be welcome as citizens in the new Russia — as long as they're of Russian descent, of course — and "white."

It isn't that he's a "racist," or an "ethnic purist." Certainly, he believes the white race is the superior race (especially white Russians because, after all, the white race did start in Russia; and he, of course, can "prove" it). But he's not "racist," or an "ethnic purist," because he doesn't believe, like Hitler did, for example, in exterminating people simply because of their skin color or ethnicity. Nor does he believe in exterminating people because of their religious beliefs — unless, of course, they have Satan for a God, " like the Pope and the rest of the evil criminal swine in the Vatican cesspool."

And while Ivan's words and actions enrage "many" in the world (especially Catholics), they also help him unite Russia like it's never before been united. Or, more accurately, he reassembles the old Soviet Union, which fell apart many years before (2 December 1991, to be precise), into a nation that's "much" more united than the old Soviet Union ever was. He doesn't, however, restore the name, "Soviet Union," or "Union of Soviet Socialist Republics." It's just "Russia." The greatest nation in the world! The greatest "family" in the world!

And it must, of course, be protected — which means that it must have a big military — no, a "huge" military! Bigger and stronger and greater than ever before! The biggest

182

and strongest and best military in the whole world!

Therefore, in an astonishingly short time, using Russia's "huge"wealth of natural resources to the maximum, Ivan turns Russia into, for the first time in history, a "true" military superpower, complete with a large fleet of huge aircraft carriers that are bigger and better than anything America possesses.

And Russia's military keeps growing — including its arsenal of nuclear, lethal chemical, and biological weapons...oh, yes, Ivan doesn't hesitate to admit that Russia is not only building bigger ("much" bigger) nuclear weapons than ever before, but that it's also building lethal chemical and biological weapons and won't hesitate, for a moment, to use them should the need arise. For example, should anyone ever invade Russia again, such as the French and Germans did in the past, Russia will use "everything" in its arsenal to "annihilate" the invaders — including annihilating the home countries of the invaders. Never again will Russia allow herself to be raped and pillaged by "immoral pigs" like the French and Germans — "NEVER!!!"

And Ivan also builds another "Iron Curtain" — only this time, it's not to keep people in; it's to keep people out. If anyone wants to leave Russia, they're free to do so.

But no Russian wants to leave the new Russia. (Except for thousands of Jews and millions of Moslems; many of the latter heading for the WIC countries bordering Israel, so they can join their fellow Moslems in the destruction of Israel; the former heading for Israel, so they can join their fellow Jews in defending Israel from WIC — but, of course, as Ivan is quick to point out, the Jews and Moslems aren't "true" Russians, since they put their religious faiths ahead of being Russian; and because of that, their leaving will be of "great benefit to the new Russia.") In fact, thousands —

tens of thousands — hundreds of thousands — millions — from around the world want to become citizens of the new Russia because they see it as a new "paradise," and Ivan as a new "messiah" in a world that's deteriorating at a frightening rate.

Most of the world's population, though, don't see the new Russia as any kind of "paradise," or Ivan as any kind of "messiah." They see the new Russia as a new dictatorship, ruled by an egomaniacal tyrant (and also, rumor has it, a deranged pervert with a fondness for cocaine and twelve and thirteen-year-old virgins of both sexes) who's just as bad — if not worse — than Stalin ever was (and don't forget the birthmark he's rumored to have). The gossip, for example, is that there are "many" Russians — "true" Russians — who want to leave Russia, but anyone who applies to leave — or even talks about leaving — is immediately found guilty of treason, given fifty lashes, and shipped to the new Russia's new Siberian Gulag.

Ivan, of course, "emphatically" denies this. He loudly declares that there isn't any new Gulag — that that prison system has been shut down, and will stay that way — and no one is being charged with treason in the new Russia, because Russians — "true" Russians — are great people who simply don't commit treason. And no one — for "any" reason — is ever subjected to whipping. It's all just vicious lies from Russia's many enemies, such as "the filth" in the Vatican and all the rest who are guilty of crimes against Russia — but especially America who, among other crimes, cheated Russia out of Alaska in 1867.

The history books show that Russia wanted to sell Alaska, and that America offered $7.2 million for it, and Russia accepted. It was a fair and honest deal, America insists. It didn't cheat Russia out of anything.

Ivan, however, simply doesn't see it that way. He accuses America of dirty dealing, claiming that he has "indisputable proof" that America, using prostitutes and drugs, blackmailed Russian officials into selling Alaska for the absurd price of $7.2 million, or a little less than two cents an acre — "much" too low a price, even by 1867 standards, Ivan insists.

He then demands that America give Alaska back to Russia — and also compensate it for all the natural resources America took from it, such as timber and oil — or else there might be "big" trouble between the two countries — BIG!!! trouble...

America, however, isn't scared of Ivan and the new Russia. America isn't scared of "anyone." It is, after all, the biggest country in the world — at least, in size. China has the biggest population, with about 1.5 billion, but its area is only about 3,700,000 square miles — whereas, America's area is over 16 million square miles (with a population of over 800 million)...but, of course, this isn't the old America. This is the "new" America.

And it isn't the "United States of America," anymore. Many call it "America," but it's now actually "officially" known as the *United States of the Americas.*

~

$\mathfrak{P}$es...the *United States of the Americas*: North America, Mexico, Central America, South America, and the West Indies are all joined together into one huge country.

It happens something like this: In 1994, America, Canada, and Mexico sign the *North American Free Trade Agreement*, or *NAFTA*, an economic partnership between the three countries. In the years following, South American, Central American, and West Indies' countries gradually join, until every country in the Western Hemisphere is a member, including Cuba, which quickly becomes "decommunized," or "deCastroized," after the death of Fidel Castro from a heart attack (or some other "natural" death).

The political union begins when, shortly following the completion of the economic union, Canada breaks apart. This occurs when French-Canadian separatists in the province of Quebec — after many decades of struggle — manage to get enough votes to separate Quebec from Canada...no, this isn't quite accurate.

It should really be: This breakup occurs after council manipulations make it possible for the French-Canadian separatists to get enough votes to separate Quebec from Canada, since council manipulations of the Canadian federal government (which the council has, of course, been manipulating, in one way or another, for many years) has weakened it severely and made it possible for the separatists to gain the strength needed for a successful separation (and, of course, the council has also been manipulating the French-

Canadian separatists; had it not, there wouldn't have been any separation because the separatists, on their own, couldn't separate cream from milk). Had certain English-Canadians had their way (or, more accurately, had the council "allowed" them to have their way), the Quebec separatists would've been destroyed in 1970, when they — members of the violent separatist group "FLQ," to be precise — kidnaped and killed a government official (or, more accurately, when the council manipulated the FLQ into kidnaping and killing a government official; we wanted to see how "the people" of Canada would react to such cowardly act, and how they'd feel about the government action that followed; it was a little "experiment," so to speak).

The council, however, didn't want the separatists destroyed because it wanted to keep Canada politically weak, since it saw a time in the future when it might want Canada to break apart, in order that it — or the pieces that remained after the breakup — could become part of America.

And that time comes. The council orchestrates a Quebec separation, and Canada is destroyed. There are many Canadians who feel that Canada can still exist without Quebec, but they're only fooling themselves — or else they're ignorant, or just plain stupid, or a combination of both — because Quebec is an "integral" part of Canada — politically, economically, and physically.

Take the latter, for example. When Quebec separates, it also "physically" separates Canada, in that, it stands between the Atlantic provinces and the rest of the provinces. This, naturally, makes the citizens of the Atlantic provinces — New Brunswick, Nova Scotia, Prince Edward Island, and Newfoundland — feel isolated and, even worse, "unwanted," or, more accurately, "more" unwanted, since they've felt for many years that the other provinces (particularly Ontario, the most powerful province) simply don't give a shit about them. Therefore, when America offers them a chance to become citizens of America, most jump at the chance. (America also offers statehood to all the other provinces and territories of the broken country, but they all reject the offer — although it's clearly evident that "many" citizens are more than just a little interested.)

The four new states, plagued by years of high unemployment and neglect/indifference by the federal government, suddenly find themselves thriving like never before as American investors begin "major"moves into the region (the council makes certain of that). There are quickly more jobs available than can be filled locally, and people from other parts of America begin moving to the region — which, of course, creates even more prosperity. And the general feeling is: "We should've done this years ago! To hell with Canada!"

The council then goes to work on the new country of Quebec, manipulating the country's new government — a collection of some of the most corrupt politicians to ever hold office anywhere in the world (they really don't need much manipulating) — and before long, Quebec is openly a dictatorship (although, of course, the Quebec government vigorously denies this, claiming that it's really a democratic government — but its enemies are trying to make it look like a dictatorship). Non-French citizens, for example, are openly discriminated against (they can't, for instance, hold government jobs, and they have to pay three times what French citizens pay for business licenses, and all business signs have to be in French only), and dissenters soon find themselves facing the new military of the new country of Quebec; a military that's been armed and trained by France (who makes certain that Quebec receives a generous amount

188

of arms, including armored vehicles, artillery, helicopter gunships, multirole jet planes, guided anti-tank weapons, and surface-to-air missiles; in a short time, the new country of Quebec has a strong, well-armed military with about 50,000 regular personnel, and a militia with over 150,000 personnel).

Canada — or what remains of it — protests to both Quebec and France about this military buildup — especially after Quebec's military begins attacking aboriginal separatists in northern Quebec with helicopter gunships and jet fighter-bombers. France responds by saying that Quebec has the right to defend itself against internal terrorism, and Quebec insists that it absolutely "needs" to use such extreme force against the aboriginal separatists — the "terrorist" aboriginal separatists — because they're using extreme force against the Quebec government; the aboriginal terrorists have, after all, killed half a dozen police officers in sniper attacks, and a further dozen in bomb attacks — plus they've also destroyed millions of dollars worth of property with bombs.

The aboriginals insist they're totally innocent, that they're being framed (which, of course, is true; the council is behind the shootings and bombings). Quebec, however, has "proof" — "absolute" proof — that they're guilty. Firearms, ammunition, and explosives have been found in aboriginal residences; plus, it has signed confessions from two aboriginal men who took part in the shootings and bombings. Unfortunately, however, they're no longer alive. One committed suicide in prison (stabbed himself in the heart three times), and the other was shot while trying to escape custody (hit by over a hundred rounds of machine gun fire).

Enraged by Quebec's actions — especially the helicopter gunship and fighter-bomber attacks — aboriginals all over Quebec begin a fierce war against the Quebec government/military. And surprisingly, they quickly become very well-armed; it seems they've somehow been able to obtain from somewhere a large quantity of military weapons (including heavy machine guns, grenade launchers, mortars, guided anti-tank missiles, and shoulder-launched surface-to-air missiles).

Quebec immediately accuses both Canada and America of supplying these arms to the aboriginals. Both countries (if what remains of Canada can really be called a "country"; it's really now only "half" a country — or even less), of course, deny the accusations, pointing out that "all" the weapons are of foreign manufacture; mainly of Russian and Chinese origin. Case closed!

Quebec, however, isn't satisfied — at least not with Canada's denial. It insists that Canada is involved in supplying arms to the aboriginals and it simply won't put up with it!

The separation agreement Quebec and Canada signed states that Canadians can "freely, without any restraint whatsoever," use the St. Lawrence River/Seaway, as well as Quebec's highways, rail lines, and airspace, to travel from Canada's western half to its eastern half and vice versa — as long as Canada pays its fair share for the maintenance of the Seaway, highways, and rail lines, of course.

Now, however, Quebec says that this part of the agreement is no longer valid because Canada no longer has an eastern section and, if Canada wants access to the Atlantic Ocean through Quebec, it must negotiate a new deal. And that new deal will definitely cost Canada more than the old deal — "much" more — because Canada is guilty of aiding the aboriginal terrorists.

Canada immediately condemns this action, accusing Quebec of "deliberately and maliciously" trying to sabotage its economy, and again denying "any" involvement in supplying weapons to Quebec's aboriginal separatists. Quebec responds by accusing Canada of "deliberately and maliciously" trying to destroy its economy by supplying arms to the aboriginals. And it claims it has "irrefutable" proof that Canadians in "high places," both in government and the business world, are indeed supplying arms to the aboriginals and, until that ends — and until Canada surrenders these people to the Quebec government for prosecution — Canadians won't be allowed to pass through, or over, Quebec — and that includes trucks, ships, and planes of foreign countries carrying exports and imports to and from Canada. American ships loaded with Canadian wheat bound for Europe, for example, won't be allowed to pass through the St. Lawrence, nor will American ships loaded with European goods destined for Canada be allowed through the waterway.

This is shocking beyond belief! Canada is certain America won't put up with this kind of behavior from Quebec; it'll "quickly" set Quebec's totalitarian government straight! Therefore, Canada is more than a little surprised when America says it'll respect Quebec's decision, declaring that it doesn't want to get involved in a Canada-Quebec dispute. It will, however, of course, allow Canadian exports and imports to be shipped through and over it, so Canada will still have easy access to the Atlantic.

Canada then appeals to the United Nations — and is again more than a little surprised when the great majority of UN members also don't want to get involved in a Canada-Quebec dispute. And a number of members — thirty-two, to be precise — are actually even openly hostile to Canada. These members include France, Spain, Portugal, Russia, and all the WIC countries (they haven't yet left the UN). They side with Quebec in accusing Canada of supplying arms to the aboriginal "terrorists." And one country — Somalia — also directly accuses Canada of terrorism because way back in 1993 Canadian troops serving with a UN peacekeeping force in Somalia tortured and killed a Somalian teenager. And it's true. There's no denying it. It's a "fact." The soldiers even took pictures of their sadistic party. And even though Canada has repeatedly apologized for what a few of its troops did, the incident has "irrevocably" tainted the once proud Canadian military — and Canada, as a whole.

And Canada — or what remains of it — has also been permanently harmed by the Quebec separation — especially since Quebec was "allowed" to separate. Many loyal Canadians believe that the federal government should've put its foot down and declared that no province could unilaterally separate from the country. But it didn't. It allowed Quebec — and then the Atlantic provinces — to unilaterally separate (although, it perhaps puts up some kind of resistance, such as the Supreme Court of Canada ruling that no province can unilaterally separate from Canada — which the provinces in question simply refuse to accept — and the federal government is afraid to use the military to enforce the decision, since a civil war could result from such an action).

And because of this, many Canadians are looking at Canada in a different way, and they see: a once powerful country that has become weak — and immoral, as the soldiers in Somalia have so graphically illustrated. Sure, it was only a "few" soldiers, and the incident happened many years before. But, as I've already said, their actions were enough to "permanently" taint "all" of Canada. And many once proud Canadians begin feeling ashamed, and start thinking that it'd perhaps be better to be American.

And an increasing number of Canadians do become Americans — especially as the conflict with Quebec heats up. Christ, at the rate it's going, Canada and Quebec are going to get into an all-out war! And because of inept politicians, Canada stands a very good chance of getting a severe beating from Quebec. After all, because of France — and WIC countries supplying aid though France — Quebec has a military that's certainly "much" stronger than Canada's. And Quebec's soldiers also certainly have a "much" higher morale than Canada's soldiers.

In fact, morale among Canadian soldiers is so low that many are actually deserting and going to America — which America actually encourages, in that it offers the deserters immediate American citizenship if they'll enlist in a branch of the American military for a minimum of four years.

This outrages the Canadian government. But so what? Its outrage doesn't mean anything to America — or the rest of the world. Even Great Britain, once its staunchest ally — and fellow member of the British Commonwealth — isn't concerned by Canada's problems (it, after all, has problems of its own: unemployment is rising at a frightening rate; people are starting to riot in large numbers, and police/military are beginning to have serious problems handling the outbreaks; the government — racked by scandal after scandal involving sex, drugs, and large-scale corruption — is growing steadily impotent; it appears that the IRA is going to win its decades-long struggle against the British government/military in Ireland...Great Britain hasn't been in such bad shape since it appeared that Nazi Germany was going to conquer it in World War Two).

America also announces that, for all those accepting its offer of citizenship in return for military service, it'll also give their families — including parents, grandparents, aunts, uncles, brothers, sisters, etc. — American citizenship should they want to leave Canada and live in "the greatest country on Earth." Plus, America will also pay all moving expenses and give them a substantial housing grant that doesn't have to be payed back! Welcome to America!

Hundreds — then thousands — of Canadian soldiers and their families accept the offer and cross the border. It's unbelievable! Canadians who, perhaps only a few weeks earlier, had said, "I'll "never" be an American — no matter what!" — are suddenly moving to America and becoming Americans.

Canadians still patriotic to Canada condemn those choosing America over Canada as "traitors." Those making the American choice, however, deny this. They're not traitors. The real traitors are the Canadian politicians who let Canada fall apart. They, the ones moving to America, are simply only decent, hardworking people who just want a better life for themselves and their loved ones.

And they're definitely going to find a better life in America because, while Canada has been experiencing an alarming rise in unemployment (largely due to the fact that many American-owned companies — as well as many other foreign-owned companies — and even many Canadian-owned companies — are pulling out of Canada because of the Canada-Quebec conflict), America's unemployment rate has been steadily dropping, due largely to the spectacular growth in its armaments industry, which is bigger than it's been for many years (since World War Two, in fact).

This huge growth, of course, is a result of the growing tension between Korea/China, and Japan — and China and Taiwan — and the WIC countries and Israel — and the many civil wars raging, or beginning to rage, around the world — and because Ivan is beginning to rattle his saber in the new Russia (it isn't yet *Cold War Two*, but it's getting close) — and, of course, because of the growing tension between Canada and Quebec.

Oh, yes, while America doesn't want to get involved in a Canada-Quebec dispute, it'll profit from the dispute by selling arms. It does have morals, however, and won't sell to both sides. It'll only sell to Canada since, after all, it's been America's military ally for many years (except during the Vietnam conflict, of course). Certainly, Quebec was also a part of that relationship, since it was a part of Canada. But that was then; this is now. Quebec is no longer a part of Canada, and even though Canada has lost "much" of its stature, America can't simply desert it — even though it didn't help America during the Vietnam conflict; and, in fact, even offered sanctuary to American draft dodgers and deserters (which, of course, the council was responsible for because it wanted something, should the need arise, that America could use against Canada in the future).

This brings strong condemnation from Quebec and its main ally, France. America responds by telling Quebec that, when it's fighting aboriginal "terrorists" near its border with America, it should be "extremely" careful since a bullet or some other piece of ordnance might cross that border and hit an American citizen, and if that should occur...well... America might get "extemely" angry — and should that happen, the consequences could be "severe" — "extemely" severe...

And before France can accuse America of threatening Quebec, America responds to France's condemnation of America supplying arms to Canada by reminding France that both Canada and America aided it during its time of crisis in World War Two — and that "many" Canadians and Americans lost their lives in the process. Therefore, France should perhaps think a little before condemning America for anything, or siding with Quebec against Canada, because it just might one day again need their help, especially America's, to combat an aggressor (Ivan or Russia isn't mentioned, but it's clear that it/he is what America's referring to).

And if France thinks that Quebec will come to its aid should such a situation arise, well, it might be very disappointed, to say the least, because Quebec, even though it's now a "country," isn't, by "any" means, a "powerful" country. It is, in fact, even though it belongs to the UN and *NAFTA*, a "minor" country who'd end up being "much" more of a hindrance than a help during a "major" conflict (that is, if it'd be of any help at all; it must be remembered that many French-speaking Canadians didn't want to fight to help "anyone" during World War Two). So don't bite the hand, or hands, that you one day might need to help you. And don't be so arrogant to think that you'll never need assistance in the future; just remember your pathetic performance in World War Two. You declared war on Germany, then Germany defeated you with humiliating ease, and occupied you. And you stayed occupied until the Allied forces — but especially American forces — liberated you.

Both France and Quebec are furious at the way America talks to them. But they remain silent, knowing that America is telling the truth, and also sensing that America is more than a little annoyed; there's definitely a threatening tone — an "ominous" tone — in its voice.

America then turns to Canada and tells it — addressing "the people of "the broken country" — that they'd be "much" better off as Americans than as Canadians (just look at how well the new states of Nova Scotia, New Brunswick, Prince Edward Island, and Newfoundland are doing; the unemployment rate in all four states has dropped from an average of 16% to less than 1%!). And America makes it clear that it's more than ready to grant immediate statehood to each and every province and territory of Canada.

And, for the first time, it also announces that it's ready to grant immediate statehood to any and every country in the Western Hemisphere, telling their citizens, like it told Canada's citizens, that they wouldn't be "losing" their identity — they'd be "gaining" one. They'd become members of a "new" country — the biggest — and "best" — in the whole history of the world. And just think about how much better life would be for you — and your children — and your children's children — and your children's children's children, etc, etc...you "must" think of their future...

Within a few months of the offer, the Canadian territories of the Yukon and the Northwest Territories have been granted statehood, as have the provinces of Saskatchewan and Manitoba, and the countries of Mexico, Guatemala, Belize, Honduras, El Salvador, Nicaragua, Costa Rica, Panama, Guyana, Chile, Uruguay, Paraguay, and all of the West Indies, except for Cuba — but rumor has it that it won't be long before Castro is gone — one way or another.

And within the next year, the Canadian provinces of British Columbia and Alberta become states, leaving Ontario as the only remaining province of Canada — so Ontario is now, in fact, "Canada." As well, the rest of the South American countries join the new confederation — and the world is stunned!

Hell, even the people who've joined the new confederation — or at least the "great" majority of them — are stunned. They just can't believe that they're now citizens of the United States of America (which will soon be known as the *United States of the Americas*). It's not that anyone has any regrets about becoming Americans...it's just that it feels so... "unreal" — like they've been hypnotized, or something...

And, in a manner of speaking, they have been hypnotized. For many years, these people — the "ordinary,"

197

or "common," people — of these Western Hemisphere countries have been looking at America and seeing: SUCCESS!

America is where a person can be born dirt-poor, and quickly become a millionaire — a multi-millionaire! — a billionaire! — a multi-billionaire! Anything is possible in America! It's the land of milk and honey and expensive cars and mansions and yachts and private jets and...the sky is the limit in America! All non-Americans in the Western Hemisphere — all the "ordinary," or "common," non-Americans, that is — want to go to America and become Americans — except for Canadians.

They don't want to become Americans. They like visiting America, and even living in it — especially to escape Canada's long cold winters in places like California, Florida, Arizona, etc. — but they don't desire American citizenship. They're Canadians — proud and free! They'll "never" be Americans! Or so they say. The truth is, generally speaking, they'd "love" to be Americans. They just have trouble admitting it, that's all.

But the council doesn't want to "force" them into becoming Americans. They have to "want" to become Americans. So we break Canada apart and manipulate them into "wanting" to join America. And it works perfectly because the "great" majority of "the people" of Canada — same as the great majority" of "the people" of the world — simply don't have much — if "any" — imagination (and this includes "many" who are "highly" educated).

They see something on TV, or read about it, or hear about it on radio, or directly from another person and, without making any attempt to go past what they see/read/hear, they "believe."

And it's this lack of imagination — this "dysfunction"

198

— that makes it "easy" to manipulate people. Therefore, it isn't any problem breaking Canada apart. And when this happens, many Canadians — no longer "really" having a country to be proud of (in fact, many actually find it embarrassing being Canadian) — are drawn to America, and the offer of American citizenship and a better life — a "much" better life — in the "best" country in the world.

So now all that needs doing to make the *United States of the Americas* a "complete" country is to bring Ontario — or "Canada," as many there insist on calling it — and Quebec — and Cuba, of course — into the new confederation. Now, Cuba isn't "any" problem. It becomes part of the new supernation after Castro succumbs to a heart attack or whatever — such as Cuba's military revolting and running over him with a tank. Or maybe the council sees to it that he gets safely out of Cuba and into a friendly country — where he suddenly renounces his revolution, proclaiming Marx and Lenin to be two of the biggest peckerheads in history — and tells his fellow Cubans that Cuba should now become part of America...there are many possibilities. But they all, of course, have the same ending: Cuba becomes part of the *United States of the Americas.*

And so does Ontario — or "Canada" — or "Ontanada," as it's now being called by many — and so does Quebec. Before that happens, however, there first has to be a war...just a "little" one, of course — just enough to destroy what remains of Canada, and the new country of Quebec.

Actually, it's more of a "symbolic" war than anything — especially as concerns the destruction of what remains of Canada. Oh, certainly, despite it only being "symbolic," thousands — maybe tens of thousands — will be killed and maimed, but the main objective, as concerns the destruction of what remains of Canada, isn't to kill and maim. It's simply to destroy the federal Parliament buildings in Ottawa, because when these historic buildings are reduced to rubble, Canada will then "truly" be destroyed.

And they're "extremely" easy to destroy. Ottawa is on the Ottawa River, and the Parliament buildings sit right on the bank of the river. Directly across from them — about 1,200 or so feet across the river — is the city of Hull, Quebec. So the Parliament buildings are a "sitting duck" target. And heavy weapons aren't even needed to do the job. All that's needed is light attack craft carrying commando/demolition teams under cover of darkness (and some help from the council, of course, who manipulates Canadian forces into zigging when they should be zagging).

But, naturally, they (because of council manipulations, of course)also use heavy weapons — such as their new French-supplied 120mm mortars, 155mm howitzers, multiple rocket launchers, guided anti-tank missiles, main battle tanks, helicopter gunships, and Mirage jets — because it makes for "much" better TV coverage — which is "extremely" important. People in America — and the rest of the world — must see the destruction, death, and suffering being inflicted by this new country of Quebec with its despotic leaders who, of course, start the conflict. It must be "clearly" understood that they're in the "wrong" — they're the "bad" guys. They split — "destroyed" — the "good" country of Canada. They reneged on treaties. They're oppressing minorities — especially aboriginals — and are even using "heavy" force against them (including, rumor has it, lethal chemicals).

And now they're destroying the beautiful, old, historic buildings that used to be the seat of the Canadian federal government. And why? It's quite clear that Canada is dead, and will "never" rise again. So there simply isn't "any" need to destroy these beautiful buildings. It's just pure malice —

pure "evil." And the world watches as the new country of Quebec reduces these once proud buildings to rubble.

But they don't stop at the Parliament buildings. They also destroy other buildings (which also conveniently happen to be within point-blank range) that were important to Canada and Canadians: the prime minister's residence at 24 Sussex Drive, Rideau Hall, the Royal Canadian Mint, the Public Archives, the Supreme Court...and even the National War Memorial! Nothing is sacred to these bastards! Quebec insists it didn't mean to destroy the monument, but since the area around it has been pounded by thousands of mortar, artillery, and rocket rounds, as well as hundreds of bombs and thousands of air-to-surface rockets, it's quite clear that Quebec is lying. It meant to destroy the monument — just like it meant to destroy everything else it's destroyed.

But perhaps even worse than the destruction it causes with its heavy weapons (including deaths and injuries), is that it also occupies Ottawa and the surrounding area, and finishes the job; it actually breaks big rubble into little rubble and little rubble into tiny rubble. It's determined to "completely" destroy "every" trace of the Canadian federal government. And, using explosives, jackhammers, and bulldozers, it does — or almost does. Before it can finish the job, it makes a mistake — a "major" mistake — a "fatal" mistake.

While fighting aboriginals on the Quebec-American border (northern Vermont-Quebec), a Quebec helicopter gunship fires rockets that overshoot their target and hit an American family who are on a camping trip, killing the father and six-year-old daughter, and seriously wounding the mother and eleven-year-old son.

America immediately (so "immediately," in fact, that it almost seems like America knew when and where it was going to happen!) accuses Quebec of a "vicious act of premeditated aggression," and even goes as far as comparing it to the Japanese attack on Pearl Harbor in 1941. This, of course, is "utterly" ludicrous. But it inflames "the people" of America — especially the many ex-Canadians who have a special hatred for Quebec — or, more accurately, Quebec "separatists."

Quebec insists that it's innocent. Its troops didn't fire any rockets in that area — at least, not on that particular day — HONEST! But America has the "proof." It has fragments of French-made air-to-surface rockets, the dead bodies of two American citizens (and one them a sweet, innocent six-year-old girl; a picture of her shattered, bloody body alongside a two week-old-picture of her playing with her puppy — also a rocket victim — is shown to the country — then the world; it "really" brings forth the tears — and rage), and two seriously wounded survivors of the attack (the eleven-year-old boy has lost an arm and a leg, and has been permanently blinded; the mother has lost the lower part of her right leg, a kidney, and a lung).

Quebec keeps insisting that it didn't do it — that it's being framed by its enemies — probably the aboriginals. (This, of course, simply isn't true. Quebec isn't being framed by its "enemies"; it's being framed by the council — and it doesn't consider Quebec to be an "enemy." It's simply a piece of real estate that "needs" to be "politically relocated"— like the rest of the Canadian provinces, Mexico, and the rest of the real estate that's recently joined America — and it was decided that this was the best way to politically relocate Quebec; there isn't anything "personal" about it.)

America, however, won't be fooled by Quebec's "obvious" and "outrageous" lies. Nor will it tolerate such behavior. It, after all, "clearly" warned Quebec to be careful when operating its military near its border with America. And it also made it "very" clear that the consequences could be "extremely" severe for Quebec if American citizens were hit by the Quebec military...oh, yes, America warned Quebec, it certainly did! And Quebec didn't heed that warning — so now it must pay...

And less than twenty-four hours after the incident on the Vermont-Quebec border, America attacks Quebec with a display of force never before seen in North America. And within another twenty-four hours, Quebec's military is completely shattered, all its government officials are in American custody, charged with "war crimes," and Quebec has officially been annexed by America.

This annexation, of course, quickly turns into statehood as the "huge" majority of Quebec citizens prove that they never wanted an independent Quebec in the first place (hundreds of thousands claim they were forced into voting for independence by separatist "terror squads").(As well, at the same time Quebec is granted statehood, Ontario/Canada becomes a state — after a "democratic" vote, of course.)

Quebec's allies strongly protest America's action — except for its main ally, France, who doesn't say much. It calls America's actions "regrettable" — but that's about all.

It, after all, realizes that it might soon be needing America's help, because Ivan's saber rattling is getting louder...much louder...

~

$\mathfrak{I}$van!

...in Moscow's Ivan Square (formerly known as Moscow Square, and before that, Red Square), reviewing a parade of the new Russia's new army. It's the biggest such display that's ever been held in the square (and in the whole world, for that matter): over 750,000 troops; over 7,500 armored vehicles (including 2,500 of Russia's new tank, the T-2000, or *Ivan*, as it's being called; described by military experts worldwide as the most advanced tank in the world); over 7,500 pieces of artillery (including 1,500 of the new 280mm multiple rocket launcher; the longest-ranged weapon of its type in the world); over 2,000 of the new *SA-24* mobile, anti-aircraft missile launchers (that use the latest laser beam technology; it's rumored that the *SA-24* has a 98% kill rate); over 2,000 long-range, surface-to-surface missiles(including 200 of the newest — and deadliest — missiles, the *SS-30*, with a reported range of over 8,000 miles, carrying either a single nuclear 25 MT warhead, or five nuclear 5 MT multiple independently targetable re-entry vehicles — or "MIRVs" — or twelve nuclear 2 MT MIRVs, or chemical, or biological warheads; it's being called, *Ivan's Thunder*)...the parade takes over six hours! And all through it — "Icing the cake," Ivan says — is the new Russian air force displaying its new power, using over 10,000 aircraft, including 1,000 of the new *Mig-37* multirole jets and 1,000 of the new *SU-39* multirole jets (both of which are reported to be the most advanced multirole jets in the world), and 2,000 of the new *Mi-32* attack helicopters (also reported to be the most advanced attack helicopter in the world). But, by far, the show's biggest star is Ivan!

...who appears the next day at a shipyard in Ivangrad (formerly known at different times as St. Petersburg, Petrograd, and Leningrad) to launch two new additions to the new Russia's new navy. The first is the world's largest nuclear-powered aircraft carrier, the 1,300 foot, 116,000 ton full-load displacement *Ivan*. (In comparison, the longest American carrier is the aging nuclear-powered *Enterprise*, at 1,123 feet, and the heaviest are the aging nuclear-powered *Nimitz*-class carriers with 101,000 ton full-load displacements; as well, both the *Enterprise* and *Nimitz*-class carriers can only carry a maximum of about 100 aircraft, whereas the *Ivan* can carry a maximum of about 120.) The second warship Ivan launches is the world's largest nuclear-powered missile cruiser, the 1,000 foot, 60,000 ton full-load displacement *Nelvonovich*, which carries, among many other weapons, eight SS-30 missiles. (In comparison, the largest American missile cruisers are the aging 585 foot, 11,000 ton full-load displacement, nuclear-powered *Virginia*-class missile cruisers — and they're not armed with "anything" even close to the *SS-30*.)

Ivan!

...giving speeches to his fellow Russians — and the rest of the world — in which he repeatedly attacks Russia's five greatest enemies/threats: America, Germany, France, Italy (particularly the Vatican), and England.

America, however, is Russia's single greatest enemy/threat. It's a cancer that's threatening, not just Russia, but the entire world with its political and religious corruptness, greed, crime, violence, drug addiction, alcoholism, pornography...it's a sick nation — an "extremely" sick nation!

And it's spreading its sickness to the rest of the world,

mainly through television and the Internet — which, of course, is why he's being "forced" to strictly control Russian TV and computers — as well as printed matter and radio.

This, naturally, brings more condemnation from America and other countries in the "free" world. First, he denies the Russian people their religious freedom, and now he's denying them their freedom of speech!

Ivan responds to these charges by saying that one of the world's greatest problems — maybe "the" greatest problem — is that people have far too much freedom. Take, for example, the freedom to reproduce without any kind of regulation. This has resulted in the births of hundreds of millions of substandard people which, of course, has led to an overall decline in the quality of life on Earth. And this isn't simply a "belief," or "opinion." It's a "fact." He has tens of thousands of pages of scientific research that've been compiled by the best scientists in the world (Russian scientists, of course; it seems Russian scientists have made "all" the "important" scientific discoveries ever made).

But all this documentation — this "proof" — isn't needed to know the "truth," Ivan declares. To see the results of too much freedom, all one has to do is look at the world — especially the so-called "free" world — "so-called" because it "really" isn't "free"; it's actually an enormous prison controlled by an elite who are only interested in money and power, and have the morals of maggots.

Take the problem of crime in the "free" world, for example. It isn't "really" a "problem." It's only made to "appear" that way by this elite who actually creates crime and keeps it alive because they profit from it at all levels. They make money from various criminal activities, such as dealing in illegal drugs, while, at the same time, making money from "fighting" crime, since they're heavily involved in businesses

206

related to the judicial system. They, for instance, own construction companies that build courthouses, police stations, and prisons, as well as owning companies that supply police forces with everything police forces need, such as computers, cars, helicopters, communications equipment, uniforms, badges, guns, ammunition... "everything" and "anything" they need. And they also own law firms that defend people charged with crimes. In fact, they own, or "control," "everything" in the "free" world — crime, government, the judicial system, big business, small business — "everything" — and "everyone."

But they don't control Ivan and the Russian people — at least, not anymore. There was a time when this scum! — this filth! — these degenerates! — did have much control over the Russian people, with their grand talk of "freedom" and "democracy," as they polluted the Russian people with their evilness, like their drugs, music, violence, pornography, and religion. An American president — Ronald Reagan, one of the foulest of the elite, Ivan says — once called Russia (when it was known as the "Soviet Union"), an "evil empire." But the "real" evil empire, Ivan shouts, was the "free" world — especially America, the head and heart of the putrid, soulless beast.

But then he, Ivan, came along and changed all that! Yes, he's purged Russia of this evil — and now Russia is again strong! Just look at it! Everyone's working and living well. It's the highest standard of living the Russian people have ever experienced. There isn't any poverty, and hardly any crime — and what little there is, is mostly "minor" — and, according to Ivan, one of the main reasons for this "drastic" drop in crime, and the "huge" improvement in living conditions, in general, is (besides getting rid of the "free" world filth that was threatening Russia's very existence)

207

because of the "dramatic" drop in Russia's alcohol consumption.

It's amazing! Ivan has actually convinced the Russian people (who had a reputation for being "heavy" drinkers) to either quit drinking altogether, or to severely cut back on their liquor consumption — especially "hard" liquor, such as the old Russian favorite, vodka.

And remarkably, he's done it without having to use any kind of laws or force. All he's done is use simple patriotic motivation: The less you drink, the more you think. And the more you think, the better your life will be. And the better your life is, the better Russia's life is.

Or: The more you drink, the less you think. And the less you think, the worse your life will be. And the worse your life is, the worse Russia's life is.

Be a good Russian — a patriotic Russian! Be healthy! Build a healthy Russia! Don't drink! Don't smoke! Work hard! Hard work makes a healthy Russia!

And it's worked. The Russian people have responded with an amazing — and frightening — zeal. Of course, many non-Russians — especially those in the "free" world — don't believe it. They think it's just propaganda, or *Ivanganda*. Ivan, however, invites journalists from all over the world — but especially the "free" world — to visit Russia and see for themselves — and he'll even foot the bill!

The offer is irresistible. Hundreds of top journalists from the "free" world accept Ivan's offer. (No journalists come from countries that aren't so "free," such as the WIC countries, because their governments won't allow it; in fact, WIC governments try to suppress all information about Ivan and the new Russia, since he's clearly a potential threat to them.) They at first think that Ivan is simply going to put on a dog and pony show for them, and only allow them to see what he wants them to see. But that doesn't prove to be the case. Ivan allows them to go anywhere they want — except for certain military installation, of course — and talk with whomever they want. His only stipulation is that they don't bring "any" kind of "free" world "filth" with them, such as religious, political, and pornographic material (and "all" writing, art, music, movies, etc, from the "free" world is "pornographic"). Nor are they to verbally spread any "free" world "filth" — including "any" criticism of Ivan and/or Russia — while they're in Russia. Anyone caught breaking these simple rules will immediately be transported to the nearest border point between Russia and the "free" world, and have to cross the border on foot and make their way home at their own expense.

Everyone agrees to these rules and, after spending a week in the new Russia, everyone also agrees that they're...well..."stunned" by what they've found. The Russian people are indeed enjoying the highest standard of living ever seen in that part of the world. In fact, taking everything into consideration, it's probably the highest standard of living "anywhere" in the world. Certainly, Russians lack certain freedoms — what many in the "free" world would call "basic" freedoms, such as freedom of speech, religion, and reproduction. But, at the same time, they also lack poverty, homelessness, hopelessness, unemployment, huge debt, a high level of mental illness/impairment caused by "free" world stress (such as poverty, unemployment, hopelessness, debt, etc), a high crime rate (Russia's crime rate is one of the world's lowest — if not "the" lowest), a high level of drug and alcohol addiction (Russia's drug and alcohol addiction rate is one of the world's lowest — if not "the" lowest)...it's incredible!

Not one journalist, despite the lack of "basic"

freedoms in Russia — and the fact that Ivan has admitted to building horrendous weapons of mass destruction, and admits to a willingness to use them — has "anything" negative to say about the new Russia, or Ivan. In fact, many openly praise Ivan and the new Russia — and some even talk about moving to Russia!

Many in the "free" world — especially "Christians" (particularly "fundamentalist" Christians) — "strongly" condemn the journalists, and quite a number even say that they deserve to be executed because they're nothing but "Godless, treasonous filth!"

And they're "serious" — especially the fundamentalist "militants," who are composed mainly of young (15-25) white males led ("manipulated") by older (40-70), fiery, charismatic, right-wing ("extreme" right-wing) Christian militants — "radical" militants — who quickly turn these "highly" impressionable young males — these "new patriots of God and country" — into wild-eyed "true believers" of the most fanatical kind by using both hypnotic rhetoric (much of which is delivered in the form of short, snappy videotaped messages that resemble music videos much more than political/religious messages), and a "power vitamin."

The leaders claim that this "vitamin" is "natural," but, in reality, it's nothing more than a powerful amphetamine that's been concocted in third-rate laboratories in various parts of the "free" world. It's cheap crap, but it jazzes the young "patriots" with a false feeling of "power" and "intelligence" and "righteousness."

Fueled by this powerful drug and "revolutionary" and "patriotic" razzmatazz — "POWER TO THE PATRIOTS!" — from the charismatic "leaders" (who don't know they're being manipulated by the council), and also "abundantly" supplied with firearms and explosives by these leaders

(courtesy of the council, of course), these new patriots —
these "saviors" of the "free" world (but especially the *United
States of the Americas*) — create the most unbelievable —
and bloodiest — reign of terror the "free" world has ever
experienced.

Heavily-armed groups (some as small as three or four,
some as large as three or four thousand) of these new patriots
begin attacking anyone and "anything" (like businesses and
religious organizations) they consider to be "anti-Christian"
and/or "unpatriotic" and/or "pro-Ivan/Russia" — including
people of Russian "descent" (even though their ancestors
might've originally come from Russia hundreds of years
before) — and even people with Russian "sounding" names
(such as "Ivan" and "Boris," and surnames ending in "ich," or
"sky," or "ski," etc). Even people who buy and/or sell and/or
drink vodka are attacked (which, of course, is ironic, since
Ivan has caused Russia's vodka consumption to sharply
decline), as are those who buy and/or sell and/or read
anything by Russian authors. Someone possessing a copy of
a work by Tolstoy, for instance, is killed without a second
thought — as is anyone possessing a copy of the Koran, or
Moslem literature of "any" kind; even possessing an
encyclopedia containing information about Islam and/or
Russia can mean death (and torture; the new patriots love to
hear people scream and shriek)...it's "insane." But it's
happening — it's for "real." Thousands — tens of thousands
— hundreds of thousands — millions — of non-Christians, or
"anti-Christians" (since, if one isn't Christian, that means one
is "anti-Christian") and/or unpatriotic and/or people who are
pro-Ivan/Russia are slaughtered without mercy.

And no one seems to be able to stop it. Or, more
accurately, no one seems to have the courage to try and stop
it. Politicians/governments order police/military to protect

211

government/politicians, and themselves, as well as certain vital facilities, such as oil refineries, power stations and main power lines, gas lines, bridges, etc. But they're afraid to order them on the offensive against the new patriots because the new patriots have made it clear that "anyone" who openly opposes them will immediately be targeted for death — as will their spouses, children, brothers, sisters, parents, aunts, uncles, grandparents, friends, etc...these "patriots" fight dirty. They'll do "anything" and "everything" to accomplish their goal of ridding the "free" world of the "Godless filth" that's trying to destroy it.

And it appears that they possess an extraordinary skill at acquiring information. For instance, they send lists to military units and police forces that contain the names and addresses of the personnel in the forces/units — along with lists of names and addresses of their next of kin — the message clearly being: We know who you are and where your loved ones live!

But it isn't the only clear message transmitted by the lists. Perhaps even more frightening than the lists themselves, is where they came from. The new patriots might appear to be nothing more than a bunch of lunatic fanatics, but they've somehow been able to access top-secret files that are supposed to be secure — "super"secure. The lists of military personnel, for instance, come from the very top of America's military: the Pentagon.

At first it's believed that some genius computer hacker in the new patriots must've somehow been able to bypass all of the Pentagon's sophisticated computer security. But there simply isn't "any" evidence of this. The lists, therefore, had to have come from someone actually "inside" the Pentagon, and that someone has to be in a "high" position — an "extremely" high position. And, naturally, this scares the military — including the very top brass at the Pentagon, whose names and addresses, as well as the names and addresses of their next of kin, are all on the lists — since it's obvious that whomever's responsible for the lists getting into the hands of the new patriots, also included their own name, or "names." Who knows how many in the Pentagon are involved? It could just be one — or ten — or twenty — or thirty...oh, yes, perhaps the Pentagon is actually behind the new patriots? Or maybe no one in the Pentagon is behind the new patriots? Maybe the lists didn't come from the Pentagon at all? Perhaps they came from the White House? Maybe the White House — even though "everyone" working there is also on the lists — is actually behind the new patriots?

Rumors begin blazing of conspiracies in high places — in the "highest" of high places. But no one can prove anything (and who'd want to?), and politicians/governments/police/militaries maintain their defensive positions, afraid — no, "terrified" — of going on the offensive against the new patriots. Consequently, with the "free" world lacking the glue that "really" holds it together — the fear "the people" have of authority — the ranks of the new patriots grow at an "alarming" rate — and the "free" world experiences a terror it's never before known.

Many areas — some with populations in the tens of millions — suddenly find themselves without any "official" law and order — except that which the new patriots provide — and their main concern is to root out and destroy "Godless filth." Consequently, thousands — tens of thousands — hundred of thousands — millions — tens of millions — are daily victimized in some manner; robbed, beaten, tortured, raped, enslaved, killed, etc. (Tragically, many are also killed and maimed when they try to find safety from the new patriots at police stations and military bases, since military and police

simply can't allow these unfortunates into their facilities —
and harsh methods, including the use of artillery and
helicopter gunships, have to be used.) And thousands — tens
of thousands — are dying daily because they're unable to get
adequate medical treatment (it seems that many doctors,
dentists, nurses, etc, are "Godless filth"), with "many" of the
deaths resulting from infections that could easily be treated
with antibiotics; in these areas, however, antibiotics, and all
other medicine, is controlled by the new patriots, who keep
most of it for themselves — and what they do sell is priced so
high that most just can't afford it, or simply can't bear to pay
the price (for example, the price for half a dozen antibiotic
pills might be one's young teenage daughter, to be used by the
new patriots as a "secretary" — which is new patriot-speak
for "sexual slave").

Furthermore, many million in the "free" world are also
going hungry, and many (especially babies, young children,
and the elderly) are even actually starving to death — for a
number of reasons; a lack of farm workers (it seems that
many farm workers are "Godless filth"); inadequate food
deliveries due to fuel shortages and massive breakdowns in
rail and highway transport (including a lack of workers in the
transportation industry; it seems that many in that industry are
also "Godless filth"); and, of course, because most food is
controlled by the new patriots, who eat first and best, and
charge exorbitant prices for what's left. (In many areas, food
shortages and hunger have resulted in zoo animals and pets
being eaten — and there have even been cases of
cannibalism!)

And many millions also don't have regular postal,
telephone, radio, television, and electrical service, and many
millions more don't have any of these services at all. As well,
many millions also suffer from chronic shortages of gasoline,

diesel fuel, propane, natural gas, heating oil, and coal, and many millions more are unable to get any of these fuels at all and, concerning cooking and heating, have to rely on wood (and in most areas, "all" wood is strictly controlled by the new patriots).

Also, unemployment is at an all-time high (on average, it's twice as high as it was during the great depression of the 1930s; and during that depression, the unemployment rate — just in America alone — hit 25%; now it's 50% — and climbing rapidly!), and unemployment insurance and welfare programs have, for the most part, completely broken down (and much of the employment that's available is more like "slavery" than "employment" — especially since unions are, for the most part, non-existent).

And education systems have also, generally speaking, completely broken down, since the new patriots view modern education as being propaganda from "Godless filth" — which has resulted in the total destruction of many educational facilities (Harvard, Princeton, and Yale, for example, have been blasted and burned beyond recognition), and many teachers, professors, instructors, etc, have been slaughtered...but so what?

After all, who needs an education in a world where there doesn't seem to be any future? In fact, many decide there isn't even any sense in living in a world where there doesn't seem to be any future — and the suicide rate soars. Every day, rather than face another day in the hell that the "free" world has become, thousands commit suicide — often in groups, with a "party" atmosphere; sometimes a group of a few hundred or more, singing and chanting and hugging each other, will simultaneously jump from a high building or bridge, such as San Francisco's Golden Gate bridge. In fact, the Golden Gate becomes synonymous with suicide, and becomes so popular with those wanting to go to a better world that the new patriots actually take control of the bridge, so they can charge would-be suicides for the privilege of using it. And at times, the water underneath the bridge actually foams because so many are jumping at the same time, and clots of 50, 60, 70, etc, bodies are a common sight in San Francisco Bay; and on some days — particularly when it's hot, and the wind is right — the smell of these decomposing islands of flesh (perhaps as many as a hundred separate islands with a total of three, four, five, etc, thousand bodies) carries for twenty or thirty miles (it's called "Golden Gate Gas").

It's terrible — "beyond" terrible...and Ivan loves it! Watching the "free" world fall apart fills him with such enormous ecstasy that his doctor sometimes has to give him drugs to calm him down. (Yes, just like Hitler, Ivan has his own private doctor who takes extremely good care of him, making certain Ivan receives his "vitamins," and anything else of a pharmaceutical nature that he might need. Also, just like Hitler, Ivan trusts and confides in his doctor, and listens to the doctor's hypnotic advice — except it doesn't seem like "advice"; it seems more like Ivan's own thoughts suddenly coming alive from somewhere deep inside him — somewhere he can't seem to reach, or even "find," without help from his doctor.

And, the same as Hitler, Ivan also has a "special" sweetheart he confides in and listens to — especially her words of praise for her "warrior king," and her words urging him to do this...and that...and this....)

Especially enjoyable to him is when refugees from the "free" world horror seek sanctuary in the new Russia — particularly when entire "free" world countries seek sanctuary!

Poland is the first. A former member of the Warsaw Pact, under the control of the old Soviet Union, it became independent — and part of the "free" world — after the Soviet Union collapsed in 1990. But as Ivan and the new Russia became increasingly stronger while the "free" world became increasingly weaker, Poland found itself in an increasingly perilous position.

It was quite clear from the way Ivan talked that Russia would one day invade both Germany and France (especially since Russian forces definitely seemed to be moving into position for just such an attack), and when that happened...well, since Poland was between Russia and France/ Germany, Russia would have to go through Poland to invade those countries and, as it did, German forces — and perhaps French forces, as well — would also enter Poland in an attempt to stop the Russians before they could get to, first Germany, then France — and Poland would become a battleground of unbelievable proportions.

Now, Poland has a number choices. It can declare itself a neutral country and hope that Russia, France, and Germany will all respect that neutrality. Or it can stay with the "free" world and hope that the "free" world pulls out of its rapid downward spiral before it's too late. Or it can take a chance and fight a Russian invasion on its own. Or it can join Ivan's new Russia.

The first choice — neutrality — is quickly dismissed, since it's obvious that Ivan won't honor "any" country's neutrality if it stands between him and his goals. In fact, he's openly said a number of times that should conflict break out in Europe, there won't be "any" neutral countries, like Switzerland and Sweden; "all" countries will have to choose a side — and if they don't, or can't, it'll be chosen for them.

The second choice — staying in the "free" world —

217

is risky because the "free" world is growing increasingly unstable, with no signs of conditions improving. In fact, it appears that they're only going to get worse — and worse — and the weaker the "free" world gets, the stronger Ivan and Russia become. And if Ivan suddenly decides to take advantage of the situation, Russian forces will be crashing into and through Poland on their way to Germany and France and, because it's chosen to remain part of the "free" world, Poland will become a conquered nation and the Polish people will suffer greatly — as Ivan has warned a few time when he's said things like: "Any country not with Russia, is against Russia. And any country against Russia can expect no mercy — "absolutely" no mercy — should an armed conflict occur."

And, complicating matters even further, Poland's closest "free" world partner is its next-door neighbor, Germany, which was reunited in 1990 when Warsaw Pact East Germany joined "free" world West Germany after 45 years of separation following Nazi Germany's defeat in World War Two.

Now, even though today's Germany isn't the Nazi Germany of World War Two, and even though Germany and Poland have "officially" become allies in the "free" world, the Polish people, generally speaking, don't trust Germans — "any" Germans — and they still, generally speaking — even though many years have passed since the end of World War Two — harbor a hatred for what the Germans did to them in that war. Truth be told, were the Polish people strong enough, or could manage to get strong enough, they'd like — they'd "love" — nothing more than to invade Germany and kick the crap out of it like Germany kicked the crap out of Poland in World War Two...oh, yes, it'd feel so great to give those arrogant bastards a taste of some "blitzkrieg"!

And more truth be told: It'd also feel great to be strong

enough to invade Russia and pay the Russians back for their invasion of Poland in World War Two (but, of course, it simply isn't strong enough — and never will be; and it'll also "never" be strong enough to withstand an attack by Russia without "massive" help from the rest of the "free" world, so choice number three — fighting Russia — is simply out of the question). Oh, yes, Poland got it good in that war. It hadn't done anything to either Germany or Russia. Yet, before they started fighting each other in 1941, both ganged up on Poland, Germany invading from the west, Russia from the east, and Poland was divided in half. But the Germans were by "far" the worst, with their genocidal death camps, such as Treblinka and Auschwitz, to name just two.

Therefore, taking everything into consideration (such as having to give up religion in favor of Ivan's "spirituality"), and after a democratic vote (that really isn't democratic; rumor has it that Poles working for Ivan are involved in a little behind-the-scenes manipulating — including stuffing ballot boxes), Poland applies to join Ivan's new Russia — and is immediately accepted by Ivan, who calls Poland a "visionary country filled with enlightened citizens of a new world." (Ivan has been using the term *new world* with increased frequency; for example, he often prefaces a speech with, "In our *new world*..." — and he's even begun adding, "...with its *new order*..." — which, of course, sounds remarkably similar to Hitler's *New World Order* of the 30s and 40s...but no one in Russia seems to notice this — although, in all fairness, the minds of the Russian people have been turned into mush by Ivan's mesmerizing words and a powerful pharmaceutical. Or, put another way: The minds of the Russian people have been *Ivanized* and "vitaminized" into mush.

Oh, yes, the Russian people might've drastically cut

down on their vodka and cigarette consumption, but those things have been replaced by something else. And that something else is a government-supplied "vitamin" that makes people feel "much" more energetic and patriotic than usual. But it isn't like the "vitamin" the new patriots in the "free" world are taking. It's much more complicated, in that it also contains ingredients that make drinking alcohol and smoking tobacco "extremely" unpleasant — which is the real reason for the drastic drop in Russia's tobacco and alcohol consumption. As well, it's also a little more addictive than the "vitamin" found in the "free" world, and it's also being delivered to the Russian people in a different manner than the "free" world "vitamin" is being delivered to the new patriots; the new patriots are receiving their "vitamin" only in pill form, whereas the Russian people are also getting theirs — unknowingly — in their water, milk, fruit juice, and food.)

The next country to join the new Russia is Hungary, another former Warsaw Pact member. It's quickly followed by the Czech Republic and Slovakia, both of which had formerly existed in the Warsaw Pact as the country of Czechoslovakia. Next, the former Warsaw Pact countries of Albania, Bulgaria, and Romania join Ivan's new Russia. Then Slovenia, Croatia, and the rest of the Balkan countries join — which creates a situation that stuns the "free" world — especially the Roman Catholic part of the "free" world.

Ivan has made it quite clear that he considers the Pope/Vatican to be one of Russia's greatest enemies/threats. And now, with the Balkan countries joining the new Russia, the Pope/Vatican are suddenly only about 250 miles from Ivan — or, as Ivan puts it: "The Pope and the Vatican are only about twenty-five minutes by cruise missile from the new Russia."

And videotape appears in the "free" world, showing

mobile cruise missile launchers — complete with the new, super-accurate cruise missile that's being affectionately called, *Ivan's Hammer* — rolling into the Balkan section of the new Russia, and into "shifting positions" along the coast bordering the Adriatic Sea. The coast of Italy is only about 125 miles from these positions; the Vatican — and the Pope — are another 125 miles from the coast. Two hundred and fifty miles in all. *Ivan's Hammer,* capable of carrying a 500 KT nuclear warhead, or a 4,000 pound conventional high explosive warhead, or chemical or biological warheads, has a maximum range of 2,500 miles and a maximum speed of 700 miles per hour — let's say, eleven miles per minute — which means that it — or 50, 100, 150, 200, etc, of them — can indeed be hammering the Vatican in about twenty-five minutes from launch.

Extremely scary, to say the least — especially since, besides moving hundreds of launchers for *Ivan's Hammer* into the area, Ivan also moves in an aircraft carrier, with two dozen support ships, including a heavy missile cruiser, and ten heavy amphibious assault vessels with a force of 20,000 crack marines; a helicopter assault force, comprised of 300 helicopter gunships, 300 transport helicopters, and 20,000 elite air commandoes; over 500,000 regular ground troops, well-equipped with armor and artillery; and 500 fixed-wing, multirole combat aircraft...and there'll be more — "much" more — if the Pope doesn't stop his aggression against Russia, Ivan warns.

Yes, that's right...according to Ivan, the Pope, not Russia, is the "aggressor," because the Pope has repeatedly said that Ivan — and Russia — are "the greatest threats to world peace that have ever existed." And Ivan warns that if the Pope — the "criminal scum" — keeps talking like that, Ivan — and the brave Russian people — the "bravest, most righteous people in the world!" — will simply be "forced" to do something about it!

And Ivan also warns that something will also "have" to be done if Germany continues its "aggression" against Russia — such as its build- up of "offensive" forces on the borders of the Polish and Czech sectors of the new Russia. This "aggressive" behavior simply can't be tolerated, Ivan warns.

Germany, of course, replies that its forces in these areas are purely "defensive," and are there only to protect Germany from the threat of the new Russia's massive military build- up on the other side of the borders in question. (In the short time since Poland and the Czech Republic joined the new Russia, Ivan has heavily militarized these areas; 750,000 troops, 600 combat aircraft, 3,000 tanks, and 3,000 pieces of artillery in the Polish sector — and 250,000 troops, with 300 combat aircraft, 1,000 tanks, and 1,000 pieces of artillery in the Czech sector.)

Ivan replies that these forces aren't "offensive"; they're "defensive," to protect the new Russia from the "aggressive" forces Germany has been amassing. He then accuses the German government of being "a hundred times worse than Hitler and the Nazis," and orders even more troops into the Polish and Czech sectors, declaring that these border areas are now on "top-priority" alert (meaning that those stationed there should be prepared for war at "any" moment).

Then Greece, caught between the proverbial rock and hard place — Ivan's new Russia and WIC (of which Greece's old enemy, Turkey, is a member) — decides to leave the "free" world and become part of the new Russia. Then Finland, knowing that it's just a matter of time before it's going to be invaded by Ivan, decides to join the new Russia — and only a few days later, a force of over 100,000 Russian troops (including 25,000 new Finnish members), with 1,000 tanks, 1,000 pieces of artillery, and 300 combat aircraft is on its way to the Swedish border.

Then Sweden, which has been a neutral country for over a hundred years, begins talking about joining the new Russia...and suddenly, the leaders of the "free" world — but especially those in the *United States of the Americas* — begin snapping out of the paralytic state they've been in for so long (it almost seems as though they've been drugged into a state of suspended animation), and begin taking control of the "free" world before it disintegrates completely.

They start moving with a quickness and energy that surprises even them...it's like they've started taking some kind of energy drug or something — but, of course, they don't take "drugs" — except for prescription drugs, of course. And vitamins — but those aren't "drugs." They're "vitamins"... .

~

Oh, yes, the politicians in the "free" world have begun taking "vitamins." Or, more precisely, they've begun taking a "new" type of "vitamin." The old type (mainly delivered unknowingly in water, milk, fruit juice, and food) had ingredients that made one mentally sluggish, indecisive, and fearful — even paranoid (especially if one also used alcohol and/or tobacco). But the new "vitamin"...well, it gets the adrenaline pumping and pushes sluggishness, indecisiveness, and fear aside. It turns people into "super" people (much like the new patriots), and it's time to act! It's time to save the "free" world!

And the crusade is on! Politicians/governments order police/military to go on the offensive against the new patriots — and hit them hard! Don't hesitate to use heavy firepower if it's necessary — tanks, artillery, helicopter gunships, multirole jets...whatever is needed! Yes, "whatever" is needed — even fuel-air explosives, napalm, lethal chemicals...yes, even nuclear weapons if it has to come to that! These people — these savages! — must be brought under control! The "free" world must be saved! Now! Immediately!

And the "free" world's police/military respond quickly — so quickly, in fact, that it almost seems as though they knew what the politicians/governments were going to do even before the governments/politicians themselves knew what they were going to do.

For example, a few weeks before the politicians/governments suddenly decide it's time to save the "free" world, the "free" world's military has been getting ready for action — and the orders didn't come from politicians/governments. They came from "high" in the military command — so high, in fact, that no one in the "regular" military, not even the "top" generals and fleet admirals, can pinpoint the exact origin of the orders. It's almost like they came from God...a voice — a voice of "ultimate" authority (but not the voice of any recognizable politician, government official, or military personnel) — speaking in "top secret" code ("extremely" top secret code, known only to a small number of high-ranking military commanders) — over "special" phone lines (often referred to as "phantom" lines, because no one seems to know where they lead to, or from). And this voice speaking the top secret code is obeyed without "any" hesitation or question. It's a quick, "Yes, sir! Immediately, sir!" — and the short exchange is ended — and it's time for action!

First, all the police forces in the "free" world are made part of the military. Then, when politicians/governments declare a state of martial law throughout the "free" world, the military snaps into action.

Spearheaded by elite, helicopter-borne commando units supported by helicopter gunships and ground attack fixed-wing aircraft, the military makes quick work of the new patriots — so quick, in fact, it almost seems as though it knows "exactly" where to strike (which, of course, it does, since the council created them and has kept them under "extremely" close scrutiny). Repeatedly, planes and helicopter gunships pound new patriot positions with guided missiles, unguided rockets, bombs (including fuel-air and lethal chemical bombs), grenades, and cannon and machine gun fire. As well, wherever possible, the positions are also hammered with artillery and mortar fire.

Helicopter transports then move in with the

commando units who, in turn, are followed by regular infantry supported by tanks and other armored fighting vehicles. And the order is to only take "important" prisoners — and kill the rest. Hunt them down like the vermin they are! Show no mercy!

And in less than a month it's over. The new patriots have been "totally" destroyed — including two or three hundred thousand "important" prisoners who are publicly executed after short, highly-publicized trials. (One of the first things military does after martial law is declared is to restore the "free" world's electricity and communications — particularly satellite TV — because it wants everyone to know what's happening — or, at least, "part" of what's happening; it doesn't, for instance, want everyone knowing about all the innocent people — especially children — who are killed in the attacks on the new patriots.)

The military then does something totally unexpected. It seizes control from the politicians/governments (who, of course, didn't have any "real" control in the first place, since the council was doing all the "real" controlling). Thousands of leading politicians and government officials — including those at the "highest" levels, such as the President of the *United States of the Americas* — suddenly find themselves being arrested by military and charged with all kinds of offenses: treason, conspiracy to commit treason, abuse of power, conspiracy to abuse power, theft of public funds, conspiracy to steal public funds, fraud, conspiracy to commit fraud, gross financial mismanagement, gross mismanagement causing environmental damage, promoting ethnic hatred, promoting racial hatred, promoting religious hatred, spying for a foreign government, subversive activities, conspiracy to commit subversive acts, general corruption, failure to provide public safety...the charges seem endless, and many are charged with hundreds — even thousands — of crimes (the President of the *United States of the Americas*, for instance, is charged with almost ten thousand crimes, including over four thousand charges of abuse of power).

Then, after short trials (some only lasting a few minutes)in military courts that convene throughout the "free" world, everyone charged is found guilty. Not "one" politician or government official who is charged escapes "justice" — nor does anyone else who's charged, such as the tens of thousands of leading businesspeople who also find themselves being arrested, charged, and convicted for many of the same offenses as the politicians and government officials.

Those convicted argue that what the military is doing is "illegal," and "unconstitutional." The military, however, quickly dismisses these arguments, declaring they aren't valid because martial law is in effect, which overrides "anything" in "any" constitution or "civilian" law.

The convicted then protest that their rights are being violated because the military is denying them fair trials, since the military has also arrested thousands of leading lawyers and charged and convicted them of the same crimes as the businesspeople, politicians, and government officials — and because they've been convicted, they aren't allowed to defend anyone in court — not even themselves. And this is wrong — "totally" wrong.

The military, however, quickly dismisses these protests, saying that what it's doing isn't wrong — in "any" way — and that the defense lawyers being provided by the military are perfectly adequate. Certainly, they're military personnel, but they know the difference between right and wrong — and that's all that matters. And yes, the judges are also military personnel (most members of the "free" world's judicial system, including the highest-ranking judges, have also been convicted of crimes). But they also know the difference between right and wrong; in fact, they probably know much more about right and wrong than "civilian" judges because, unlike civilian judges, they haven't been corrupted. And yes, the juries are also military personnel, but they too know the difference between right and wrong. Therefore, "everyone" is getting a "fair" trial (which many don't really deserve, the military is quick to point out). And certainly, everyone who's charged is found guilty of everything they're charged with — but that's simply because they are guilty. After all, if they weren't guilty, they would've been found not guilty.

And the great majority of "the people" are ecstatic seeing all these corrupt, greedy bastards being dragged from their positions of power and privilege in handcuffs and leg irons. And they love seeing them sitting glum-faced in prisons — denied bail, being treated like common, low-life criminals — as they await trial. And they cheer as they're charged and convicted in trials held in huge stadiums, such as the Maracana in Rio de Janeiro, Brazil, with a capacity of over 200,000, and the Azteca in Mexico City, Mexico, and the Rose Bowl in Pasadena, California, both with capacities of over 100,000.

The jubilation quickly begins fading, however, when death sentences begin being handed out — especially to those who've been convicted of what most see as "minor" crimes, such as the theft of small amounts of public funds. It's one thing to see someone sentenced to death for stealing millions in public funds, but many are given the death penalty for thefts of public funds under $5,000 and, in many cases, the amounts are less than $5,000 and, in many cases, the amounts are less than $1,000. The military, however, declares that "no" crime is "minor" — especially when it involves public funds, public trust, and public safety (and "all" crimes, in one way or another, involve one or more of these things).

And dampening the celebratory spirit even more is the speed at which some of the sentences are carried out. Sentenced to death and executed less than an hour later. No appeals. No leniency. The "free" world "must" be saved, the military proclaims, and the "only" way to do this is by destroying the cancer that's killing it. And these people are that cancer. And, after being found guilty in "fair" trials in "legal" courts, they "must" be destroyed. And "the people" must understand that these executions aren't "punishment." They're "operations" to rid society of a deadly disease — exactly the same as a doctor having to amputate a gangerous leg in order to save the rest of the body.

And in a short time — less than six months — the "free" world's military does a lot of "amputating"; over five million ex-politicians/government officials/judicial officials/businesspeople/lawyers are publicly executed by firing squad, hanging, garroting, gassing, electric shock, burning, and beheading. And these executions are often mass executions, such as the one in the Rose Bowl, for instance, where the ex-President of the *United States of the Americas* and 499 of that country's highest-ranking ex-politicians/government officials/judicial officials (including all nine members of the Supreme Court) are hanged simultaneously, using a long cable stretched between large cranes. Then, after hanging from the cables like bizarre Christmas ornaments for twenty-four hours, the corpses are loaded into dump trucks by front-end loaders, and driven to the Mojave Desert, where they're left unburied for the turkey vultures to feast on. Many are horrified and outraged by such "acts of barbarism," and begin protesting.

229

The military, at first, is patient with the protestors, explaining to them that protesting is illegal under martial law, and "requesting," not "demanding," that they quit. These requests are met with even more — and louder — protesting. Again, military patiently explains that protesting is illegal under martial law — so "please" stop. It "implores" them to stop. But they won't. The protests grow larger — and louder — and violent, as some protestors, in their righteousness, begin throwing rocks and bottles at the military, who remains calm, and again asks — "implores" — the protestors to quit.

Some protestors do what the military asks. Most, however, respond with even more protest, and increased violence; rocks and bottles are joined by gas bombs; vehicles are overturned and burned; buildings — including private dwellings — are looted and torched...and "innocent" people begin getting hurt — and killed — which, of course, is really what the military wants — or, more accurately, what the council wants (that's why council agents, using the power of inflammatory rhetoric and "vitamins," are making certain that the protestors keep protesting — and protesting even harder; screaming louder; throwing more rocks, bottles, and gas bombs; burning more; looting more; wrecking more; hurting more; killing more....).

And the reason for this is so that the basic glue of society — the fear of authority — can be restored in the "free" world. What happened to the new patriots and politicians/government officials/judicial officials/ businesspeople/lawyers horrified "the people." But it didn't, generally speaking, "really" scare them — at least, not in a "personal" sense because, after all, they weren't part of any of those groups. They were "the people" — the "common" people — and they hadn't committed any crimes. They'd been the "victims."

Now, however, that's changed. Many millions of these people have committed crimes by refusing to stop protesting...hell, they committed crimes simply by protesting in the first place, since martial law was in effect, and it was made clear that, under that law, protests of "any" kind are illegal (as is — in "any" way — "supporting" a protest; supplying food to a protestor, for instance, makes one guilty of "supporting" a protest).

Oh, yes, they were warned — again — and again — and again. The military begged them to stop. But, like little children throwing temper tantrums, they just wouldn't listen. They must, therefore, be taught a lesson — a "painful" lesson — that'll again make them fear authority — like they've never feared it before.

They must learn who their master is, and that they "must" obey that master, and that "any" opposition to that master is "absolutely" futile. And this lesson (and hopefully the only one that'll be needed) takes place at the Pentagon, headquarters of the Department of Defense of the *United States of the Americas* (or, more accurately, the "official" governmental headquarters of the *United States of the Americas*, since there aren't anymore "civilian" politicians, and the White House no longer exists; it was completely destroyed in the turmoil by the new patriots — or so it "appeared" — who crashed — using a suicide-pilot — an old *Boeing 707* into it at about 500 miles per hour — with almost a full load of fuel — and about twelve tons of high explosive!). (Actually, the Pentagon is the "unofficial" headquarters of the entire "free" world...no, that's not quite accurate. It's actually the "unofficial" headquarters of the whole world — and has been since the council took control of the world in 1945 — although, even more accurately, the "unofficial" headquarters of the world is actually somewhere else — at a place unofficially called, "CC" — for "Council Command" — somewhere in the former United States of America.)

Situated on the west bank of the Potomac River in Arlington, Virginia, directly across from Washington, D.C., the Pentagon is a huge, five story, five-sided building that covers 29 acres and contains over 3,700,000 square feet (at least, "officially"; "unofficially,"the Pentagon contains over four million square feet, since its basement is a little larger than most believe). Normally, about 30,000 people work here (about 27,000 in an "official" capacity, and about 3,000 in an "unofficial" capacity). But now, with the military takeover of the "free" world, over 60,000 people work here — including about 20,000 "special" security troops who are positioned atop the building and around its almost one mile perimeter, behind thick tangles of razor wire and thousands of Claymore anti-personnel mines (nasty boxes that spray out about 1,000 ball bearings when triggered).

These troops are particularly "special" because they're "orphans." They don't have parents/family, in the sense of "biological" parents/family — at least none they know about. As far as they're concerned, their "parents/family" is the military of the *United States of the Americas.* And they'll do "anything" to protect that "family." "Anything"! Whatever their superiors order — no matter how "terrible" it might seem — they'll do it — without question. Of all the military in the world, these soldiers (and there are over half a million of them stationed around the world; many operating in an "unofficial" capacity) are the most ruthless killing machines the world has ever seen. But they're not "monsters" — not by "any" means. They don't act on their own. They're just loyal — "super" loyal — soldiers following orders; orders from superiors who are like parents to them.

Those guarding the Pentagon are armed with a large assortment of weapons, including over 100 old *M-60* main battle tanks that've been refurbished into "Anti-Personnel Deterrence Vehicles" ("APDVs"), with 150mm "shotgun" barrels designed to fire canister rounds containing either about 1,500 steel 12.7mm pellets, or about 350 steel flechettes, as well as turret-mounted grenade launchers that fire about eight 40mm grenades a second (including lethal chemical grenades, of which these troops are well-supplied; "the people" must "never" be allowed to get control of the Pentagon!).

But the deadliest weapons these troops possess are, by far, the helicopter gunships. They come in four different classes — light, medium, heavy, and super-heavy — and are horrendous killing machines (especially when used against civilians who don't have any weapons to combat them) — especially the super-heavy machines. They're old *CH-47 — Chinook* — cargo/troop transports that've been refurbished with six 7.62mm Gatling guns that can fire 6,000 rounds a minute, and six 40mm grenade launchers that can fire 480 rounds a minute — meaning that in just one thirty second pass, one of them can unleash a hail of 18,000 bullets and 1,440 grenades. (Actually, the deadliest gunships are the "dusters" — *Chinooks* that've been fitted with sprayers; one *Chinook* duster, filled with a lethal chemical, can, if conditions are right — temperature, humidity, etc — eliminate a million or more in about thirty minutes.)

And the million or so protestors around the Pentagon find out firsthand just how deadly these weapons are (except for the dusters; they won't be used unless "absolutely" necessary). They're given one final warning: Disperse immediately! If you don't, the troops will be forced to open fire!

Some of the protestors leave (including all council

233

agents), but the great majority stay, convinced that it's just another bluff. They've been given "final" warnings before — and nothing happened...the troops simply won't fire on unarmed citizens — even if some of them are throwing rocks, bottles, and gas bombs — as long as they don't try forcing their way into the Pentagon.

They're wrong, of course. The troops do open fire, and about an hour later, almost forty thousand protestors are dead, with over four times that number wounded.

The *Pentagon Massacre*, as it quickly becomes known, is videotaped by the military, and is shown around the "free" world, mainly via satellite-TV. Of course, before it's broadcast, some skillful editing is done to "enhance" the tape. For example, none of the protestors actually tried forcing their way into the Pentagon. The tape, however, shows protestors — "hordes" of them — trying to force their way into the building.

And few of the protestors were ever armed with anything — the rock, bottle, and gas bomb throwers were a definite minority. The tape, however, "clearly" shows (courtesy of computer graphics) every protestor carrying some sort of weapon, including firearms, and also makes it appear that they're "all"drug-crazed, obscenity screaming lunatics out to destroy the "free" world.

And they're also murdering butchers who have killed — and horribly mutilated — military personnel and civilians...oh, yes...the tape "clearly" shows protestors killing innocent civilians and soldiers (actually, the killers/mutilators are soldiers dressed to look like protestors ,and the civilians and soldiers being killed/mutilated are actually new patriots who were taken prisoner during the assault on them).

And the tape also shows protest leaders preaching pro-Ivan rhetoric to young, glazed-eyed protestors (obviously high on drugs), who scream approval when the leaders call for the destruction of the "free" world; as well, there are graphic scenes of these young fanatics raping young girls and old women...oh, yes, by the time the editors are through with the tape, very few who see it (and the military — or, more accurately, the council — makes certain that it's "widely" seen) have much — if any — sympathy for the protestors who were killed at the Pentagon (in fact, many who see the tape say the protestors "deserved" what they got; quite a few even say that more of them should've been killed).

And, generally speaking, the basic glue of society — fear of authority — is restored. Oh, certainly, some are slow to get the message, and the military is forced to kill a further one or two or three or four, etc, thousand protestors here and there. But, for the most part, the "free" world is again peaceful.

Actually, it's more peaceful than it's ever been because the period of turmoil has cleansed it of "much" of the anger, hate, frustration, jealousy, etc, that'd built-up over the years. For instance, all right-wing paramilitary "militias" and/or racist/white supremacist groups, such as the Ku Klux Klan, have been destroyed. Of course, many black people have also been destroyed — especially those of the Moslem faith. In fact, there aren't "any" black Moslems left in the "free" world...actually there aren't "any" Moslems of any color left in the "free" world. Those not slaughtered by the new patriots have fled to WIC countries.

Nor are there any Jews, Buddhists, Sikhs, Hindus — or "any" other "non-Christians" — left in the "free" world. (Countries predominantly non-Christian, such as Israel, India, and Japan, who were once part of the "free" world, are no longer considered to be part of that world — although they do retain certain economic, diplomatic, and military ties with that

235

world.) And it won't be long before there won't be "any" non-Christians in the whole world because, after all, the Four Horsemen of the Apocalypse — Conquest, War, Famine, Death — are riding, and the *Second Coming of Christ* is on the way, and when he gets here...well, simply put, it's the end of "all" non-Christian faiths.

But before he arrives, the Four Horsemen — particularly Death — still have a lot of riding to do. The turmoil in the "free" world has claimed about two hundred and fifty million lives — almost 25% of the "free" world's population. But that pales compared to the upcoming turmoil. Remember, before there can be a *Second Coming of Christ*, there first has to be *Armageddon*, that final great battle between good and evil, and before that happens, the Horsemen have "much" more ground to cover.

For example, the Bible says that the *Antichrist* — the *Beast* bearing the mark 666 — will appear shortly before *Armageddon*. Now, many Christians believe he'll appear in Rome — in the form of a Pope (many Christians have, in fact, believed that every Pope was/is the *Antichrist*). And that could indeed be arranged. The council could turn a Pope into the *Antichrist*.

This might sound "absolutely" unbelievable. But it should be quite clear by now that the council has the power — and skill — to do the "absolutely" unbelievable. Actually, the council doesn't even classify turning a Pope into the *Antichrist* as being something "absolutely unbelievable" because, in fact, it'd be quite simple.

We could, for example, replace an existing Pope with an imposter, complete with a 666 tattooed somewhere on him. Or we could simply take an existing Pope and force him to play the role...perhaps with the assistance of one or two or three of the multitude of drugs and other methods of persuasion at our disposal.

It would, however, be even easier — and much more convincing — to simply have the *Antichrist* come to Rome from somewhere else and conquer it, destroying the Pope and Vatican in the process. Someone, let's say, like...Ivan...who just happens to have a large military force assembled and ready in the Balkan sector of the new Russia, just 125 or so miles from Italy on the other side of the Adriatic Sea (plus a large naval battle force in the Adriatic itself); as well, he also has a large force in the Slovenia sector of the new Russia, on Italy's northeastern border. And Italy simply doesn't have the necessary strength to stop Ivan from invading and occupying it. And it can't expect "any" help from other "free" world countries, including the *United States of the Americas*, since the turmoil the "free" world has experienced has greatly sapped its strength — especially as regards its "international" strength (or so it "appears" — it must be remembered that "everything" is being orchestrated by the council).

But, of course, Ivan isn't going to start a war with Italy. Never! Italy is the one who's going to start the war. Oh, yes...Italy, even though its military strength is "nothing" compared to Ivan's, is actually going to attack the new Russia.

In early August 1964, communist North Vietnamese torpedo boats attacked American warships in the Gulf of Tonkin, off North Vietnam's coast. The warships weren't damaged, but the attack was enough justification for America to adopt the *Gulf of Tonkin Resolution*, which made it "legal" for America to attack North Vietnam — as well as expanding its military presence in Southeast Asia. (The "fact" is, of course, that North Vietnamese torpedo boats never attacked the American warships — the North Vietnamese weren't stupid; the council was responsible for the "attack" — it was

237

a simple way of getting America "much" more involved in the Vietnam conflict.)

And that's what happens with Italy and Ivan. An Italian frigate fires a missile at a Russian destroyer (at least, that's what Ivan claims). The missile is shot down by the destroyer and no damage is done to the Russian warship. Ivan, however, declares the *Adriatic Sea Resolution*, which gives Russia the "legal" right to "defend" itself against Italy's "unprovoked aggression" — or, more precisely, the Pope's unprovoked aggression, because it's the Pope who's "really" responsible for the attack. He wants to destroy Russia because Russia is the only country that has the courage to stand up to the corruptness of the Pope and Vatican, Ivan claims.

The idea of the Pope and Vatican — and Italy — trying to "destroy" a military behemoth like Russia is beyond ridiculous — but so what? In that part of the world, and at that time, with the "free" world just emerging from years of severe turmoil, and no American military forces in the area (they've all been withdrawn from Italy and the Mediterranean, in general, to help take care of domestic problems), Ivan can damn well do as he pleases, and it pleases him to attack Italy — and the Pope and Vatican — in "defense" of Russia.

Ivan begins the attack by hitting key Italian military installations with a devastating barrage of about 2,000 cruise missiles, each carrying a two ton high explosive warhead. Russian forces in the Slovenia sector (over 350,000 troops with 1,000 tanks, 2,000 pieces of artillery, 300 helicopter gunships, and 250 fixed-wing aircraft) then attack northeastern Italy, at Gorizia and Monfalcone. At the same time, the battle force in the Adriatic (which now includes two aircraft carriers with 190 combat planes, three heavy missile cruisers, eight missile destroyers, twenty-four missile frigates, sixty heavy rocket assault craft, and sixty heavy marine and

238

air commando assault craft, carrying 50,000 marines, 25,000 air commandoes, and 200 helicopter gunships) begins attacking eastern Italy at a number of points. And also, at the same time, from the Adriatic coastline sector of the Russian Balkans, a large force (over 750,000 troops with 2,000 tanks and 4,000 pieces of artillery, supported by 400 helicopter gunships and 1,000 fixed-wing aircraft), is beginning its attack on Italy.

Italy doesn't stand a chance — especially since, for a number of years prior to the attack, its military has been "completely" infiltrated by Ivan's secret agents (who are, of course, actually council secret agents; the council has had agents working in the Italian military since the beginning of World War Two). These agents make certain that, shortly before the attack, the Italian military begins "malfunctioning." Computers suddenly begin spitting out gibberish, or quit working altogether; there are sudden power outages, including emergency generators refusing to start; telephone communications — including radio/wireless communications — become clogged with static, or frequencies are jammed, or systems quit working altogether; fires begin erupting in fuel and ammo dumps — and fire fighting equipment won't start; important military staff — including "top" staff — suddenly mysteriously disappear, or become violently ill, or suddenly go "crazy" from huge doses of powerful hallucinogenic drugs that they've unknowingly received; troops receive misleading and/or conflicting orders that have them going in the wrong direction, or in circles; radar in anti-aircraft missile batteries quit working, making the missiles useless; interceptor aircraft suddenly won't start, or their pilots have disappeared, or have become too sick or crazy to fly; safes containing top-secret orders — orders "essential" in emergency situations — turn out to be empty when opened...it's "complete" chaos!

239

Then cruise missiles — flying at seven hundred miles per hour — begin arriving with their 4,000 pound high explosive warheads. And their accuracy is "amazing" (the reason later given for this is that they were equipped with an advanced guidance system, but, in reality, Ivan's agents planted radio-homing devices on the targets prior to the attack).

Fixed-wing aircraft and helicopters with guided missiles and "smart" bombs then begin hitting targets with pinpoint accuracy (also mainly because agents planted homing devices before the attack). Then troops begin arriving by land, sea, and air (including thousands of "undercover" troops who secretly entered Italy before the attack), and, because there's so little opposition, it's all over in about thirty-six hours. And amazingly, considering the awesome amount of firepower at Ivan's disposal, the casualty rate is extremely low. The Italian military only suffers about 50,000 dead and about three times that number wounded, while the civilian population only sustains about 1,000,000 wounded and about 200,000 dead — including the Pope and a few hundred other high-ranking Vatican officials whose *Boeing 747* mysteriously blows up over Corsica as they attempt to flee to France. (Russian casualties are "minimal"; a few hundred dead, and a few thousand wounded, with most death/injuries resulting from accidents occurring during the attack — such as collisions between helicopter troop transports.)

Ivan then celebrates his victory by doing something even more shocking than invading and occupying Italy.

Vatican City, an independent state covering 108 acres in northwestern Rome, is the spiritual and governmental center of the Roman Catholic Church. Located here is the largest, and most famous, Christian church in the world: St.

Peter's Church. Ivan orders this church — and "every" other building in Vatican City — to be destroyed (including all the "decadent" artwork by all those "morally corrupt" artists, such as Michelangelo and Leonardo da Vinci), and replaced with the headquarters of Russia's Mediterranean sector.

This action "outrages" the citizens of Rome and they begin protesting. (Because Ivan has "complete" control of communications, as well as "everything" else in the area, other Italians — and the rest of the world — don't find out about the destruction until it's over; when it's finished, Ivan releases to all corners of the world a beautifully produced video of the demolition, titled: *The End of Evil.*) Ivan, however, has established martial law in Italy, making "any" kind of protest illegal. Therefore, when people begin protesting the destruction of Vatican City, his troops kill fifty or sixty thousand or so, and arrest another fifty or sixty thousand or so who, after being convicted of violating martial law in short group trials (two or three thousand at a time), are shipped off for "rehabilitation" to various locations in Russia (such as coal mines in Siberia) for fifteen or twenty years.

Of course, no protestors appear in *The End of Evil*. In fact, it's just the opposite. The two hour piece of propaganda is filled with many scenes of mobs of Italians cheering the Vatican City's destruction (of course, the "Italians" are actually Russian military personnel). As well, individuals of both sexes tell horror stories of being sexually molested as children (including such depravity as being forced to eat feces) by high-ranking Vatican officials — including a number of Popes. And as further proof of the sexual depravity in the Vatican, the film shows tons of pornographic material — pictures, magazines, videos — that were found in locked vaults — along with business records showing that the Vatican was involved in a huge, world-wide pornography business.

And also found in locked vaults underneath Vatican City are business records showing that the Vatican was also "heavily"involved in the worldwide trafficking of drugs — and found along with the records are tons of cocaine and heroin (that's actually just a few dozen large, clear plastic bags filled with icing sugar, and hundreds of empty boxes — just like police often do when they have a "huge drug seizure"; and the tons of pornography is actually just a few hundred pornographic pictures, a few dozen porno magazines, a few dozen pornographic videos, and hundreds of empty boxes; and the business records are nothing more than a few thousand pages of fabricated "proof," and hundreds of empty boxes).

As well, more business records are found that prove — beyond "any" doubt — that the Vatican was financially involved — in a "major" way — in both the arms industry and the birth control industry!

And — even more shocking — records are found that "clearly" prove — beyond "any" doubt — that the Vatican was "really"...yes, of course...the Vatican was "really" the "Mafia" — and the Pope was "really" the supreme "Godfather"!

Oh, yes, *The End of Evil* is a work of propaganda genius — and ends on an ominous note — especially for Israel.

It shows Ivan on Pantelleria, a 32-square mile ex-Italian island that sits in the Mediterranean Sea, in the Strait of Sicily, about eight miles from the ex-Italian island of Sicily, and about fifty miles from the North African WIC country of Tunisia.

Now, providing they have the necessary military strength, whomever/whatever controls the Strait of Sicily —

and the much narrower (and dangerous) Strait of Messina (between Italy and Sicily) — also controls shipping to the eastern end of the Mediterranean — at least, in the sense of "straight-through" shipping.

Shipping can bypass these two straits by using two ships and an overland detour through Italy or Tunisia — except, in the case of Tunisia, shipping to or from Israel won't be allowed, since it's a WIC country. Therefore, a detour through Italy would be the only choice — that is, of course, if those in power in Italy will allow it. And if they don't, Israel could be in "big" trouble. And with Italy now a part of the new Russia, Israel is indeed now in "big" trouble — "extremely" big trouble — especially since America has abandoned the Mediterranean — because Ivan now has the military strength/position necessary to control the entire Mediterranean Sea. After all, there are only two entrances/exits from/to that body of water. One is the Suez Canal, which runs through Egypt, a WIC country on the eastern end of the Mediterranean. And the other is the Strait of Gibralter, on the western end, between Spain, an ally of America's, and Morocco, a WIC country. It's about 32 miles long and from 8 to 23 miles wide — "extremely" easy to block if one has the military strength Ivan has.

But he doesn't want to rely on military strength alone. Oh, no, he doesn't want to appear as a "bully." He wants to show his highly-refined diplomatic side. Therefore, after some clever "diplomacy," an agreement is reached between him and WIC. He'll sign a non-aggression treaty with WIC, of which a part will say that Ivan/Russia has a 50-year lease on 50,000 acres (5 by 15 miles) in Morocco, right beside the Strait of Gibralter, that Ivan/Russia can use for a military base — with no restrictions whatsoever on the kind of weapons that can be kept on that base.

And on Pantelleria, in the final scene of *The End of Evil*, Ivan sits at a big table with representatives from every WIC country — it ends up being called the *Pantelleria Summit* — and signs the agreement. (WIC, of course, doesn't really want to sign this treaty — at least, not including the part about the Russian military base in Morocco. But, at the same time, they also don't want Ivan as an enemy — especially after seeing how easily he conquered Italy — and what he did to Vatican City.) And planes and ships loaded with construction workers, material, and equipment immediately begin leaving Russia for Morocco — accompanied, of course, by tens of thousands of military personnel.

The citizens of Israel realize this is the beginning of the end...it's only a matter of time before Ivan completely isolates them, and the WIC forces on their borders begin attacking. Consequently, they begin final preparations for the last battle.

Actually, everyone in the world is getting ready for the last battle because it definitely appears that it's finally going to really happen — there's going to be a World War Three — and it'll probably be a "nuclear" war — and if it is...well, that's it — THE END!!!

This isn't true, of course. It won't be THE END!!! — at least, not for everyone. But it will indeed be the end for many...it is, after all, the *Second Coming of Christ,* and one only has to read a little of the Bible to know how much destruction and death precedes that event...hell, the people of the world haven't really seen anything yet...the Four Horsemen are still really only trotting.

For example, Korea and China still haven't attacked Japan. And China still hasn't attacked Taiwan, Vietnam, Thailand, and India. And India and Pakistan haven't yet started fighting. And the newly united tribes in southern

Africa haven't yet started the final assault on the whites in that region...oh, yes, the world's people haven't really seen anything yet....

~

The Russian base in Morocco is impressive; generous docking facilities for the largest Russian warships; two long runways that can accommodate the largest Russian planes, plus hardened hangers for 500 combat aircraft; state of the art long-range radar; about 500 heavily protected gun and missile emplacements (including, it's rumored, emplacements for *SS-30* missiles); first-rate permanent barracks and facilities for 200,000 troops, plus temporary barracks/facilities for 300,000 troops...but there's a problem — a "big" problem.

All the "free" world has to do to nullify the base is build a similar one across the strait in Spain. There is, of course, the British military stronghold at Gibralter, a peninsula on Spain's southern coast. Britain acquired the rocky 1,300 acres when it signed the *Treaty of Utrecht* in 1713, and has kept control of it ever since, despite numerous attempts by Spain to regain control of it (including a three year blockade in the late 1700s).

Gibralter — or *The Rock*, as it's commonly called — has been heavily fortified over the years by the British (including over ten miles of well-protected tunnels), and has often been referred to as the *Key to the Mediterranean* — and at one time it definitely was. But not anymore.

Ivan's Moroccan base — which is "much" bigger, "much" more heavily fortified, and "much" better positioned than the *The Rock* — is now the *Key to the Mediterranean*, and the British base is a relic. (Actually, it's been a relic for many years — ever since 1945, in fact, when atomic weapons made their first appearance. One nuclear device and *The Rock* is vaporized. Of course, this also applies to Ivan's Moroccan base, and "every" other fixed-position military base in the world. There are claims that some bases are "nuke proof," but these claims simply aren't true. There isn't "one" fixed-position military base in the world that's "nuke proof," and there "never" will be — although some are definitely more "attack resistant" than others — especially as concerns a "non-nuclear" attack.

Gibralter, however, isn't one of them. It's simply too small. The defenders don't have room to maneuver, unlike Ivan's base, which has plenty of room for maneuvering. And while Gibralter's huge tunnel system provides excellent protection, there's a "serious" downside, in that all an enemy needs to know is where all the entrances, exits, and air vents are — and *The Rock* can be turned into *The Tomb*.)

No, that's not quite accurate...yes, Gibralter is a relic — but, no, Ivan's base isn't really the "key" to the Mediterranean; it's really only "half" a key. What's needed for a "complete"key is a similar base on the other side of the strait in Spain.

Now, Spain is a member of the "free" world. At the moment, however, that world isn't nearly as strong as Ivan's world — especially since Ivan made the deal with WIC. Spain, therefore, is now in an "extremely" precarious position — especially in its southern region.

Ivan, however, assures Spain that he doesn't have "any" intention of attacking it. But he does have a proposition for it — a "business" proposition. And, naturally, it's "top-secret." Three of Spain's leading military officers (remember, the "free" world is now "totally" under military control) meet with Ivan at the Moroccan base to hear Ivan's offer, which is: Russia and Spain will sign a non-aggression treaty, part of which will give Ivan/Russia a 50-year lease on 50,000 acres (5 by 15 miles) beside the Strait of Gibralter for a military base (with no restriction on the kind of weapons that can be kept on that base.) As well, Ivan will do something special for Spain.

Ivan knows that for centuries Spain has been trying to get *The Rock* back from England, but, for one reason or another, hasn't succeeded. This has been humiliating for Spain. And because of this, the Spanish, generally speaking, hate the English with a passion, and would love to see them humiliated. Consequently, as part of the non-aggression treaty, Ivan promises that he'll return *The Rock* to Spain. He doesn't say how he'll accomplish this; he simply guarantees that he'll do it.

Now, the Spanish would certainly like to have *The Rock* back, but they don't like the idea of Ivan/Russia having a 50,000 acre military base in their country (today, it's 50,000 acres...tomorrow it's 100,000...then 200,000...500,000...1,000,000... 5,000,000...until one day the whole country is under Russian control). At the same time, however, they don't want to be conquered — and humiliated — like the Italians were. And they don't have any doubts whatsoever that Ivan can conquer Spain just as easily as he conquered Italy — especially when a Russian naval battle group just happens to arrive at the base while they're meeting with Ivan.

The naval force is impressive, to say the least. Just this one group is much bigger — and has "much" more firepower — than Spain's entire navy...hell, it packs "much" more firepower than Spain's "entire" military — and it's just "one" battle group of "one" branch of the Russian military.

The group is composed of 85 warships (175 ships in all, if the various support ships are included). And, by far, the most impressive are the two nuclear-powered *Ivan*-class aircraft carriers, the two nuclear-powered *Nelvonovich*-class missile cruisers, and a large "mystery" ship. It's about the same size as an *Ivan*-class carrier and, in fact, looks like a carrier...yet, at the same time, doesn't look like one...

Ivan is more than happy to tell them about the mystery ship. In fact, he's going to tell the entire world about it. The camera crew in attendance isn't just there to record the signing of the non-aggression treaty between Spain and Russia; it's also there so Ivan can introduce the world to the *Archangel*.

It's a "cruise" ship, Ivan tells the Spanish military elite, who look mystified. It certainly doesn't look like a cruise ship — at least, not like any they've ever seen. For one thing, cruise ships are usually white, with colorful trim. But the *Archangel* is an ominous dark grey without any colorful trim.

Of course, the *Archangel* isn't that kind of cruise ship. It's a nuclear-powered warship (1,200 feet long; 110,000 full-load tons), equipped with 80 cruise missile launchers, 40 on each side. Under each launcher is a vertical magazine that can hold eight missiles (exactly like a single-stack small arms magazine works). This means the *Archangel* can carry — with fully-loaded launchers (one in the launcher and eight in the magazine) — a total of 720 cruise missiles (as well as substantial numbers of surface-to-air, anti-ship, anti-missile, anti-torpedo, and anti-submarine missiles).

Just try to imagine, Ivan tells his Spanish guests (and the rest of the world), seven hundred and twenty missiles; each with a maximum range of 2,500 miles and a maximum speed of 700 miles per hour; each able to fly at a fifty foot altitude, following the ground's contour, thus avoiding ground-based radar; each pre-programmed for a certain target;

each armed with a 500 KT nuclear warhead (equal to over 500,000 tons of TNT) — a total of over 350,000,000 tons of TNT; each taking only 10 seconds to launch — meaning that all 720 missiles can be launched in just two hours; and all done while the *Archangel* is moving at her top speed of 35 knots — and also while fighting off attacks from enemy aircraft, surface ships, submarines, and ground-launched missiles (although, of course, she never operates alone; she's always escorted by one or two *Ivan*-class carriers, one or two *Nelvonovich*-class cruisers, and at least half a dozen missile destroyers, a dozen missile frigates, and a dozen submarines)...oh, yes, just imagine the *Archangel* pumping out those nuclear-warheaded cruise missiles....

The Spanish generals can indeed imagine it...no, that's not true. They can't "really" imagine Spain being reduced to a smoldering radioactive rubble in two hours by an explosive force equal to over 18,000 times the force of the bomb that was dropped on Hiroshima. And then there are Ivan's *SS-30* missiles, which can hit Spain from Russia itself — or from anywhere in the world. It's a grim picture, to say the least — much too grim to "really" see or imagine.

But Ivan isn't threatening Spain...oh, no, he'd never do that. He wants to be allies with the great country of Spain. And he's certain that the majestic country of Spain wants to be Russia's ally...doesn't it?

Yes, of course it does. It's simply an offer that Spain can't afford to reject. Therefore, Ivan begins building the Spanish base across from the Moroccan base — much to the dismay of the "free" world — especially Great Britain — particularly when Ivan begins saying things like, "The British base at Gibralter is the single biggest threat to peace in the Mediterranean," and, "Great Britain's refusal to return Gibralter to its rightful owner, Spain, is an act of intolerable aggression," and — even more ominous — "Great Britain's base at Gibralter is a malignancy that should be removed — even if it means radical surgery."

But, of course, Ivan isn't going to attack the base...oh, no, he's not going to start a war with Great Britain. The "corrupt" British "warmongers" are going to start a war with Ivan.

Ivan begins "preserving peace" in the Mediterranean when he orders his warships to stop British warships from passing eastward through the Strait of Gibralter. This, of course, enrages Britain. It angrily declares that the strait is "international" waters, and demands that Ivan withdraw his order. Ivan responds to Britain's demand by declaring that the strait isn't international waters, and that's all there is to it! Case closed!

The British can't believe it. They're simply not used to this kind of treatment — or, perhaps more accurately, they're not used to being so impotent. There simply isn't any way they can fight Ivan — at least, not without "much" aid from the *United States of the Americas* — especially "direct" aid ("combat" aid). And America won't supply any of that at this time. It'll supply as much as it can spare in the way of arms and equipment (which isn't really that much, since it's building up its military, and simply can't spare much — no matter how much Ivan is humiliating Britain — or how much he's threatening it). But it simply can't get involved as a combatant because, at the moment, it just isn't strong enough (or so it "appears").

Therefore, Britain — and the rest of the "free" world countries in that part of the world — will simply have to survive the best they can...and, if they can't survive — if Ivan invades and conquers them like he did Italy...well, there just isn't anything America can do about it at the present time...sorry....

Consequently, there isn't really anything Britain can do when Ivan makes his move against *The Rock* — or, more precisely, when he responds to Britains's attack...oh, yes, Britain attacks Russia. A British submarine fires four torpedoes at a Russian frigate that's patrolling a dozen miles from Gibralter, and all the torpedoes hit, sinking the frigate with the loss of all hands (or so Ivan claims; in reality, no Russian ship of any kind is sunk, and the "dead" sailors being pulled from the water are, in fact, nothing more than crude dummies).

Ivan calls this an "unbelievable, totally unprovoked act of the most hideous aggression," and demands that the British immediately surrender Gibralter to him — "Immediately!"

The British, of course, refuse, insisting that they didn't fire any torpedoes; that they didn't even have any warships of any kind in the area at the time. Ivan, not one to mince words, calls them "lying, corrupt swine," and repeats his demand — and is again answered with a loud, "No! Never!"

Ivan then gives them a time limit — which, naturally, they ignore. There simply isn't any way they'll allow Ivan to push them around! They're British, damnit, and they're going to stand their ground! They didn't back down from Hitler and Nazi Germany — and they're sure as hell not going to back down from Ivan and Russia!

Oh, yes...that indomitable British spirit! Ivan loves it — or, more accurately, he loves smashing it! And, exactly ten seconds after his time limit expires, he starts smashing; two hundred cruise missiles — half with high explosive warheads, half with hideous fuel-air warheads; five hundred 500mm ship-to-shore artillery rockets with 1,000 pound high explosive warheads especially designed to penetrate rock and concrete; a thousand 450mm ship-to-shore mortar rounds with 1,000 pound high explosive rock/concrete penetrator warheads; five thousand 200mm ship-to-shore artillery rockets with 200 pound high explosive rock/concrete penetrator warheads; three hundred 2,000 pound fuel-air bombs; six hundred 2,000 pound high explosive bombs; a thousand 1,000 pound high explosive bombs; two thousand 150mm high-velocity, air-to-surface rockets with 100 pound high explosive rock/concrete penetrator warheads...every Russian combat aircraft and warship in the area takes part in the awesome display of firepower — which is exactly what it "really" is: a "display."

The destruction of the base is really only the secondary objective of the horrific bombardment. The base can "easily" be conquered with only 10% — or less — of the firepower Ivan uses. But he wants a "demonstration" — "another" demonstration (Italy was the cake; Gibralter is the icing) — of Russian firepower, so he can film it and show America, France, Germany, and everyone else what they can expect if they launch "unprovoked attacks" against Russia.

And, of course, the film is shocking — beyond shocking — "far" beyond — especially the end, when, after letting the base cool down (so much heat is produced in the bombardment that rock actually melts), marines and air commandoes land and make certain that all the entrances/exits to the base's tunnel system are "completely" blocked, making it "impossible" for those trapped inside to escape (many of the base's personnel have survived the hellish bombardment by retreating into the tunnels). They then seal all of the tunnel system's air vents — after pumping in a few tons of a lethal chemical. The approximately 15,000 British personnel in the tunnels don't stand a chance. *The Rock* is turned into *The Tomb*. Ivan then, as promised, turns the base over to the Spanish.

And after seeing the film, Sweden, Norway, Denmark, Liechtenstein, and Austria decide that joining Ivan's new Russia is "definitely" the smart thing to do. This leaves the Netherlands, Belgium, Luxembourg, the United Kingdom, Germany, France, and Switzerland to face Ivan/Russia (Portugal, like Spain, has signed a non-aggression treaty with Ivan).

Now, Switzerland has been a "neutral" country since 1874, and refuses to side with "anyone" and, for the moment, Ivan is content to leave it alone. In fact, it's last on his list of European countries he plans to make part of the new Russia.

First on his list are France and Germany. But before he launches full-scale offensives against either country, he first needs to do some additional maneuvering. He has strong forces in the Polish, Czech, and Italian sectors of Russia who are ready to attack on a moment's notice. And he has strong naval forces in the Mediterranean Sea, the North Sea, and the Baltic Sea who are also ready to attack on a moment's notice.

It isn't enough, however. He also needs naval forces in the Bay of Biscay and the Balearic Sea. But before they can be put in place, he needs bases for them, in Spain, on both ends of the Pyrenee Mountains that sit on the Spain-France border.

Yes, Ivan would like to have a further 100,000 acres from Spain for military bases. And Spain, of course, doesn't hesitate to lease him the land. They want to keep him happy. Construction on the bases begins immediately, as does construction on 50,000 acre bases in Austria and Denmark. And while these bases are being built, Ivan invades and conquers the French Mediterranean island of Corsica — or, more precisely, France lets him have it, because it simply isn't worth fighting over. In fact, many French citizens don't believe France itself is worth fighting over — especially since it's so obvious that Ivan can't be defeated (particularly after seeing how easily he conquered Italy). It'd be far better to surrender to him now, than to have the country — and people — ravaged by war.

Of course, there are also many French citizens who don't agree with this. They believe it'd be better to fight Ivan, and have France totally destroyed by war — and die fighting — than to willingly become part of the new Russia. Or so they say. In reality, this kind of talk is only bravado from those who've never experienced war, or who'll be able to flee France if war begins, or who won't be in combat if war does occur, such as high-ranking military personnel — although, Ivan has made it quite clear that no military personnel — not even the highest-ranking — can escape combat when fighting Ivan. He will, in fact, if at all possible, attack high-ranking military personnel before attacking "regular" troops — just like he did in Italy.

Of course, France and Russia don't have to fight at all, Ivan says — as long as France is willing to make reparations for Napoleon's 1812 invasion of Russia. France argues that today's France isn't responsible — in "any" way — for what Napoleon and France did well over 200 years before. Besides, France adds, the Russians gave Napoleon — and France — a humiliating defeat. And Ivan also now has Corsica — Napoleon's birthplace — so that should be the end of it.

No, no, no...it isn't the end of it, Ivan tells them. Certainly, he now has Napoleon's birthplace and, yes, the Russians did indeed give Napoleon and France a humiliating defeat and, yes, the invasion of 1812 is indeed old history. But France still owes Russia, because the invasion was a traumatic experience that's still impacting the Russian people in a "major" way.

255

Naturally, those in power in France (or "appearing" to be in power; remember, the council is the "real" power there — as it is everywhere else) don't agree with this. Ivan, however, doesn't care whether or not they agree. He knows — for a "fact" — that he's right and they're wrong — and that's all that matters. And if France wants to fight about it — so be it. Ivan — and the brave Russian people — are more than willing to fight for what's right. And there isn't "any" question about who'll win. It's quite clear that France — even though it has nuclear weapons (or "appears" to) — can't stand up to Russia's military might.

However, if France wants to avoid bloodshed, all it has to do is take a map of France, and draw a line from the Bay of Biscay to the city of Bordeaux to the city of Montpellier, and let Russia have everything south of that line, including Bordeaux and Montpellier. Simple as that — nothing to it!

Ivan then informs Germany that it still owes reparations to Russia for Hitler's 1941 invasion, and to pay that debt, all it has to do is draw a line from the city of Karlsruhe to the city of Bayreuth, and let Russia have everything south of the line, including the two cities; and draw a line from the city of Hamburg to the city of Szezecin in the Polish sector of Russia, and let Russia have everything north of the line, including Hamburg. Simple as that — nothing to it!

Germany, of course, doesn't agree with him. It gives the same argument France gave; it's old history, and Russia gave Hitler — and Germany — a humiliating defeat. And Ivan tells Germany the same thing he told France: yes, it's old history, and yes, the Russians did indeed give Hitler and Germany a humiliating defeat, but the invasion was a traumatic experience that's still "greatly" impacting the

Russian people.

Germany still doesn't agree, of course. But Ivan doesn't care. In a well-publicized speech, he orders a ten percent increase in armaments production and adds ten million personnel to Russia's military. If France and Germany want a fight — then let the fighting begin. He, after all, has "all" the top cards. And his hand gets even better when the countries of the Netherlands, Belgium, and Luxembourg decide to join him. It's a move that horrifies France and Germany because, while these countries aren't "major" powers, they are in "major" key positions, and with Ivan's military in these countries, France and Germany — and the United Kingdom — are now "really" in precarious positions (as is Switzerland).

As Ivan begins constructing 50,000 acre military bases in Belgium (one on France's border; one on Germany's border), France swallows its considerable pride and yields to Ivan. He can have the land he wants in southern France (about 45,000 square miles; roughly 20% of the country). This, naturally, outrages many of "the people" of France — especially those living in the area. But if the alternative is war with Russia...well, as long as Ivan keeps his word....

And Germany also swallows its considerable pride and gives Ivan what he wants (about 40,000 square miles; roughly 25% of the country). And, naturally, this outrages many of "the people" of Germany — particularly those living in the area. But if the alternative is war with Russia...well, as long as Ivan keeps his word...

And he will indeed keep his word, Ivan assures them. All he wants is the property he asked for — and, of course, land and air "access" routes across both countries. His military, for example, must be able to travel by both land and air from his territory in southern France through/over France to Belgium, and vice versa; and from Belgium to his territory in southern Germany, and vice versa.

Germany and France protest that he didn't mention this before. Ivan replies that he just took it for granted that they'd understand his need for such access routes. And, naturally, they do. They simply don't have any other choice but to "understand" — and "agree" — unless, of course, they're prepared to go to war. Which they're not. Ivan's military is simply too powerful (or so it "appears"; remember Sun Tzu's words: "All warfare is based on deception"; an *Archangel*-class cruise missile ship, for example, can carry 720 cruise missiles — but it doesn't have to carry even one to "appear" to be "dangerous").

And soon, Russian military convoys are a daily sight in France and Germany. Many are only a few dozen or so vehicles with only a few hundred troops. Others, however, are five hundred or more vehicles (many towing heavy weapons) with ten thousand or more troops. And also a daily sight are Russian military aircraft of all types crisscrossing the skies above both countries. Sometimes it's only a single aircraft, or half a dozen, or a dozen. But often there are ominous formations of five hundred aircraft or more, which, along with the convoys, makes the citizens of France and Germany extremely nervous, to say the least. And large numbers begin leaving both countries for Great Britain (many so desperate that they cross the English Channel in small rowboats and rafts made from inner tubes, oil drums, and anything else that'll float; the British have blocked the "Chunnel," fearing that Ivan will use it to invade England).

Most, however, consider England only a temporary stop. Their goal — including that for many English — is the *United States of the Americas*, since it's quite obvious that it's the only country that'll — hopefully — have the strength necessary to defeat Ivan when the time comes.

But many Germans, French, and British — and people from other European countries — simply refuse to leave their homelands. Many claim they'd sooner fight and die than succumb to a tyrant. And many, for one reason or another, simply can't leave (they just can't afford it, for instance). But they certainly aren't the only ones in the world who are stuck in such a position. Nor are they, by any means, in the worst position.

The Taiwanese, for example, are in a "much" worse position. And in an even worse position are the Japanese. In Taiwan's case, the enemy — mainland China — just wants to make Taiwan — and its people — a part of mainland China. It doesn't want to slaughter the Taiwanese, or enslave them, like it — and Korea — wants to do with the Japanese.

In the worst position of all, however, are the Israelis. They're completely surrounded by an enemy who "vastly" outnumbers and outguns them, and who wants to "annihilate" them — "totally." WIC wants to kill "every" Israeli — men, women, children; "all" ages — "everyone."

Yet, despite being in this hopeless position (especially since Ivan has stopped "all" Israeli shipping and air traffic in the Mediterranean), the Israelis aren't despairing. In fact, it's just the opposite. They're actually in a celebratory mood. They, as a people — and as individuals — have accepted their fate. They just don't stand a chance; that's a "fact." WIC simply won't negotiate with them — in "any" way. It's determined to destroy them — "all" of them — and that's final!

But even if WIC was willing to negotiate, and allow them to leave Israel, they don't have anywhere to go. No one in the "free" world — the "Christian" world — wants them. Ivan doesn't want them in his new Russia. The Chinese won't accept them. No African nation — not even any that aren't part of WIC — will accept them — not even their old friends, the white South Africans. They're simply "doomed" — unless, of course, the *United States of the Americas* suddenly comes to their aid. Unfortunately, however, America simply isn't in the position to fight WIC at this time — especially since WIC is allied with Ivan. So, Israel is "clearly" on its own — and is "clearly" doomed.

It isn't, however, going to go without putting up a fight. And it's going to be a fight the world will "never" forget — especially the Moslem world. And it isn't going to wait for WIC to attack...oh, no, Israel is going to launch a preemptive strike, just like it did in the Six-Day War, way back in 1967...only this time, it's going to strike "much" harder....

h, yes...Israel launches the most devastating preemptive strike in history. In fact, it's the most destructive attack of any kind in history.

First, Israeli agents (and council agents, of course) inside WIC disable major communications systems and radar installations — especially those designed to spot incoming Israeli missiles. Following this sabotage, Israel fires nuclear missiles (with 10 KT warheads) at the WIC cities of Damascus, Baghdad, Cairo, Alexandria, Istanbul, Ankara, Amman, Jidda...and the holiest of all WIC cities; birthplace of Mohammed, the founder of Islam — Mecca.

This is immediately followed by the firing of fifteen smaller nuclear missiles (with 5 KT warheads) against WIC primary, medium-range military targets.

And the results are "devastating," to say the least. In the space of a few hours, Israel has hit the Moslem world with 165 KTs of nuclear destruction. Or, putting it another way: The Moslem world has just experienced about 11 times the nuclear blast intensity that was experienced at Hiroshima in August 1945. And about 4 million are dead, with about four times that number wounded.

And Israel isn't quite finished its preemptive strike. It still has primary, close-range military targets to hit. This is accomplished by multirole fixed-wing aircraft, attack helicopters, and long-range artillery. This last stage kills about 150,000 troops, wounds about three times that number, and destroys many weapons and much equipment/supplies.

In all, the WIC force that's been assembling against

261

Israel for the past number of years has, factoring in "everything" (such as the nuclear destruction of cities far from the actual combat zones), experienced a "staggering" loss of strength; perhaps as much as 90%. And it'll take at least five years of vigorous rebuilding, with "much" help from Ivan — and no more major Israeli strikes (especially nuclear ones) — to regain that strength — and morale.

The Israeli action has plunged the morale of the Moslem people from an ecstatic high to an unbelievable, mindnumbing low. One moment they're only a few days from launching the war that'll finally "permanently" destroy Israel and less than twenty-four hours later, they're the victims of the most savage attack in history; one that's even destroyed Mecca, their most sacred city. It's utterly humiliating — "far" beyond utterly humiliating — especially since they can't retaliate with a nuclear counterattack because they don't have any nuclear weapons. (It isn't that the council has anything against the Moslems; it's simply that a nuclear-armed WIC just isn't part of *Operation Return*.)

They do, however, attempt a retaliatory action with a ground and air attack by conventionally-armed troops. But because it's an attack filled with intense rage and hatred (and also because of council manipulation, of course), it's a dismal failure. The few WIC aircraft that can take off are blown out of the sky almost as soon as they leave the ground. And none of the ground troops — severely lacking tank and artillery support — even make it through Israel's outer defenses; over a hundred thousand are killed and twice that number wounded in the futile attack — humiliating WIC even further.

Israel, of course, is still doomed. It's scored a "major" victory, but it's still trapped — and it doesn't have anymore nuclear weapons. It does, however, still possess an awesome conventional military force (Israeli losses in the action are minimal; a dozen or so aircraft destroyed, a hundred or so troops killed and a few hundred or so wounded), and it also has the capability to survive without external help for many years. In fact, it could survive indefinitely without external aid — if it didn't have to fight a major war.

But, of course, it's going to have to fight a "major" war, since as soon as WIC can regroup, it's going to attack — in a "major" way. And the rebuilding of the WIC forces begins immediately, with Ivan coming to WIC's aid in every possible manner (with the exception of supplying them with nuclear or biological weapons, of course). But it isn't "free" aid. Oh, no...Ivan expects certain things in return. For example, he wants billions of barrels of oil, and permanent title to the base in Morocco — plus an additional 10,000 square miles!

And he also wants permanent title to 10,000 square miles in Somalia, on the tip of the Horn of Africa; permanent title to 25,000 square miles of northern Afghanistan; permanent title to 5,000 square miles in Tunisia, opposite the island of Pantelleria; and permanent title to 20,000 square miles in Algeria, Libya, Sudan, Saudi Arabia, Oman, Iraq, Iran, and Indonesia.

Naturally, WIC isn't happy about giving Ivan/Russia all this "strategic" property since, should it ever have to fight Ivan/Russia (a very real possibility, despite any treaties that might've been signed — especially considering Ivan's views on religion), these pieces of land — which Ivan will immediately begin turning into massive military bases — will give Ivan/Russia a "huge" advantage over WIC. But it simply doesn't have any other choice. It has to regain its strength so it can destroy Israel; that's all that really matters at the moment — destroy Israel! Kill "every" Jew! The Moslem people "must" have revenge for what the Jews have done —

especially their destruction of Mecca! They must "all" die! This is what Allah wants! This is what Allah demands! Revenge! Revenge! REVENGE!!!

WIC, therefore, accepts Ivan's terms, and Ivan immediately begins sending huge amounts of aid to WIC and, in doing so, quickly gains total control of France, Germany, Spain, and Portugal — without having to use any military force. This is because Ivan's aid deal with WIC is "exclusive," in that, no one else can send aid, or do any kind of import/export trade with WIC, without first being approved by Ivan. This, Ivan claims, is a necessary security precaution, both for Russia and WIC. And because of this, any country who isn't part of Russia...say, like France, Germany, Spain, and Portugal...well, they might find that trying to do business with WIC is a long, complicated — and expensive — process.

Ivan, for example, has the power to stop their ships anywhere in the Meditteranean, board them, check out their cargoes, and charge them a high "approval," or "security," tax (say 50% of the cargo's value — or 75% — or 90%...whatever Ivan wants). Or he can simply seize — or *Russianize* — the ships and cargoes. Or he can let his military use the ships for target practice. And the same applies to aircraft flying over the Meditteranean. If the proper taxes haven't been paid, and the proper approval received, Ivan's planes will force them to land and the aircraft and contents will be seized — or they'll be used as targets.

Consequently, since this aid/trade with WIC will mean a "major" economic boost for France, Germany, Spain, and Portugal, it only makes sense to become part of Ivan's new Russia. Certainly, it'll mean the loss of certain freedoms, such as freedom of speech and religion — but "many" in these countries are questioning the importance of such freedoms — and "many" are even saying that such freedoms aren't

264

important at all; that, in fact they're actually detrimental to a "good" life.

They (particularly council agents, who are at "every" level of society) point out that the new Russia is doing "much" better — "far" beyond simply "much" better, in fact — since Ivan took control, and that all the countries that've joined the new Russia are also doing "far" beyond simply "much" better since joining. Even Italy, who didn't voluntarily join — who was invaded and conquered by Ivan/Russia — is doing "far" beyond simply "much" better. Certainly, Ivan destroyed Vatican City and banned all religion, and imposed severe restrictions on speech/expression. But the people are "thriving"...everyone is employed and receiving excellent wages; food is plentiful, good, and cheap; there is excellent free medical/dental care; taxes are low; crime is almost non-existent; alcoholism is almost non-existent (instead or wine, most Italians are drinking grape juice...which is heavily fortified with "vitamins," of course); drug addiction is almost non-existent (except for the "vitamins," of course); political corruption has completely disappeared (of course, so have all the politicians; remember, they were eliminated when the military took over the "free" world)...conditions are so good, in fact, that "many" Italians are starting to believe that perhaps Ivan has actually been sent by God, and that the destruction of Vatican City was what God wanted. After all, if God wasn't on Ivan's side, why would He allow him to destroy Vatican City?

Soon, only Switzerland and Great Britain aren't part of Ivan's new Russia in that part of the world. And they're both suffering greatly because of it — especially Britain, where the national unemployment rate is about 60% (in some areas, it's 95%; in comparison, the unemployment rate in Ivan's new Russia is 0% — everyone who is employable is working); unemployment insurance and social welfare systems have, for the most part, collapsed; crime is rapidly increasing (especially violent crime); there are major shortages of everything, including electricity, heating and cooking fuels, basic foods (people are beginning to kill each other over crusts of bread), and medicines (people are again beginning to die from simple illnesses and infections)...conditions are "quickly" becoming as terrible as they were during the time of turmoil before the military takeover...no, they're getting even worse (in fact, conditions are getting so bad that "many" who fled from France, Germany, Sweden, Poland, etc, to escape having to live in Ivan's new Russia, have returned — or are trying to return — to where they came from).

But the British military leaders declare that Britain will Never! join Ivan's new Russia! NEVER!!! Not after what the bloody bastard did at Gibralter! No, Britain will sit firm and wait for the *United States of the Americas* to finish regrouping, and then it'll be just like the old days, in World War Two, when Britain and America (the "old" America, that is) joined together to defeat Hitler. Oh, no, Britain will Never! succumb to the likes of that bloody bastard Ivan! NEVER!!! NEVER!!! NEVER!!!

Enter the "Ivanites." Actually, they've been on the scene ever since Ivan took over Russia and turned it into "paradise." But they've had to stay "underground," since they were hunted during the great turmoil when anyone thought to be pro-Ivan/pro-Russian/anti-Christian was slaughtered; and after the military takeover, they were "officially" declared "illegal" and persecuted (even saying "anything" positive about Ivan is a serious offense, punishable by execution).

Now, however, they're beginning to surface — and in greater numbers than non-Ivanites ever imagined. It appears that almost every Brit under 21 — both male and female — is an Ivanite — even those in the military! And, even more shocking, it also appears that they're "extremely" well-armed — mainly with weapons that are clearly from Ivan's new Russia. Somehow that bloody bastard has managed to smuggle large quantities of automatic rifles, machine guns, rocket and grenade launchers, mortars, etc, etc, into Britain, and now the Ivanites have started a bloody, full-scale civil war!

And before long, with a series of brilliant moves (aided by council manipulations inside the British military, of course), the Ivanites gain control of a substantial amount of territory bordering the English Channel in the southern counties of Kent (about 1,200 square miles), East Sussex (about 550 square miles), West Sussex (about 500 square miles), and Hampshire (about 750 square miles) — including, in the latter county, the important naval base at Portsmouth and the major commercial seaport of Southhampton.

With this territory (totalling approximately 3,000 square miles) under their control, the Ivanites declare it to be an independent country — *Ivania* — and apply to Ivan for admission to the new Russia. And, of course, Ivan immediately recognizes the new country and welcomes it to the new Russia, and instantly begins sending huge amounts of military aid to the new Russia's latest addition — including "direct" aid.

In less than a week, from Russia's new French-sector, over 300,000 troops — equipped with 1,000 tanks, 1,000 pieces of artillery, and 400 helicopter gunships — arrive by air and sea in *Ivania*. As well, thousands of aircraft operating from the French-sector and aircraft carriers in the English Channel provide intense air support, and cruise missiles from *Archangel* hit major radar installations and communications

267

centers (although most of these have already been neutralized from the inside by council agents, as have other areas inside the British military; it's Italy all over again). And, to show those loyal Brits who have trouble accepting the "fact" that it's "really" the end of the United Kingdom, Ivan makes certain that historic British landmarks, such as Buckingham Palace, Westminster Abbey, the Tower of London, and St. Paul's Cathederal, are "completely" destroyed.

And in just a few weeks, it's all over. The United Kingdom (including all of Ireland) is *Ivania*, and, shortly thereafter, Switzerland joins Ivan's new Russia. It doesn't really have any other choice. Ivan has it "completely" surrounded — "totally" isolated — although most Swiss don't see joining the new Russia as a negative. They've been eager to join for quite awhile, especially the younger Swiss, who see Ivan as the only hope for the future — especially now that China is on the rampage — or, more accurately, now that the "new" China is on the rampage.

Shortly after Israel's nuclear attack on WIC, Wung Hung's new China begins a massive military campaign on eight fronts; Japan (aiding Sung Dark's new Korea); Taiwan (which only lasts about a dozen hours because the Taiwanese military — no longer receiving any aid from America — decides it's ridiculous trying to fight mainland China); India (aiding Pakistan); Vietnam; the Philippines; Indonesia (careful not to infringe on Ivan's new sector there); Malaysia; Thailand (aiding Myanmar). And rumor has it that Wung Hung's long-range plans include conquering Ivan's new Russia and turning the survivors into slaves (who'll find themselves living under conditions even worse than existed in Pol Pot's Cambodia).

Wung Hung, of course, vehemently denies any such plans, and says the new China wants to be friends with the new Russia. And the new Russia and the new China sign a non-aggression treaty. But Ivan doesn't trust Wung Hung. He feels that Wung Hung does indeed plan on turning the new Russia into a slave state, and he's going to make certain that such a thing will "never" happen. But he's not going to use military force against China — at least, not in a conventional sense, because he can't really afford to, since he's going to need all the conventional military strength he can muster in his upcoming wars with WIC and America.

Nor is he going to use nuclear or chemical weapons, because they're simply too obvious. He wants — "needs" — something "subtle"...something that doesn't look like a "weapon"...oh, yes, he's going to use biological warfare. And his weapon of choice is the bacterium *Yersinia pestis*, which causes one of the deadliest diseases ever experienced by humans: bubonic plague — or, as it's often called: *Black Death* — which, between the years 1347 and 1351, claimed about 75,000,000 lives.

And, to make certain that the casualty rate is as high as possible, Ivan chooses to use the "pneumonic" form of the plague, which has a mortality rate of about 99.99%.

Of course, the great danger of using such a weapon is that it may backfire and end up doing as much damage — or maybe even more — to the user as it does to those it's being used against...hell, just one person being exposed to such a deadly disease could conceivably result in the death of the entire human species.

Ivan isn't a fool, however. He's not going to use such a weapon without some safeguards, such as possessing a vaccine for the disease, and having the ability to keep the disease confined to a certain area.

Now, regarding the latter, there's a definite problem, since the primary target country, China, and the secondary target countries (Mongolia, Korea, Japan, Vietnam, the Philippines, Indonesia, Malaysia, Thailand, Cambodia, Laos, Myanmar, Bangladesh, India, and Pakistan) make up quite a large area, with many miles of both inland and coastal borders, some of which border on Russia itself (including the Russian forces in Indonesia.)

However, the people of these countries are quite "distinctive" — in a "racial" sense. A non-native of these countries — a "white" person, if you will — wouldn't have any trouble identifying them as being from somewhere in that large area. Therefore, the disease is introduced into the approximate geographic center of the area — say, Hanoi, in Vietnam — and is then carried outward in all directions to all the other regions of the area by Chinese military personnel — especially high-ranking ones who do a lot of travelling.

Then, when it's discovered that the *Black Death* is again on the rampage, and people begin trying to flee the area by land, sea, and air, those outside the area — the new Russians, the WIC nations (except for those, such as Indonesia, that'll be hit by the disease), and America (which now includes Australia and New Zealand) — will know who to fire their guns, missiles, torpedoes, etc, at — because, in order to keep the disease from leaving the area, "everyone" — "all" men, women, and children — trying to flee the area will have to be destroyed, since it'll simply be too dangerous to medically examine them first...oh, yes, I know...this all sounds beyond terrible — "far" beyond terrible. But it must be remembered that this is the *Second Coming of Christ*, an event that, according to Biblical prophecy, is preceded by events that are far beyond terrible.

So Ivan introduces the *Black Death* into the area and, in less than a year, it kills over two billion (plus at least 200,000,000 more die from other diseases, such as cholera and typhus; and over 100,000,000 more die from starvation; and over 200,000,000 more die from internal strife — in all, Ivan is responsible for the deaths of over 2,500,000,000 in that part of the world!).

Then, with the new China no longer a threat to him, Ivan now devotes his attention to the destruction of WIC. First, he helps WIC regain its strength, so it can destroy Israel. He could simply start attacking WIC now, instead of helping it rebuild, but that just wouldn't be the smart thing to do.

By helping WIC rebuild, he's providing the people of his new Russia with "much" employment, and people who are working (and receiving good wages and benefits) are a happy people (even if they don't have freedom of speech/expression/religion, etc,etc). As well, it'll give him time to develop the property he acquired from WIC in the aid deal into strong military bases, so when WIC finally destroys Israel (and it will, that's for "certain"), Ivan will be in a "much" superior military position — especially since, in destroying Israel, WIC will also suffer a great loss of military strength. Israel might not have anymore nuclear weapons, but it's conventional arsenal (and lethal chemical arsenal) is still "huge," and before it and all its people go down, Israel is going to lay another huge beating on WIC.

Then, after Israel is destroyed and a much weakened WIC is celebrating its victory, Ivan attacks and destroys WIC — and the Moslem faith, as well. He eradicates "every" piece of Moslem writing (including "every" Koran) and "every" mosque in the former World Islamic Confederation...and is fully prepared to kill "every"Moslem unless, of course, they renounce their faith and become citizens of his new Russia. And "many" do, deciding that becoming part of Ivan's new Russia is better than death. (This might sound absolutely unbelievable — especially to Moslems. But we do have the

271

power to eliminate Islam — and any other faith — from the world; many believe that ideas/beliefs can't be killed, but that simply isn't true. Ideas/beliefs can indeed be killed — especially if one can actually get inside the ideas/beliefs and do the killing from the inside. Or, put another way: Kill the ideas/beliefs by "imploding" them.)

So then, there's just Ivan's new Russia and the *United States of the Americas* — and it's time for the world's final war.

And America is more than ready. While Ivan is expanding his new Russia into Europe, the *United States of the Americas* is building up its military strength in a "huge" way — and moving into position to confront Ivan (and also to keep the *Black Death* from spreading to America; it has an anti-plague vaccine, of course, but it's much better to stop plague-carriers before they can make it to America).

This involves a massive build-up in Alaska to counter Ivan's forces across the Bering Strait (which, despite all his rhetoric about taking Alaska back from America, he's badly neglected; American forces now outnumber Russian forces in that area by an across-the-board strength of ten to one), and an even bigger build-up in the Pacific, with a strong line of warships and island bases stretching from Alaska to Australia, as well as an equally-sized build-up on the east coast of the *United States of the Americas* (including Greenland and Iceland). The most massive build-up, however, is in southern Africa.

At about the same time Ivan is destroying the British base at Gibralter, the *United States of the Americas* is sending its first personnel to southern Africa (South Africa, to be precise); over 750,000 troops with 3,000 fixed-wing aircraft, 5,000 helicopter gunships, 5,000 armored fighting vehicles, 5,000 pieces of artillery, and the support of over 400 warships, including 40 large amphibious assault ships, 10 large aircraft carriers, 10 guided-missile cruisers, and 6 cruise missile ships similar to Russia's *Archangel*-class vessels.

This force quickly establishes beachheads at Cape Town, Port Elizabeth, and Durban, and demands that the blacks and whites immediately cease fighting. (In the preceding few years, a bitter war has been raging between blacks and whites in South Africa, with the whites suffering about thirty thousand casualties, and the blacks, because of the much superior firepower of the whites, sustaining about two million casualties — not counting the six million or so who've succumbed to starvation, and various diseases, such as AIDS, cholera, and typhus.)

The whites do as they're ordered. Many blacks, however, don't seem to understand what "immediately" means, and continue fighting. This, unfortunately, results in over half a million of them falling victim to the American troops who, never having experienced combat, are extremely eager to show their superiors just how well they've learned their lessons.

Then, following the stabilization of the three beachheads, forces of the *United States of the Americas* turn South Africa into a colossal military base, with tens of thousands of military aircraft of all kinds, thousands of military ships of all types, and tens of millions of military personnel of all kinds.

As well, while this activity is taking place in South Africa, American air, naval, and ground strike-forces begin moving north into Namibia, Angola, Botswana, Zimbabwe, Zambia, Malawi, Mozambique, Madagascar, Tanzania, Zaire, and Kenya...which, tragically, results in the deaths of millions of blacks.

This is terrible — "beyond" terrible — "far" beyond

terrible. But it simply can't be avoided because the American landing in South Africa has destroyed black unity, not just in South Africa, but also in the neighboring countries. And tribal warfare breaks out again (as does "intertribal" warfare), and "many" more blacks kill each other than are killed by the American forces who, in fact, only kill blacks — "reluctantly" — in self-defense. (But it should be noted that the great majority of blacks die, not as a direct result of military action, but from starvation and diseases, such as AIDS, cholera, and typhus; and it should also be noted that, sadly, the American forces simply aren't able to offer "any" kind of humanitarian aid — not even a slice of bread or an aspirin! — since "all" their energy must be used strictly for military matters.) They're not there to kill blacks. They're there to prepare for war with Ivan. They are, in fact, the primary strike-force in the upcoming war, with one group going up the west coast of Africa, one up the middle, and the third up the east coast.

As well, in America, there's a huge force (over 5,000 ships, including over a hundred large aircraft carriers, a couple hundred guided missile cruisers, and a hundred or so cruise missile vessels) ready to cross the Atlantic and attack the Europeon sector of the new Russia; and in Australia, there's another equally massive force ready to cross the Indian Ocean towards the Persian Gulf sector of the new Russia; and in Alaska is another huge force ready to drive into northeastern Russia.

This enormous assemblage of military power doesn't frighten Ivan, however. He, after all, also has an immense military force. As well, he also has the tremendous advantage of being in the defensive position. The forces of the *United States of the Americas* have to come to him. And when they do, he's going to slaughter them! By the hundreds of thousands! By the millions! By the tens of millions! And then he's going to invade the *United States of the Americas* and conquer it! Then the whole world will be his! Oh, yes...he's going to be the first person in history to rule the whole world! He's going to be the greatest conquerer in history!

But, of course, he doesn't even come close to ruling the world. Nor does he even come close to invading the *United States of the Americas*. No, Ivan and his mighty military machine are soundly defeated by the *United States of the Americas* (aided, of course, by tens of millions in the new Russia who suddenly begin seeing Ivan as a "bad" guy). (Although, his forces do indeed kill a few million American troops — but this simply can't be avoided; it is a war, after all. The great majority of them, however, are simple soldiers with basic skills who are expendable... yes, I know, this sounds beyond terrible, but it's the truth.)

Of course, it must be remembered that Ivan's defeat isn't just the result of a colossal military action. What "really" defeats Ivan is the fact that he's our creation (without his knowledge) and is "completely" controlled by us.

For example, his top military staff — "all" of them — are, to one degree or another, council agents, as are "all" his top scientists and technicians. But perhaps the most important council agents in the new Russia are Ivan's girlfriend and his personal doctor...no, there isn't any "perhaps" about it; they are "definitely" the most important council agents in the whole operation (just like Hitler's girlfriend, Eva Braun, and Theodor Morell, his doctor, were in the council's manipulations of Hitler). (It should be noted, however, that "none" of these agents have "any" kind of "intimate" knowledge of the council — except that it's "all" powerful; it is the *Big Brother* of Orwell's *1984,* and there isn't "anyone" or "anything" that can fight *Big Brother*.)

They make certain that Ivan takes his "vitamins," as

well as their "advice," which they make seem are his own thoughts/ideas/ visions...oh, yes, Ivan believes he's a genius — a "super" genius — the most brilliant person who's ever walked the face of the Earth...no, he's not just a "person" — he's a "god" ...no, he is "God"...no, he's "beyond" God; he's "super" God...oh, yes, Ivan loses all touch with reality.

Therefore, he doesn't realize when his huge military machine begins malfunctioning exactly like the Italian, British, and Moslem militaries did just before he attacked them. In fact, he spends his last few weeks in such a fog that he has trouble remembering his own name, and by the time tens of millions of his troops at Megiddo and surrounding area are vaporized by a ten megaton thermonuclear device, he actually can't even remember his own name at all; in fact, in his last days, he's reduced to a drooling, toothless, hairless, crawling, shell of a man with the mind of a three-month-old who can't even feed himself and needs to wear diapers...oh, yes...Ivan is finished! The Antichrist has been defeated! (And it's "proven" that he was indeed the Antichrist because, after his hair falls out, the number 666 is found on his scalp.)

And then, appearing on TV screens around the world, wearing a long, white, flowing robe, and surrounded by a halo of golden light...oh, yes! It's Him!!! It's Jesus Christ!!! It's the *Second Coming*!!!

But what then?

Judgment Day, of course. Although, since that requires the resurrection of billions of dead, the council will have to postpone that event for awhile — for forever, in fact, because, while we might be all-powerful, we're not quite that all-powerful; so Christ will simply say that *Judgment Day* will happen when God decides it's the right moment.

In the meantime, Christ will rule the world — and "everyone" will obey him! Oh, yes...there'll be absolutely no nonsense — "none" — from "the people"; it simply won't be tolerated. People who get caught stealing ("anything"), for instance, will simply be eliminated. There won't be anyone "paying a debt to society" by sitting in a prison cell, because there won't be any prisons...no, this isn't quite accurate; the whole world will, in fact, be one huge prison.

Yes, that's correct. The whole world will be a prison — except, of course, there won't be any cells, bars, fences, etc (except, of course, for "temporary" accommodations, such as execution waiting rooms). There'll just be *God's Law*, and the *Holy Police* to enforce them without mercy...or maybe there'll be a "real" *Second Coming*? Or a "real" alien invasion? Or maybe an alien invasion is already underway? Hell, maybe the council is actually being controlled by aliens? It is, after all, a possibility — at least, we believe it is.

But, whatever...we do know for certain that something "major" has to happen soon, or the people of Earth will soon find themselves caught in the biggest sociological/environmental disaster of all time...actually, they're already caught in it; at the moment, however they're still on the outer rim of the whirlpool — they still have a chance of avoiding the center.

Or, then again, maybe something "major" doesn't have to take place? Maybe we can just let things go along pretty much the way they have been for another ten or twenty or thirty years, or more...hell, most of the present council will probably be gone in ten years, or less, and there'll be a new council, and who knows what they'll do? Ten or twenty or thirty, or whatever, years from now, maybe the council will mutate into a *Fourth Reich*, complete with a new Hitler...who knows? Much stranger things have happened.

But I must admit that recently I've been feeling an increasing disinterest in what happens to the world and its people because, after all, I'll be gone fairly soon, as will the other council members. So why should it matter to us what happens? For the sake of our children?

Well, for one thing, the next council will be composed of our children (two of them, in fact, are my sons; their mothers, who I never actually met in person, were artificially inseminated with my sperm) who've been in training to serve on the main council since birth. And, for another thing, they too will one day be gone. Hell, one day the whole damn Earth will be gone — burned to a crisp by the sun as it grows huge before its own death — and that's a "definite" reality.

But, as I've said before a few times, like T.S. Eliot said: Humankind can't bear much reality.

Which is tragic...yes, beyond tragic — "far" beyond tragic. The world would be so much better off if people could just accept more reality — "much" more. And also be less stupid — "much" less stupid.

But I very much doubt this will happen — at least, not on a "large" scale — although, who knows? After all, anything is possible...right?

Well, if that's true, then it also has to be true that some things just aren't possible....